Date Due

FEB 28 '68			
JUL 31 '68			
DEC 11 '68			
DEC 17 '69			

JOHANNES BRAHMS

JOHANNES
BRAHMS

HIS WORK
AND PERSONALITY

BY

HANS GAL

TRANSLATED FROM THE GERMAN BY
JOSEPH STEIN

NEW YORK: ALFRED·A·KNOPF

1963

72019

L. C. catalog card number: 63–9122

THIS IS A BORZOI BOOK,

PUBLISHED BY ALFRED A. KNOPF, INC.

FIRST AMERICAN EDITION

Originally published in German as *Johannes Brahms: Werk und Persönlichkeit*. © 1961 Fischer Bücherei KG, Frankfurt am Main.

Preface

SEEN with a certain detachment, the life story of any great person is seldom more than a background: indispensable for understanding his development, but beyond that hardly of any basic significance. For this reason I have confined to a minimum whatever is biographical in a narrow sense. The depth and aura of Brahms, as a character as well as an artist, justify a presentation centered on problems of personality and artistic creation; from these problems, however, all kinds of side lights will inevitably fall on the story of his life.

Concerning the bare facts of Brahms's life we are in a more fortunate position than with any of the great musicians of the more distant past. In his comprehensive, multivolume, and factually almost exhaustive biographical study, written at a time when direct sources of information were still readily available, Max Kalbeck compiled and presented everything of biographic significance. Also, all accessible correspondence carried on by Brahms with friends, colleagues, and performing artists has been presented in publications. Added to all this material, there also exists an almost unlimited literature of old and new biographies, articles, all types of essays, personal reminiscences, and other contemporary expressions. Under these circumstances the present monograph lays no claim to producing new factual material. It rests its case solely on an intensive, lifelong engagement and a thorough acquaintance with Brahms's work.

I considered it proper to use one personal source of information in addition to the above-mentioned material, even though it was of necessity dependent on memory: the word-of-mouth communications from my teacher Eusebius Mandyczewski, who during the last two decades of Brahms's life was one of his most intimate friends. When I first went to him, about twelve years after the master's death, his completely flawless memory was still under the immediate influence of his great friend. Until his death in 1929 I remained in close contact with him and have cherished his numerous sayings concerning Brahms's personal traits, his judgments, and his attitude toward all kinds of musical questions. Also, as his sole collaborator in publishing the Breitkopf & Härtel edition of Brahms's complete works, I had innumerable opportunities to discuss with him anything bearing upon the object of our enterprise. If I thus consider myself presumably the last surviving bearer of a direct Brahms tradition, I do so in all humility and without overestimating this circumstance, but nevertheless with a sense of obligation to pass on my experiences to the best of my ability.

For reasons of space, detailed discussions of individual works have necessarily been limited to a small selection which was yielded up naturally by the context; but the entire selection is always concerned with instances which, for one reason or another, are characteristic and illustrative of Brahms's creative work. I have made every effort to avoid insofar as possible anything that is strictly technical. Wherever I failed in living up to this intention, I beg the friendly reader's indulgence.

Contents

Plates

PLATES

The musical examples on pages 164 and 227 are from the Collected Works of Johannes Brahms.
Edition of the Society of the Friends of Music, Vienna. With permission from the publishers, Messrs. Breitkopf & Härtel, Wiesbaden.

JOHANNES BRAHMS

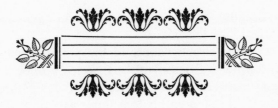

Biographical Sketch

I<small>N</small> 1826 Johann Jakob Brahms, father of the composer, a somewhat rebellious scion of peasants from the region between Hanover and Holstein in Lower Saxony, finished his apprenticeship with a village musician. Twenty years of age, he wandered into the nearest big city, Hamburg, to seek his fortune. Acquainted with several instruments, he played the keyed bugle in the militia band, performed for weddings and other celebrations, and in cafés and cabarets. He also applied himself with diligence and perseverance to his principal instrument, the double bass, learning it sufficiently well to hold his own in theatre orchestras and ultimately in the Hamburg Philharmonic Concerts. In 1830 he married his landlady, Christiane Nissen, seventeen years his senior. Johannes, born May 7th, 1833, was the second child of this union, which at first was a very happy one, although many years later it foundered—probably largely because of the great disparity in ages. Johannes had by then long left home.

The external circumstances of the paternal household, though narrow and impoverished, seem to have been orderly and respectable. The father took it for granted that his son would follow in his footsteps, especially since the latter showed signs of talent at a very early age; it was considered equally natural that whenever the opportunity presented itself, he would be taken into the bands in which his father was employed. It was a real disappointment that the boy showed great interest in an instrument as unlucrative as the piano rather than in the more practical orchestral instruments which his father could teach him. A friendly and capable musician, O.F.W. Cossel, declared himself willing to give Johannes some lessons and, since the Brahms household did not have one, to permit him to practice on his piano. The youngster applied himself and at ten years of age was already capable of playing in public. He came close to falling into the hands of an enterprising agent who promised the parents mountains of gold and a career for their son as a prodigy in the United States. Fortunately this was prevented by Cossel and his teacher, Eduard Marxsen, a capable pianist and composer who from then on took the talented boy in hand. Under his guidance Johannes developed into a thoroughly competent pianist. The extraordinarily high level of his first published compositions, created between his eighteenth and twentieth year, testifies to a schooling that could hardly have been better. In the higher sense of developing his artistic individuality, Brahms was just as much self-made as all really great men are. Yet he remained ever grateful to his mentor, and he expressly asked him for advice and criticism even at the time he composed his *German Requiem*. One of the greatest of his works, the Piano Concerto in B-flat major, is dedicated to his "beloved friend and teacher Eduard Marxsen."

A coincidence brought the young musician to wider public notice during the spring of 1853. The Hungarian violinist Eduard Reményi, a refugee from the suppressed 1848 revolution, proposed to take Brahms on an improvised concert tour as accompanist. Reményi appears to have been more of a talented gypsy fiddler than a serious musician—Brahms himself quotes him as saying: "Totay vill I blay de Kraitzer Sonahda to mak all de fur fly!"—but he was already an experienced globe-trotter and uninhibited sponger who never hesitated to cultivate advantageous connections nor to exploit them to his profit. Together with his accompanist he called on a successful compatriot, the violinist Josef Joachim, who as a boy had started his concert career under the auspices of Mendelssohn and now held the post of Royal Concertmaster in Hanover. At first sight, there arose between Joachim and the youthful Brahms a profound attachment which developed into a lifelong friendship. "Brahms," Joachim wrote at that time to a friend, "has an exceptional talent for composing and a nature which can develop to its fullest bloom only in the most perfect seclusion; pure as diamond, soft as snow . . . . His playing shows that intensive spark, that (I might say) fatalistic energy and rhythmic precision which prophesy the artist, and his compositions already contain more of finished significance than I have ever encountered in any musical student of his age." A letter of introduction by Joachim led the two itinerant musicians to Weimar and into the presence of Liszt, who, as court conductor to the grand duke, lived with the Russian Princess Wittgenstein in the Altenburg and surrounded himself with a coterie of young talent, among them Joachim Raff, Karl Klindworth, and Peter Cornelius.

Brahms, timid and awkward, felt most uncomfortable in this brilliant and somewhat exalted circle despite Liszt's friendly encouragement. He took leave of Reményi, who seemed entirely in his element there, and departed for Göttingen at Joachim's urgent invitation. That summer, during a walking tour along the Rhine and a sojourn with well-to-do musical amateurs in Mehlem, near Bonn, he finally decided to pay his respects to Robert Schumann in Düsseldorf. Joachim, who revered the master above all others, had long proposed such a visit. The meeting, which took place in September, had fateful consequences; it determined both the outer and inner development of the young artist.

As editor of the *Neue Zeitschrift für Musik,* which he had founded, Schumann had for more than a decade been one of the leaders of public opinion in the musical life of Germany. In this journal, which had long since passed into other hands, he now published an article under the heading "New Departures." As an act of friendship on the part of a mature and highly regarded master on behalf of a youthful beginner, it is unique in the annals of music history—a monument to the man who wrote it, to his enthusiasm, his warmth, and his almost uncanny artistic intuition and prophetic foresight.

Years have passed—almost as many as I had devoted to the editing of this journal (ten, to be exact)—since I have last allowed myself to contribute to its pages, so rich in memories for me. In spite of my strenuous productive activity I have often felt the urge; many a new significant talent appeared on the scene; a new force in music seemed imminent, as witnessed by many aspiring artists of recent times, even though their work is known to a rather narrow circle only. I felt, in following the progress of these select ones with the keenest of interest, that one day there must suddenly emerge the one who would be chosen to express the most exalted spirit of the times in an ideal manner, one who would not bring us mastery in gradual developmental stages but who, like Minerva, would spring fully armed from the head of Jove. And he has arrived—a youth at whose cradle the graces and heroes of old stood guard. His name is Johannes Brahms; he came to me from Hamburg, where he worked in obscure tranquillity but was initiated into the most intricate secrets of the art by a knowledgeable and inspiring teacher. He had been recommended to me shortly before by an honored and well-known master. Even his outer appearance showed all the attributes which signal to us that here was a chosen one. Seated at the keyboard, he started to unfold miraculous new realms. We were drawn into a circle of ever growing magic. Added to this there was the playing of a genius, transforming the piano into an orchestra of mourning and rejoicing voices. There were sonatas, or rather veiled symphonies—songs whose poetry one could understand without knowing the words, even though a deep melody pervades them all—individual piano pieces partly of a demoniac nature but all of the most agreeable form, sonatas for violin and piano, and string quartets—each so distinguished from the others that they seemed to issue forth from different sources. And then it was as though he, like a thundering stream, would unite them all into a waterfall, bearing a rainbow over the rushing waves, met on the shore by fluttering butterflies, and accompanied by the voices of nightingales.

Once he waves his magic wand over hosts of massed choirs and orchestras who lend him their forces, we will experience wondrous insights into the world of spirits. May the highest Genius strengthen him; this may well be expected because he is also possessed of another genius—that of modesty. His contemporaries salute him in his first flight into the world, where no doubt suffering will await him, but also laurels and the palms of victory. We bid him welcome—a forceful warrior.

There reigns at all times a secret bond of kindred spirits. Those of you who form part of it—close your ranks more tightly

7

so that the truth of art will shine forth with ever growing clarity, spreading joy and blessings everywhere.

The impact of such an utterance must have been extraordinary, especially at a time when serious critical publications were comparatively scarce. In a single stroke it brought the young musician reputation, a publisher, and the most attentive respect of the entire musical world of Germany. It goes without saying that there was no lack of jealousy, especially when one considers the displeasure with which many professional musicians and aspiring students alike must have read these words. Both Schumann and his protégé were, however, prepared for this. The effect on Brahms of being thrust into the limelight in this manner was conditioned by the peculiarity of his character: a sense of deep responsibility weighed on him with frightening acuteness, and never again was he to know joyous, carefree, naive happiness in the act of creation. Schumann's prophetic revelation of his future greatness weighed upon his soul as a categorical imperative. Now he would have to justify the confidence placed in him; he would have to aim at nothing less than the supreme achievement, the unattainable, with the full knowledge and the ever mounting, ever deepening realization of the superhuman arduousness of his task.

Meanwhile, of course, there was great happiness and rejoicing. Johannes, back with his family after his first successful excursion into the world, was able to put his first published works under his friends' Christmas trees. He wrote to Schumann, showing extraordinary self-critical seriousness for a twenty-year-old:

I herewith take the liberty of sending you your first foster children (which owe their right of world citizenship to you), very concerned about whether they are still entitled to the enjoy-

8

ment of your lenience and love. In their new garb they appear to me far too orderly, almost pedantic. I still cannot get used to seeing these innocent children of nature in such decent clothing. I look forward with infinite joy to seeing you in Hanover, so that I can tell you in person how much my parents and I are beholden to your and Joachim's excessive kindness for the most blessed time of our lives. I found my parents and teachers superlatively happy and am spending the most joyous times in their midst.

And to Joachim:

I am thinking of coming to Hanover on January 3rd, and for this reason I am not bothering to send you the sonata and the first book of lieder. I am also not telling you of all my wonderful new experiences. My parents, my teachers, and I are in seventh heaven. . . . We long for you to share our joy!

All the prerequisites of a rapid and brilliant rise to fame seemed at hand. That things turned out differently was not only due to external circumstances; it was a peculiarity of Brahms's personality that he was unable to forge ahead except by force of character, perseverance, and driving energy in the face of obstacles. At times he confessed himself envious of great masters such as Mozart and Schubert, to whom everything seems to come without effort, or of his friend Dvořák, to whose talent he paid extravagant tribute while acknowledging that his results often were not commensurate with his inspired ideas.

At first, plunged into a catastrophic maze of conflicting feelings, Brahms found himself in a situation that sent him off the track for years. In February, 1854, Schumann's mental disturbance became acute. Ultimately leading to his death after two years of progressive disintegration, it had been casting its shadow for years. Schumann's wife, Clara, expecting the birth of their eighth child, was in despair.

9

Brahms rushed to Düsseldorf to be at the revered woman's side, and he remained there until her husband's death. Both he and Joachim were permitted to see Schumann occasionally at the institution near Bonn where he was confined. Since at times there seemed to be some improvement, the relapses were all the more terrifying. Clara, whose visits were forbidden by the physicians in order to avoid all possible agitation for the patient, did not see him again until just before his death. A joint letter from her and Johannes to Joachim gives, in a few lines, a shattering picture of the situation. On July 29, 1856 she wrote: "I saw him yesterday. Let me be silent about my own despair, but I did perceive a few loving glances; I shall carry them with me all my life! Pray God he may have a peaceful end. It cannot last much longer." And Brahms added: "I am writing this just in case you wish to see him once more. I would like to add, however, that you must think it over carefully; it is a very, very horrifying and pitiful sight. Schumann is very thin, and there can be no question of conversation or even consciousness." Many years later Brahms wrote to his friend Julius Otto Grimm: "To me, Schumann's memory is holy. The noble, pure artist forever remains my ideal. I will hardly be privileged ever to love a better person; neither, it is to be hoped, will I have to come again so horrifyingly close to such a terrible fate and share such suffering."

Through her husband's illness Clara found herself in a precarious financial position. It became necessary for her to resume her career as a concert pianist, so successful during her younger days, which had been abandoned except for rare occasions since her marriage. It was an accomplishment of the first order to regain within a very short time, through her driving energy and remarkable talent, her former place in the musical world. Brahms, who lived close by, devoted himself entirely to helping and supporting her and her children. Whatever he required for his own modest needs he earned by giving lessons.

This must have been a period of passionate inner struggles for him. Clara, fourteen years his senior, was a beautiful and fascinating woman to whom he was devoted with tender respect. Their constant, intimate nearness must have been dangerous for him, especially because of his extreme youth. When she had to go to Rotterdam on a concert tour, for example, he followed her within a few days because he could not stand her absence. Clara's feelings for him were, no doubt, at first of a rather maternal nature. As time went on, however, a change must have taken place, natural enough for a still young, imaginative woman confronted by a young man of genius who worshipped her. When Brahms showed his friend Hermann Deiters his Piano Quartet in C minor, Opus 60, which was conceived in Düsseldorf at that time but completed very much later, he expressed himself in a manner that could hardly be misunderstood: "Just picture to yourself a man who is going to shoot himself and who then has no other choice left." A number of years later, when he was about to publish the work, he sent it to Theodor Billroth with this remark: "This quartet is only communicated as a curiosity, say as an illustration to the last chapter of the Man with the Blue Jacket and Yellow Vest." He made a similar remark to his publisher Simrock. The allusion to Goethe's *Werther* and to his own situation at that time of passion is so transparent that it needs no further elucidation.

Beyond this, the matter has remained a mystery. All we know is that shortly after Schumann's death Brahms managed to struggle free of Clara. He returned to his parents in Hamburg. Working tirelessly, he waited for an improvement in his external circumstances and his position in the world without actually undertaking anything positive to achieve that end. His friends of the Schumann circle had their secure berths: Joachim in Hanover, Grimm in Göttingen, and Albert Hermann Dietrich in Bonn. At first, on Clara's recommendation, the only thing Brahms was able to find was a modest connection with the court of the Prince of Detmold. For several years he spent a few months there each winter, teaching piano to a princess and her ladies-in-waiting, leading a choir, and occasionally being allowed to use the court orchestra. His income from these activities was barely sufficient for his simple needs; he eked it out by giving piano lessons in Hamburg. The Detmold activities gave him but little satisfaction. Brahms was no courtier. He wrote to Joachim:

Her Highness's amusements leave me no time for thinking about myself. I am all the more thankful when they occupy me fully, and I have many an advantage which up to now I lacked. I have so little practical knowledge! The choir rehearsals point up many of my shortcomings and are most useful to me. My things really are written with an appalling lack of practicability! I have rehearsed quite a variety of them, fortunately with sufficient confidence right from the first moment.

During the Düsseldorf years he had accomplished little, but now one work followed another in rapid succession: chamber music, piano compositions, vocal music, and his first orchestral attempts. The crowning work of this period, his monumental Piano Concerto in D minor, was ready for its debut only after untold difficulties, scruples, and changes. He played it for the first time in Leipzig in 1859. The failure of this performance left scars for a long time to come, despite the apparent indifference with which he reported the concert to Joachim:

There is nothing further to write about the event, since nobody breathed a word about the composition. . . . This failure leaves me completely unaffected. . . . Still, once I have improved its anatomy, the concerto will please; and a second one will certainly turn out better. I honestly believe this is the best thing that could have happened. It forces me to buckle down, and it builds up my courage. After all, I am still experimenting and groping my way.

Brahms's letters of this period often reflect a certain misanthropy and a growing dissatisfaction. The years flitted by, and he had the feeling that he was not progressing. In Hamburg he remained an outsider, probably because of provincial narrowness and jealousy. He gave up his now-burdensome position in Detmold even though it was limited to only three months a year. At last, in the fall of 1862, he decided on an adventure: he took a trip to Vienna, the opposite pole of the German musical world. In retrospect this journey seems to have been an instinctive action.

In Vienna he instantly established contact with the leading musical circles and found the most eminent musicians to take a lively interest in his work. Quickly making friends, he appeared as pianist and successfully introduced his music on the concert stage. Most important, he was enchanted by the charm of the city and its environs, by the friendly, informal atmosphere, the excellent yet inexpensive eating places, and by the extraordinary, inherent musicality and receptivity of a people for whom music, through centuries of tradition, had become a vital necessity. He was to become acquainted soon enough with the less admirable side of life in Vienna—its palpable lack of seriousness and of perseverance in work, its capriciousness, and its lack of reliability as far as loyalties and consistency are concerned. But he retained his predilection for Vienna in spite of occasional disappointments, and, except for one extended interruption, Vienna became his home for the rest of his life. The first impression was indeed decisive. In November, 1862, he wrote to Grimm:

Well, this is it! I have established myself here within ten paces of the Prater and can drink my wine where Beethoven drank his. Since I can't have it any better, I find things quite cheerful and attractive. Of course, hiking through the Black Forest with one's wife, as you are doing, is not only still more cheerful but also more beautiful.

And to his parents he reported about his first concert, given at the instigation of his Viennese friends:

I had much joy yesterday. My concert came off very well. The quartet [the Piano Quartet in A major] was well received, and I had extraordinary success as a pianist. Each number won rich applause. I sensed much enthusiasm in the audience. . . . I played as unconcernedly as though I were at home among my friends. The public here is much more responsive than ours at home. You should see their attention and hear their applause! I am very happy I gave the concert.

In Vienna Brahms enjoyed the limitless freedom of a strolling visitor while he waited for a decision back home in Hamburg that to him seemed of infinite importance. Friedrich Wilhelm Grund, for many years conductor of the Philharmonic Concerts, was getting ready for retirement, and Brahms, who counted heavily on becoming his successor, had entrusted his Hamburg friends with taking the necessary steps on his behalf during his absence. It was the bitterest disappointment of his life to learn that he had been passed over and that his friend, the singer Julius Stockhausen, had been appointed to the conductorship. He never quite got over the mortification. Perhaps it was a tragic characteristic of his profound nature that he could never forgive, never forget. His unconcealed bitterness came to the surface in a letter to Clara Schumann, written in Vienna, November 18, 1862:

For me this was a much sadder event than you can possibly imagine, perhaps even sadder than you can understand. I am an old-fashioned character, not at all cosmopolitan, and am attached to my native city as to a mother. . . . Now along comes this enemy of a friend [Avé-Lallemant, who seems to have played a rather ambiguous role in the whole affair] and, probably for good, pushes me aside. How rare it is for one of my kind to find a permanent position! How happy I would have been to find one in my native city! Now here, even though much beauty gladdens my heart, I still feel very keenly, and always will, that I am a stranger and cannot find repose. If I can't find hope here, where shall I? Where may I and can I? You experienced it with your husband and know full well that they would prefer to let us go altogether, to have us fly around in empty space. And yet one craves to belong and to earn that which makes life really worth living; one dreads loneliness. Working in close harmony with others—the happiness of family life—who is so inhuman as not to have a longing for all this?

Klaus Groth, a writer from Lower Saxony whose poems Brahms had set to music and with whom he was friendly, tells us in his *Erinnerungen an Johannes Brahms* ("Reminiscences of Johannes Brahms") of a significant incident that took place many years later at the fiftieth anniversary celebration of the Hamburg Philharmonic Society. In the preceding festival concert Brahms's Symphony No. 2 had been performed under his direction. Now one of the speakers was rash enough to say that, in the case of this illustrious son of the city of Hamburg, the proverb *nemo propheta in patria* had been proven false. Brahms angrily whispered to his neighbor: "This they exemplify by my case! And on two occasions the conductorship of the Philharmonic Concerts was filled by strangers while I

15

was passed over! If I had been chosen at the right time, I would have become an orderly citizen; I would have married and lived like others. As it is, I am a vagabond."

His anger was certainly genuine and his bitterness justified. But perhaps fate was kinder to him than he himself could, or would, have realized. It is doubtful whether he could have long tolerated the extremely provincial musical conditions in Hamburg at that time, and, in the event he had stayed on, whether his success as musical director would have been of much help to him as a composer. One thing cannot be disputed: the measure of his renown rose rapidly to its zenith as soon as he had established himself in Vienna. For his Hamburg disappointment he was partly compensated by an offer to take over the directorship of the Vienna *Singakademie*, an oratorio society founded a few years earlier. Joyfully accepting the offer, he wrote to the society's board: "It is a peculiar sensation to give up one's freedom for the first time. Still, whatever comes from Vienna sounds twice as sweet to a musician's ear; and whatever calls to Vienna presents twice the temptation."

The new musical director started his service in the fall of 1863 with enthusiasm. But his success was not without reverses. Faced with occasional difficulties, such as irregular attendance at rehearsals or differences of opinion concerning program policy, Brahms soon lost his joy in work which could never have become the focus of his interest. After a single season he resigned his post as choir director of the *Singakademie*. Eight years later, when called to the conductorship of one of the oldest and most respectable musical institutions, the Society of the Friends of Music, he stuck to his post for three years before relinquishing it in anger and profound disillusionment. The artistically uncompromising nature of his programs had given rise to opposition. Writing about a concert in which, after Bach's Cantata No. 8 ("Dearest God, when shall I die?"), Cherubini's Requiem in C minor was performed, Eduard Hanslick, the leading music critic of Vienna and a warm friend of Brahms, wrote: "Vienna does not lack a public which reveres and seeks out the serious beauty of music. But here, as elsewhere, one does not go to concerts for the express purpose of attending his own funeral—first Protestant and then Catholic." And it was probably on a similar occasion that Hellmesberger, the witty concertmaster of the Vienna Philharmonic Orchestra, quipped: "When Brahms is in extra good spirits, he sings 'The grave is my joy'."

Brahms had by then a well-established and large circle of friends and admirers, but he no longer accepted any close ties. From a practical point of view this was no longer a necessity for him. Within a decade of starting his activity at the *Singakademie* he had moved into the very first ranks of living creative artists. In the universal wealth of his output, which embraced all branches of absolute music, two works, extraordinarily disparate both as to content and significance, contributed most to the rise to European fame—even to popularity—of an artist who so far had merely been regarded with respect and earnest expectations: the *German Requiem*, which, after a spectacular success in the Bremen Cathedral on Good Friday, 1868, was performed wherever a chorus and orchestra could be found; and the *Hungarian Dances,* which were composed as piano duets and which soon appeared on every piano and invaded the world market in countless arrangements for all conceivable instruments and combinations.

By that time Brahms's mode of life had settled into a certain routine. The first months of each year, generally from January to April, he went on concert tours as both pianist and conductor, performing primarily his own

17

works. These trips took him through all of Germany—to the Rhineland and to Leipzig, to Breslau, Berlin, and Hamburg, and frequently to Holland and Switzerland as well. His income from this activity was more than enough to cover his personal needs and, in addition, to take ample care of his Hamburg relatives. He hardly touched his rapidly increasing royalties from publications, and soon a respectable capital had accumulated. Summers, which for several years he spent in Baden-Baden close to Clara Schumann and later in the Austrian or Swiss Alps, were entirely devoted to work. In later years he took an occasional spring trip to Italy, which he loved dearly. Autumn and the first half of winter were devoted to the completion and to the supervision of the printing of the compositions which the summer had brought to fruition. Brahms was an outdoor man like Beethoven, and he preferred to compose while taking walks, working in his head without ever jotting down any sketches.

In Vienna he lived in modest comfort in an austerely furnished three-room apartment which was kept in good order by his landlandy, Mrs. Truxa. In his summer places, whether Baden-Baden, Wiesbaden, Rüschlikon, Thun, or later with overwhelming preference the Austrian towns Pörtschach, Mürzzuschlag, or Ischl, he set great store by undisturbed solitude, for which reason he avoided hotels whenever possible. He urgently needed society, but never closer than at the periphery of his existence, and his friends knew that he was not to be disturbed when he was working. After Wagner's death in 1883 he was considered indisputably the greatest living master, and he was overwhelmed with honors and decorations, about which, however, he cared mighty little. When the University of Cambridge offered him an honorary degree, he declined the distinction because his presence would have been required at the ceremony, and he did not wish to make the trip to England. Shortly thereafter he did receive an honorary doctorate in Breslau. It was this occasion which gave rise to his *Academic Festival Overture.* On his sixtieth birthday there were celebrations and music festivals everywhere, all of which he avoided as far as possible. In Vienna the Society of the Friends of Music caused a commemorative medal bearing his portrait to be struck. Hamburg, his native city, invested him with the freedom of the city; in his letter of acceptance to the mayor, however, he was unable to suppress a covert remark in which his pique about the old slight still reverberated.

This period from his middle forties to his sixtieth year was the most fruitful one of his life. At last entirely free and joyous and without frustrations, he gushed forth music in a full stream. Then, however, twilight set in rapidly. Death took a heavy toll among his friends: Ernst Frank, Rudolf von Beckerath, Elisabeth von Herzogenberg, Philipp Spitta, Hans von Bülow, and Billroth had passed away, and in the spring of 1896 Clara Schumann, now seventy-six years old, lay on her death bed. Joachim wrote him: "My head spins at the thought of losing her; yet we have to get accustomed to the idea." Brahms replied on April 10, 1896, in a pathetic letter, one of those rare utterances in which unfettered emotion flowed from this withdrawn personality into his pen as otherwise only into his music:

Now then, I cannot consider truly sad that which your letter mentions. I have often thought that Mrs. Schumann might survive her children as well as myself, but I have never wished it. The thought of losing her can no longer frighten us—not even me, the lonely one to whom all too few still remain alive. Once she has left us, will not our faces light up with joy whenever we think of her—of this glorious woman, whose presence we

19

were privileged to enjoy for a long lifetime—with ever increasing admiration? Only in this way can we mourn her.

Clara died on May 20. The deep emotion with which Brahms at that time brooded over this personality whose love, enthusiasm, and never-failing sympathy for his work had accompanied him all his life, impelled him to create his last gigantic composition, the *Four Serious Songs,* set to biblical texts. Approaching the end of his own days, he set down in them thoughts which, in their depth, individuality, and fatalism, constitute a creed such as was probably never before uttered by a great master as a farewell offering. He completed them on May 7, 1896, his sixty-third and last birthday. Two months later he wrote to Marie, Clara's daughter:

If shortly you receive a book of "serious songs," please don't misunderstand my motives in sending it. Quite aside from the dear old habit of writing your name at the heading, these songs concern you particularly. I wrote them during the first week of May. Similar texts have often haunted me. I had been in hopes of not having to expect worse news of your mother. Yet in the depth of the soul something may speak, and urge you on almost unconsciously, and that something may materialize as poetry or music. You cannot play through the songs now because the words would be far too distressing for you. But I beg you to consider them as a very personal offering to the memory of your beloved mother and to keep them as such.

He himself avoided these songs. He could make up his mind neither to attend their public performance nor even to have them sung for him in private. The letter just quoted amply explains this.

From his summer stay in Ischl Brahms had gone to Clara's funeral; he missed a train connection and just barely managed to get to Bonn, but only after the service had already begun. The agitation occasioned by this, together with a cold contracted on the trip, was blamed by him for an attack of jaundice which appeared soon thereafter. It was only at the urging of his friends in Ischl that he finally consented to consult a physician. The result of the examination was a death warrant—of which, however, he was not told. He suffered from an advanced case of cancer of the liver, the same condition which had caused his father's death twenty-five years previously. In order to give the patient the illusion of a cure, his physicians sent him to Karlsbad for treatment. Richard Heuberger reports that the specialist, Dr. Schrötter, whose opinion he asked, replied sadly: "The poor fellow! It does not matter one bit where he is going to spend his money."

The following winter was passed in a steady and relentless decline, but on March 7 Brahms dragged himself to a concert of the Vienna Philharmonic Society to hear his Fourth Symphony under Hans Richter's direction. Here he became the object of a spontaneous ovation on the part of both audience and orchestra. This was his last public appearance. He died on April 3, 1897.

A few personal utterances may throw some characteristic side lights on this last phase of his life. In a letter written in Vienna on September 2, 1896, to Joachim, who had sent him an urgent invitation to play his Piano Quintet with him and the other members of his quartet, Brahms replied:

Under absolutely no circumstances! Even if you were four lovely, lovable loves instead of being serious and dignified gentlemen! I am here for only twenty-four hours and leave for Karlsbad today. So forgive me if, in the meantime, I just send my heartfelt thanks, look forward to next December, and beg for a Haydn quartet in your program.

Or, in another letter to Joachim, dated March 24, 1897:

I feel more and more miserable. Every word, whether spoken or written, is an effort for me. Since we last saw one another here, I haven't gone out a single evening; in fact, I have not set my foot down once.

From Berlin on March 30, 1897, Heinrich von Herzogenberg wrote to Joachim: "It is tragic that a forceful personality like Brahms is condemned to observe with a clear mind every phase of the destruction of his body. Like Prometheus bound, he is learning in belated but bitter discipline to bow before physical suffering . . . . Sickness and death in themselves are not evil as long as a person can reconcile himself to them and continue in inner harmony. Let us hope that his powerful soul, his great heart, will succeed in this."

The following day he continued: "This morning I received the enclosed note from Arthur Faber in Vienna." The message, written by one of Brahms's most faithful friends, reads: "March 28. The revered master has been confined to bed for two days now and is very, very weak. Fortunately he does not suffer much pain and has not given up hope of recovery." Herzogenberg adds: "The end comes much more rapidly than we had thought possible. Brahms flat on his back! Who can still think of recovery? . . . For thirty-five years I have asked myself with every note I composed: 'What will Brahms think of this?' It was the thought of him and his judgment that has made me whatever I am today. He was my ambition, my impetus, my courage. And now my lodestar is to be extinguished!"

Herzogenberg wrote in another letter to Joachim, dated April 12, 1897: "I was at the funeral of our beloved Brahms in Vienna. I could not bear to remain home; I had to witness the unbelievable with my own eyes. The extent of our loss cannot be measured. I felt at the open grave as though it would swallow up everything we hold dear, all the meaningful human beings who are still left, all the music we carry in our hearts. I myself would like to collapse, to lie down in sleep, and just dream."

He who leaves such friends and receives such tributes has led a rich life.

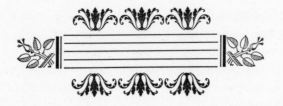

Background,
Environment,
Attitude toward the
World, and External
Appearance

THE WORLD in which we live today has thoroughly cured us of any illusion that we can decisively influence our destinies. We have learned to accept the fact that blind, powerful forces over which we have no control can play with us at will. The nineteenth century, on the other hand, may be characterized as the most placid and stable period that ever existed on the European scene, once the Napoleonic upheavals had been overcome. Wars and revolutions were violent but brief episodes, transient as thunder and rain storms, and they hardly threatened the life and existence of the individual. The value of money scarcely fluctuated, prosperity and economic progress appeared to be inescapable, and the security of justice unshakable. This orderliness, this security, may well evoke suspicion on our part; yet it was enviable. The course of a successful man's life in that period was of almost trivial uniformity; it could be practically reconstructed from a set of surveyable given conditions. For the unexpected to happen, erratic tendencies had to exist in the individual himself, as, for example, was the case with Wagner. Brahms, on the other hand, almost fearfully clung to conformity in his attitude toward the world.

Hidden behind his seeming normality there lurked, however, a never-ceasing, gigantic strain in his battle for accomplishment and for the conscious and logical development of all the forces of his personality, his intellect, and his talent—a Faustian struggle for perfection. If the distance between a fully developed intellect and its origins, i.e., the educational foundations received during its childhood and early youth, were measurable, it would be phantastically large in the case of Brahms. What his parental home and his formal education—he never went beyond primary school—had to offer was but a bare minimum for intellectual subsistence. Yet as a mature man he had not only an encyclopedic knowledge of his own field, surpassing that of any trained music scholar at the time, but also a general education that in breadth and solidity was second to none.

When, barely twenty years old, he embarked on his first

venture into the world, he was a timid young man who was somewhat withdrawn in his behavior but whose appearance, it seems, had something appealing about it. Joseph Wilhelm von Wasielewski, who met him during the summer of 1853, described him as an "attractive, blond-haired youth." Slender, with shining blue eyes, he appeared to be of an almost girl-like delicacy, an impression further heightened by his high-pitched voice. Brahms evidently had suffered some vocal disturbance during adolescence, and his voice never attained full equilibrium in the masculine register. Even in later years it tended to break when he was excited, although, according to his biographer, Max Kalbeck, he finally brought it under control by determined exercising. Hans von Bülow, at first skeptical, wrote to his mother after having made Brahms's acquaintance: "I have gotten to know Robert Schumann's young prophet pretty well; he has been here [with Joachim in Hanover] for two days and spent all his time with us. A very lovable, candid soul who really shows something of God's grace—in the good sense of the word —in his talent."

Blond Johannes was a romanticist: Novalis, Brentano, E. T. A. Hoffmann, and Jean Paul were his idols. And his early works, those which he submitted to Schumann, were romanticism in its purest form. Romanticism in art, just as *Sturm und Drang*, is basically a phenomenon of puberty; it is the natural expression of youth and has a youthful and spontaneous effect, so long as it conforms to the artist's status as a youth and so long as it goes hand in hand with genuine freshness of invention and intensity of expression. The romanticism of Schubert, Weber, and Schumann is incomparably charming and natural, while that of Liszt is already in danger of turning rancid. Wagner found his way out of the romantic extravagance of his

Lohengrin, which came perilously close to Liszt's manner, into a mode of composition that was tightened and fortified by polyphony into the style of *Der Ring des Nibelungen* and *Die Meistersinger.* In his early years Brahms knew neither Liszt nor Wagner nor, for that matter, Schumann or Chopin. He had been brought up very conservatively by his teacher Marxsen. "Only since my absence from Hamburg," he wrote Joachim, "and especially during my stay in Mehlen [in the summer of 1853] did I get to know and worship Schumann's works. I feel like doing penance to him for this." It was understandable that after Schumann's sensational article Brahms was widely regarded as his pupil and disciple and also that, as a result, he was exposed to certain animosities and prejudices. His friend of later years, Theodor Billroth, the celebrated surgeon who, while working in Zürich, became the amateur music critic of the *Neue Zürcher Zeitung,* mentioned Schumann's article in connection with the performance of one of Brahms's works and added: "This inspired annunciation, which is by no means free of excessive enthusiasm, probably did Brahms more harm than good. Not that it would have led him into wrong paths or impeded his further development, as might easily have been the case with many another young artist, but it can readily be seen into what a vulnerable position it has placed him in the eyes of a large segment of the public."

A character is steeled by the resistance it encounters. Young Johannes soon outgrew his girl-like delicacy; he became cool and critical, and learned to see the world as it is. His personality and behavior soon were no longer to everyone's taste. Even Joachim, who loved him dearly, perceived that his friend was not always "soft as snow." In a letter of 1854 to Gisela von Arnim he wrote:

27

With Brahms, who stayed with me for a few days, sleeping on the black couch, I could not feel perfectly at ease, even though I again recognized his good, even extraordinary, qualities. . . . Brahms is the most intransigeant egotist imaginable, although he himself does not realize it. Everything oozes out of his sanguine nature quite spontaneously, but at times with a lack of consideration (not a lack of reticence, which would suit me fine!) that causes injury because it betrays uncouthness. . . . He recognizes the weaknesses of people with whom he deals, and he exploits them. . . . All he craves is to indulge without interference in his music and his faith in a more sublime world of phantasy, and his manner of keeping all the unhealthy sensations and imaginary sufferings of others at arm's length borders on sheer genius. He is unwilling to make even the slightest sacrifice of his intellectual inclinations: he does not wish to play in public—even though he makes divine music—simply because of his disregard for the public and because of laziness. I have never heard piano playing (with the possible exception of Liszt's) that satisfied me as completely as his—so airy and clear, so blessedly cool and innocent of all passion. Also, his compositions, so rich and ruthlessly rejecting all earthly woes, are such an effortless game in the most complex disguise. Never have I encountered such talent. He has surpassed me by far.

And two years later:

I consider myself fortunate to be able to do him greater justice. Poor old Schumann in his enthusiasm showed more courage than all those who mocked his prophetic guise. . . . Brahms has two personalities: one predominantly of childlike genius (it is to this one that, because I love it more than I can say, I begrudge not a single one of your thoughts) and the other of demoniac cunning which, with an icy surface, suddenly breaks forth in a pedantic, prosaic compulsion to dominate. Perhaps, as he gets more recognition, the latter will gradually vanish and will be used by him only as defensive shell when necessity arises.

The depth of insight shown by this judgment is astonishing, since, although far more mature and experienced, Joachim was but two years older than Brahms. Anton Rubinstein, who had no immediate incentive to regard Brahms with sympathy, judged him less favorably. "As for Brahms," he wrote Liszt, "I find it difficult to describe accurately the impression he made on me. For the drawing room he is not graceful enough, for the concert hall not fiery enough; for the countryside he is not primitive enough, for the city not cultured enough. I have but little faith in such natures."

In later years the paths of the two artists crossed frequently—in Baden-Baden at Clara Schumann's and also in Vienna, where Rubinstein was in a certain sense in direct competition with Brahms as pianist, conductor, and composer, even though Rubinstein's accomplishments as pianist surpassed all his others, just as the compositions did in the case of Brahms. There was never a close approach between the two.

Brahms rejected at all times and with abrupt obstinacy anyone who was alien to his nature. This included Rubinstein as well as Liszt. Just as he met both Joachim and Schumann with open heart and overflowing sentiment, so he withdrew into himself at his first encounter with Liszt in the Altenburg. If his reaction at that time was purely instinctive, he was soon to be in a position to justify it to himself; and his rejection of everything for which Liszt stood remained with him for life.

It now becomes necessary to touch upon the disagreeable subject of musical politics in the 1850's, when Brahms entered the scene. Franz Liszt, the greatest and most brilliant virtuoso of his time, had grown weary of the nomadic life when he established permanent residence in Weimar in 1848 and assumed the musical leadership of the court opera house and court orchestra. His ambition as composer had up to that time remained unfulfilled. He himself considered as byproduct of his pianistic activities whatever he had contributed to the virtuoso literature of his instrument. Yet he did believe himself destined to creative production in the grand manner. In addition he felt a call to serve, both as music director and opera conductor, the trends in which he believed. Tireless as a propagandist, always eager to foster any new talent that seemed remarkable to him, he established in Weimar the headquarters of a "Neo-German school" whose constantly re-emphasized goal was to liberate music from formalistic narrowness into a realm of poetic expression. His own chief contribution toward that goal was his twelve symphonic poems, composed during the Weimar period, in which he aimed to replace the abstract, classical principle of form with a free structure compatible with the poetic argument. This had been tried years before by Berlioz, who in this respect was Liszt's primary inspiration. Liszt had welcomed Wagner's first musicodramatic works with enthusiasm. In 1850 he staged the world première of *Lohengrin* while Wagner, who in 1849 had been involved in the revolutionary events in Dresden, lived as a political exile in Zürich. The performance made an extraordinary impression and had the most far-reaching consequences for the composer, whose works gradually gained ground in Germany at a time when, because of his stay abroad, he was without direct contact with German musical life. It was during this period that Wagner published his controversial articles on esthetics and cultural politics: *Art and Revolution, The Work of Art of the Future, Opera and Drama, Art and Climate,* and *Judaism in Music.* Their general impact should not be overestimated—the public interested in these subjects was not numerous—but they did

furnish an intellectual and esthetic argument for the movement headed by Liszt. The phrase "Music of the Future"
which was coined by him, became the device, and the
Neue Zeitschrift für Musik, founded by Schumann but
now edited by Franz Brendel, became the mouthpiece of
the group. Wagner and Liszt were probably the first to
utilize modern methods of publicity systematically for
propaganda purposes in the field of music. The literature
devoted to their cause would fill a small library. Hanslick,
its most determined adversary, probably did not exagger-
ate when he wrote in 1862: "Liszt's and Wagner's compositions have the force of military commands. As soon as
any work by one of these gentlemen appears, a small literature of explanatory articles, brochures, etc. follows in its
footsteps."

It will be readily understood that under such circumstances Schumann's article about Brahms, which the journal could not possibly reject, contained a good deal that
hardly corresponded to its basic party line—the more so
since Schumann had distinctly divorced himself from it
long before. A few months previously when Brahms, together with Reményi, paid his visit at the Altenburg, Liszt
certainly had no reason for receiving him other than with
the utmost hospitality, especially since Brahms arrived
with a recommendation from Joachim who, while concertmaster in Weimar, had belonged to his circle. What happened on that occasion can only be conjectured in very
broad outlines; Brahms never expressed himself on the
subject. As far as can be determined from contemporary
reports, Brahms, timid and nervous, declined to sit down
at the piano, whereupon Liszt put one of the manuscripts
which Brahms had brought along, the Scherzo in E-flat
minor, on the piano with the remark: "Well, in that
case I'll have to play it myself," which he proceeded to do

31

with bravura, to the admiration of everyone present. This incident recalls a similar one told by a friend and pupil of Liszt's, Count Géza von Zichy, one-armed pianist and composer of Hungarian nationalist operas, in his memoirs about his first encounter with Liszt. He had brought, for purposes of criticism, a ballade of his own composition which Liszt immediately sight-read from the manuscript not only with incredible virtuosity but with the most brilliant additions and embellishments. The young composer, beside himself with admiration, was rendered supremely happy by Liszt's remark: "I know that this was what you had in mind." If Liszt had attempted anything of this sort with Brahms, he would have been sadly mistaken. Anyone who at the age of eighteen is capable of writing a piece like the E-flat minor Scherzo—this was the very earliest of the works then published by Brahms—is beyond the stage where he can be told, no matter by whom, what he had had in mind. But quite aside from such a purely hypothetical construction, the negative attitude displayed by young Johannes appears entirely understandable. Over against Liszt's genuine kindness and friendliness, there were also his glitter as an elegant man of the world and his somewhat histrionic manner of putting himself in the limelight, both of which went thoroughly against the grain of the young fellow. The story that Brahms once fell asleep while Liszt played his recently composed Piano Sonata in B minor, as reported by an eye witness, the American pianist William Mason, may well have been invented but, if true, might have been interpreted as a not necessarily demonstrative action on the part of the young man, weary as he was from his travels. His critical attitude would have found expression in a rather more embarrassed manner had he stayed awake during the performance, because this sonata contains everything that to him was distasteful in Liszt's music, in which he was unable to discern anything but false pathos, formless improvisation, vacant invention, and that which he was wont to describe by the disrespectful word "swindle." Thus he wrote Clara Schumann from Hamburg in 1860: "Yesterday Otten was the first to introduce works by Liszt into a decent concert: *Loreley*, a song, and *Leonore*, by Bürger, with melodramatic accompaniment. I was perfectly furious. I expect that he will bring forth still another symphonic poem before this winter is over. The disease spreads more and more, and in any event lengthens and ruins the ass's ears of audience and young composers alike." In 1869 he wrote from Vienna to Hermann Levi: "The public here may well be praiseworthy but, being a child, it needs strict discipline; its schoolmasters, our worthy colleagues, disclosed their utter shabbiness so completely at the new swindle by Liszt that I hid my head in shame." (Liszt's oratorio *Saint Elizabeth* had been performed under Herbeck's direction.) And on another occasion, in a letter to Reinthaler written in Vienna in December, 1871: "On the thirtieth we will have to live through Liszt's *Christus*. The whole thing is so monumentally boring, stupid, and senseless that I can't understand how all the necessary swindle will be carried off this time."

On the other hand Brahms remained full of enthusiasm for Liszt as a pianist. "Whoever has not heard Liszt," he said to Kalbeck, "cannot even speak of piano playing. He comes first and then for a long space nobody follows. His playing has something unique, incomparable, and inimitable." In his opinion, Liszt's unquestionable genius was directed too late, and probably never with the necessary concentration, toward creative work. Speaking to Eusebius Mandyczewski, he once exclaimed: "The prodigy, the itinerant virtuoso, and the man of fashion ruined the composer before he had even started." What he resented even more than Liszt's music was his influence on the younger generation of progressive musicians. It is not easy to give the layman an idea of the things which were at stake—of the esthetic principles to which the progressive segment of the musical world subscribed a hundred years ago. How some of the artistic doctrines of our time will appear a hundred years hence, remains to be seen. A certain distance is necessary for seeing things in their proper perspective; this is true of the absurd as well as of the sublime. The numerous scores of symphonic poems which at that time came into being under Liszt's ægis and under his benevolent protection are now gathering thick layers of dust and cobwebs, and the names of their creators are forgotten. Today it can scarcely be understood how, for example, the following—the description of the movements of Joachim Raff's symphony *To my Fatherland,* which in 1863 was awarded a prize by the Society of the Friends of Music in Vienna—could be printed in a program without evoking mirth:

> *First movement:* Allegro. Image of the German character: ability to soar to great heights; trend toward introspection; mildness and courage as contrasts that touch and interpenetrate in many ways; overwhelming desire to be pensive.
>
> *Second movement:* Allegro molto vivace. The outdoors: through German forests with horns a-winding; through glades with the sounds of folk music.
>
> *Third movement:* Larghetto. Return to the domestic hearth, transfigured by the muses and by love.
>
> *Fourth movement:* Allegro drammatico. Frustrated desire to lay a foundation for unity in the Fatherland.
>
> *Fifth movement:* Larghetto—allegro trionfale. Plaint, renewed soaring.

The absurdity does not consist so much in the writing of

music for this type of program but rather in the unshakable doctrine that one cannot and must not make music
but with such a subject tailored for the purpose if one
wishes to be taken seriously as an artist and that, with the
emphasis placed on the subject, the musical substance as
such becomes secondary. Out of an essentially justified
reaction against the superficial formalism employed by
moderately talented scribblers, there inevitably arose a
theory which threatened to destroy any vestige of inherited
feeling for form which may still have survived.

It was necessary to deal with this subject in some detail
because it bears on a state of feud in which Brahms was
involved for many years, and because it was responsible
for the only action in Brahms's life which must be branded
completely ill-advised, imprudent, and futile. Evidently
his feelings and oversensitivity must have played a part in
impairing his usually mature and cool judgment. "My fingers often itch," he wrote to Joachim, "to start a scrap and
to write anti-Liszt articles. But who am I? I can't even
write greetings to my dearest friend because I don't know
what to write—or whatever other excuses my inherent laziness dictates to me." Joachim shared his feelings completely but was more circumspect: "The folks in Liszt's
camp are far too well versed in writing, too much on
guard, too coarse, and too sophistical. Liszt knows only too
well how to arouse enthusiasm and how to exploit it for
his own ends; consequently an honest fight with these
bacchantes and sycophants is not possible. And it is really
not necessary. Their uncouth fanaticism and their false
harmonies will dig their own graves for them."

Brahms now had a bug in his ear; the matter pursued
him constantly. And Joachim at long last agreed to join
him in organizing the issuance of a public declaration by
all the opponents of Liszt's clique. This declaration, drawn

up in March, 1860, by Brahms, Joachim, J. O. Grimm, and Bernhard Scholz, reads as follows:

The undersigned have long observed with dismay the behavior of a certain group whose mouthpiece is Brendel's *Neue Zeitschrift für Musik.*

The above-mentioned journal constantly spreads the notion that all serious, striving musicians are basically in agreement with the party line pursued by it, that in the compositions of the leaders of said party they recognize works of artistic value, and that the contest for and against the so-called Music of the Future has been concluded, especially in northern Germany, in its favor.

The undersigned consider it their duty to protest against such a distortion of the facts and to declare that, for their own part, they do not recognize the principles represented by Brendel's journal. They can only deplore and regret as being contrary to the innermost essence of music the productions of the leaders as well as followers of the so-called Neo-German school, who partly apply these principles in actual practice and partly force the adoption of ever new and more outrageous theories.

It was planned to collect two dozen signatures of prominent musicians, including those of Niels Gade, Robert Volkmann, Woldemar Bargiel, Carl Reinecke, Ferdinand Hiller, Carl Grädener, and Theodor Kirchner. Quite aside from the lack of judgment shown in this entire enterprise, it was incredibly careless to circulate this sort of thing in writing. Because of an indiscretion which has never been fully cleared up, the entire declaration was printed in the Berlin *Echo* with only the signatures of the four proponents affixed to it. Outside of the embarrassment that ensued, the only result was that the opposition was nettled in the extreme; and Brahms was the one who had to bear the consequences. It was a wholesome lesson for him;

never again did he write a single word for publication. What he had to say he said in his music.

This singular episode was only a symptom of the irritable uneasiness under which he labored during his Hamburg years. His inner development continued unabated. He matured to manhood and mastership, and he worked tirelessly to fill the gaps in his general education, with a constantly increasing awareness of everything that came within his horizon. He was an avid reader. As a conductor he had gained a good deal of experience while in Detmold and also in Hamburg where he directed a women's chorus. Still, he felt like a fish out of water. His music, honored in full recognition of its value by his closest friends, such as Joachim and Clara Schumann, did not evoke any discernible response elsewhere. He was isolated. The fact that the "musicians of the future" produced more noise than music did not alter the circumstance that to him the "musicians of the present" around him, such as Hiller, Scholz, Bargiel, or Volkmann, seemed equally inadequate. On the occasion of Ludwig Spohr's death he wrote to his friend Berta Porubszky in October, 1859:

Spohr is dead! He was probably the last of those who still belonged to an artistic period more satisfying than the one through which we now suffer. In those days one might well have looked about eagerly after each fair to see what new and beautiful things had arrived from one composer or another. Now things are different. For months and years I have hardly seen a single collection of music that gave me pleasure, but a great many that almost caused me physical pain. At no time has any art been so mistreated as is now our beloved music. Let us hope that somewhere in obscurity something better is emerging, for otherwise our epoch would go down in the annals of art as a pit for trash.

Brahms was not suited to be a party leader, since no

37

party existed which he could have led with a good conscience. For this reason it became a vital necessity for him to escape from the narrow circle in which he felt himself entrapped and to go out into the wide world which opened up for him in Vienna. For the first time in his life he had the sensation of being appreciated to an extent commensurate with his merits, both by the Viennese musicians and by the public at large. What he brought with him already represented a rich selection of significant works of all types. He arrived as an accomplished personality, an artist of mature characteristics. It is not difficult to be received in Vienna with open hospitality; the fact, however, that Brahms took root there, as Beethoven had done seventy years previously, attests to a genuinely mutual sympathy. As Beethoven was honored by the aristocracy, who were at that time of decisive influence in musical life, so now it was the educated, open-minded middle class who honored the guest as a superior musician, a genuine artist, and an interesting and stimulating personality and who made his life in Vienna pleasant and comfortable. And, just like Beethoven, he did not always make it easy for his friends to remain friends. Brahms was entirely egocentric—one will recall Joachim's sharp criticism—and in no wise inclined to make concessions or sacrifices. Billroth wrote on one occasion: "He makes it difficult for anyone to remain fond of him." Brahms was a keen observer, always alert to his own advantage, and had already acquired a sophistication which served him well in his struggle for existence, especially since he invariably maintained and defended his standpoint with unshakable firmness.

For the first time he made friends with musicians who were in the "enemy camp." He wrote to Joachim in December, 1862:

Wagner is here, and I shall probably be considered a Wagnerian largely because of the contradictions to which any intelligent person must be provoked by the irresponsible manner in which musicians here rail against him. I am also particularly in touch with Cornelius and Tausig, who claim not to be, nor ever to have been, followers of Liszt and who moreover can accomplish more with their little fingers than other musicians with their heads and all their fingers.

Of his relationship with Wagner at that time we will speak later on. Carl Tausig, a Liszt pupil and a brilliant pianist, was an excellent partner: Brahms played his own just completed F Minor Sonata for two pianos with him at a concert at the Vienna *Singakademie*. Competition with Tausig stimulated him not only to renew his piano practice, which he had been wont to neglect, but also to write his most brilliant piano composition, the *Variations on a Theme of Paganini*. The fact that his friendship with Peter Cornelius cooled off rather soon is to be regretted for both of them. Evidently the difference in temperament of the two was too great. The delicate and very retiring Cornelius, who lacked all energy and initiative, made a meager living in Vienna as music teacher. The general public took no notice of him in any way, although he was one of the most sensitive and original musicians of his time. No doubt he resented the rough and unconcerned manner with which Brahms was accustomed to look after his own interests. "With one person I am now definitely through," he wrote in his diary, "and that is Mr. Johannes Brahms. He is a completely selfish and autocratic individual. I have no longer gone to visit him this year [1864]. He came to me. May he walk the path of his glory! I will henceforth neither disturb nor accompany him."

The beardless Brahms was described, at thirty years of age, as still very youthful in appearance. His friends were vastly amused when he was once refused admittance to the gambling casino in Baden-Baden because he seemed too young to the doorman.

The Swiss writer Josef Viktor Widmann, who later became an intimate friend of Brahms, described his reaction when he first saw him on the concert stage in Zürich in 1865:

Brahms, then in his thirty-third year, immediately gave me the impression of a gigantic personality, not alone because of his powerful piano playing with which no virtuoso technique, no matter how brilliant, could be compared, but also through his personal appearance. It is true that the short, somewhat stocky figure, the almost straw-blond hair, and the protruding lower lip which imparted an almost sarcastic expression to his beardless face, were conspicuous features which might rather displease. His whole presence, however, seemed suffused with power. The broad leonine chest, the Herculean shoulders, the mighty head which he occasionally threw back with an energetic toss while playing, the pensive, well-formed forehead radiant as if by some inner illumination, and the Germanic eyes which sparkled a miraculous fire from between their blond lashes—all betrayed an artistic personality which seemed charged to its very finger tips with the power of genius.

Ten years later and at the height of his fame he was described by Georg Henschel, the celebrated concert singer, conductor, and composer of lieder:

His solid frame, the healthy, dark-brown color of his face, the full hair, just a little sprinkled with gray, all make him appear the very image of strength and vigor. He walks about here [on vacation in Rügen] just as he pleases, generally with his waistcoat unbuttoned and his hat in his hand, always with clean linen, but without collar or necktie. These he dons at the *table d'hôte* only. His whole appearance vividly recalls some of the portraits of Beethoven. His appetite is excellent. He eats with great gusto and, in the evening, regularly drinks his three glasses of beer, never omitting, however, to finish with his beloved coffee.

Henschel also tells an amusing anecdote particularly characteristic of Brahms. The occasion was a music festival in Cologne. At an informal get-together of half a dozen prominent composers in a bistro after the concert, one of them exclaimed, pointing toward Henschel: "Now just look at that lucky fellow Henschel! He can both sing and compose, and we," describing with his hands a circle which included Brahms, "we can compose only." Instantly from Brahms, whilst his countenance bore the expression of the most perfect innocence, came, "And not even that." One can almost see the sarcastic lower lip so frequently mentioned in descriptions of his appearance. But he was probably not often in a position of taking one of his colleagues seriously.

Since his financial situation vouchsafed him the necessary liberty and independence, his whole life became organized to serve the exclusive purpose of creating. As far as his personal needs were concerned, he lived as modestly as at the time of his youth. But he had to have quiet, comfort, and free access to the outdoors. In Vienna he frequented with preference the ordinary taverns, the folksy eating places which served simple and wholesome food. He was sufficiently well treated with fancy dishes when he was invited out. And his sentiments as son and brother were just as unassuming as his material requirements. To him a family signified a bourgeois patriarchal unit into which one is born and to which one gives no further thought. He did have tender feelings for his mother, whose death in 1865, even though it may not have been the immediate incentive, no doubt helped to inspire his *German Requiem*. In its fifth movement, which was added later, the phrase "I will comfort ye as a mother comforteth" is, in its delicate yet virile feeling, one of the most glorious moments in a work rich in magnificence. Much in the emotional life of this skeptical, modern human being was of elementary simplicity, just as his lifelong preference for folk music, the influence of which extended deep into his soul, complemented the often intricate and unusual structure of his melodies. His relationship with his father cannot be characterized better than he himself did it in his letter of congratulation on receiving the news that the old man was contemplating remarriage:

Dearest father, when I opened your letter and found three handwritten pages, I looked with some trepidation for the news that caused you to write that much. I was indeed greatly surprised that I had not thought of it before. Dearest father, a thousand blessings and the warmest wishes for your well-being accompany you from here. How gladly would I sit at your side, press your hand, and wish you as much happiness as you deserve, which would be more than enough for one earthly life time. This step is nothing but a handsome testimonial to yourself, and tells us how much you have merited the happiest of family lives.

Later on he remained on the best of terms with his stepmother and throughout his life generously provided for her and her son from a previous marriage, as he did for his own brother and sister. In view of his own modest requirements, his increasing prosperity afforded him pleasure mainly because it permitted him the luxury of adequately looking after his relatives and at the same time quietly doing a great deal of good for others. Any friend, such as Stockhausen or Theodor Kirchner, who, because of old age or sickness, found himself in difficulties, could count on him at all times. Clara Schumann, who had great worries concerning her children and grandchildren, had to allow him to press a birthday present of fifteen thousand marks upon her; he would do no less, in spite of embarrassed protests.

He was no psychologist, and the recipients of his largesse did not always really enjoy the good things he had intended for them. It is touching to read of the joy with which Brahms reported to Joachim about an excursion through the Alps with his father, who had at last accepted his invitation to come to Vienna and to whom he proudly wanted to show the beauty of the mountains (Vienna, August 1867):

Through my father's visit and through the little trip which we undertook together, I experienced the greatest happiness I have known in a long time. Not the least of this happiness was the enjoyment my father derived from everything new that he saw. Until then he had never even seen a mountain, let alone looked down one. You can well imagine how great his astonishment was. Also it was by no means unimportant to him that he saw the Emperor, first here with the Pasha, and then again in Salzburg with Napoleon. Now I am again settled down and will remain here quietly, but my soul is refreshed like a body after a bath. My good father hasn't the slightest idea how much good he has done me.

He actually succeeded in dragging his father up the Schafberg in the Upper Austrian Alps, which after all is almost 6000 feet high. An eye witness quotes the conversation on the summit: "Oh, father! Isn't it magnificent here? The air! And the view!" But the old man only nodded and said: "Yes, but my dear Johannes, never do that to me again."

It is curious to think how long Brahms toyed with the idea of getting permanent employment, even at the time of his greatest prosperity. In spite of his unfavorable experiences in Vienna at the *Singakademie* and at the Society of

43

the Friends of Music, which should have taught him a lesson about the disadvantages of such a position, there evidently existed a deeply rooted compulsion to find a definite sphere of activity as a nucleus for his work, as all his famous predecessors of the past generation had done. In this connection it is perhaps not irrelevant to mention the enormous debt which the development of musical life in Germany in the first half of the nineteenth century owed to those great musicians who, in addition to their creative work, devoted their best efforts to the burgeoning opera and concert life in the medium-sized cities, e.g. Weber and later Wagner in Dresden, Spohr in Kassel, Mendelssohn in Leipzig, Marschner in Hanover, and of course Liszt in Weimar. The court theatres and the community concert associations provided the financial means and the opportunities for performance, while the musical enthusiasm and the ambition of prominent musicians furnished the vital energy necessary for giving such institutions an ideal artistic climate. According to the opinions prevailing when Brahms grew up, only this type of practical activity could give an artist a legitimate place in society, but on the other hand part of this social responsibility lay in guiding the public performance of music—and thereby the audience which had confidence in him—toward genuinely artistic goals. It is a paradox that Brahms, who always referred with extreme misgivings to the commercial value of his music, became the first composer of serious music to whom a flourishing economy, a public eager to buy, and an increasingly lively publishing industry were able to offer the independence necessary to live for his creative work without being disturbed by such time-consuming side occupations. It is understandable that at first he could not conceive of such an ideal situation, which no one save a few successful opera composers had ever enjoyed before. Thus he always showed interest in positions that were about to become vacant. At times he even became involved in negotiations, which fortunately never achieved results— fortunately because they could only have led to mutual disappointment, for Brahms had by then become far too great for such a relationship of dependence. A letter written by him to Theodor Billroth in September, 1876, refers to an affair of this type; it was in connection with an opening as music director in Düsseldorf:

You will have heard from Faber that I have received a call to Düsseldorf. I have wished so long and so ardently for such a position, for regulated activity, that I now must give it serious consideration. I am reluctant to leave Vienna, and I have a great many objections to Düsseldorf. You will no doubt say that every affair has its good side, too. Because of this one, I made up my mind to come out with a symphony [his First Symphony, which for a long time he had hesitated to publish]. I thought I'd have to produce something decent as a farewell to the Viennese. I dislike writing far too much, else I would now go into detail about how the manner and form of the invitation to Düsseldorf pleased me very much. . . . My principal reasons for not going are of a rather childish character and must remain secret. Perhaps the good eating places in Vienna, perhaps the poor, uncouth manners of the Rhinelanders (especially those of Düsseldorf), and—and—in Vienna one can remain a bachelor without difficulty; in a small city a bachelor is a caricature. I no longer wish to marry, and yet I do have some cause to fear the gentle sex.

Two years later he still inquired of Elisabeth von Herzogenberg (the Herzogenbergs lived in Leipzig at the time) about the post of cantor at St. Thomas'. An amusing element entered into the negotiations, since in Leipzig he was under suspicion of leading a "dissolute life." In this connection he wrote to his publisher Fritz Simrock:

For years I have had the habit of saying, when I leave the restaurant earlier than others, "I must now go to Schwender or to Sperl [popular amusement spots in Vienna]." Perhaps once a year or so I might actually get there, but only together with old man Lachner or Nottebohm. Now I have gotten used to saying instead, "I am going to the Wagner Club." I hope this will rehabilitate me.

The Herzogenbergs anxiously waved him off; Leipzig did not seem to them the right environment for their revered friend. And thus the matter fizzled out, as had so many before it. He had long become resigned as far as such plans were concerned when, sixty years old by then, he was offered the directorship of the Hamburg Philharmonic Concerts, once so passionately coveted. In his letter of reply to Senator Scheumann of Hamburg, the old anger about the slight of long ago burst forth once more:

There is but little that I have desired so long and so ardently in its time—that is, at the right time. It has taken a long time before I got used to the idea of having to go along other paths. If things had gone according to my wishes, I would perhaps celebrate an anniversary with you today; but in that case, you would now still have to look around for a younger capable talent. May you find him now, and may he serve your cause with as much good will, tolerable competence, and devotion as would have

Your respectful and obedient servant,
J. BRAHMS

Aside from a few exceptional cases, Brahms was surprisingly sure of his instincts in whatever decisions he made. In other words, his experience as a thinking person who was certain of himself enabled him, in all difficult situations, to do whatever most closely harmonized with his character and his goals. "Mrs. Schumann told me today," Joachim wrote him in April, 1875, "that you are giving up your position in Vienna. What a pity! But you always know best what to do. No doubt you are doing the right thing. . . ." One thing he definitely did not know: indecision.

Just as more recent impressions always tend to obliterate earlier ones, so the image which the world preserves of any famous figure is that of its later years. Brahms's outer appearance changed so radically in his middle forties that it is hard to find a connecting link between the face of the romantic youth at the time of the *German Requiem* and the *Song of Destiny* and the prophet's head of the symphonic writer. This transition was well described by Henschel, who came to Vienna on a concert tour in the fall of 1878:

At the end of the concert we were receiving, in the artists' room, the congratulations of friends, when suddenly I saw a man unknown to me, rather stout, of medium height, with long hair and full beard, coming. In a very deep and hoarse voice he introduced himself "Musikdirektor Müller," making a very stiff and formal bow, which I was on the point of returning with equal gravity, when, an instant later, we all found ourselves heartily laughing at the perfect success of Brahms's disguise, for, of course, it was he.

To his friend Bernhard Scholz, now musical director in Breslau, Brahms broke the news more gently: "But the worst is that I will arrive with a large beard. Prepare your wife for a terrible one, for nothing that has been suppressed for so long can possibly be beautiful." Joseph Viktor Widmann also tells of his surprise at the metamorphosis: "I was so taken aback by the unexpected appearance of the Jovian head that I blurted out a request to know the reason for this change. 'With a shaved chin, people take you either for an actor or for a priest,' Brahms

47

replied, contentedly stroking his mightily cascading waves of beard."

The desire to preserve an incognito may well have been a deciding motive; in a world as hirsute as that of Brahms's time, he apparently felt uncomfortably conspicuous with his smooth-shaven face. Against this rather obvious interpretation one cannot help feeling that somehow the beard was an inherent part of his broad dignity and Olympian grandeur. It is worthy of note that he himself referred to it as having been "long suppressed," as though he sensed that the beard had been part of him for a long time. With it he now definitely became "Herr *von* Brahms" in Vienna; restaurant employees there are very apt to bestow nobility on anyone whose appearance is sufficiently dignified.

His doubtful reputation with respect to Schwender and Sperl was not entirely without justification insofar as he liked to frequent popular places of amusement. Ever since his first visit to Vienna he adored the Prater, not only for its lush meadows and glades but also for the Wurstelprater with its shooting galleries, side shows, and merry-go-rounds. He was a regular patron of the Prater coffee houses, especially the Czarda, where a gypsy band held forth. It is odd that the solemn North German, who never quite lost his Hamburg accent, grew so fond of the brighter and friendlier people and landscape of the South that he never wanted to live anywhere but in Austria. "When I cross the Austrian border on my way home, I always feel like embracing every railway conductor," he said to Mandyczewski. Similar outbursts were frequently heard from him. But he was particularly enamored of the population in Upper Austria, whom he came to know at his favorite summer vacation homes of later years. Thus he wrote to Clara Schumann from Ischl in 1891: "I can report only good things about myself. It is extremely beautiful and agreeable here, and, as I have said many times before, the lovable and well-mannered people here are thoroughly to my taste." And to Elisabeth von Herzogenberg: "The fact that half of Vienna comes this way does not disturb me one bit. After all, I do not dislike Vienna in the least. Now if it were half of Berlin or Leipzig, I should run away. But half of Vienna is attractive and can show itself." And in another letter to Clara: "There are no more delightful people or children anywhere. I never go out without a joyful heart nor without the sensation of having had a refreshing drink when I pat a few of the darling children on the head. In Baden I rejoice in the people, but never in Bavaria and even less in Switzerland. I speak of those people I encounter in the streets—who to me can be far more important than the majority of those I meet in homes. I am grave enough at home and am glad to see a friendly face when I go out. And now I think of yours, the friendliest and most beloved of all, and send greetings with all my heart." It is always wonderful when such a loving tone rings out, be it in his prose or in his music.

The image of the master, as the world knew it at the time of his greatest fame, took its final form when he was in his fifties. With uncommon clarity Widmann describes Brahms and his manner of living from 1886 to 1888, when the composer established his summer residence near Thun. Brahms was in continuous and intimate contact with him and his family, close by in Berne, and the poet wrote:

Wide awake at the first break of dawn, he brewed his first breakfast on his Viennese coffee machine. A faithful lady admirer from Marseilles furnished him excellent mocha for it, and in such abundance that from the very beginning he was able to share it with my household, thereby indulging in the pleasure of being simultaneously host and guest while visiting us in Berne. The morning hours were devoted to work which,

49

in his quarters in Thun where a large arbor and a lodging of several spacious rooms permitted him to walk about pensively and undisturbed by anyone, turned out particularly well. . . . For his noon meals Brahms went to some outdoor restaurant whenever the weather permitted. He always disliked eating at the *table d'hôte* and avoided it whenever possible for the simple reason that he did not like to get dressed up. He felt most comfortable in a striped wool shirt without collar and without a necktie. Even his soft felt hat was more often carried in his hand than worn on his head. When on Saturday of each week he would come to Berne to spend the week end with me, usually staying until Tuesday or even Wednesday, he would carry a leather traveling case which resembled an itinerant mineralogist's specimen bag filled with rocks, but which primarily contained the books I had lent him the previous week, which he brought back to be exchanged for others. In bad weather an old, brownish gray plaid, held together in front by an enormous pin, hung over his shoulders and completed his queer, unstylish appearance, causing people to stare at him in astonishment.

Hanslick, in his memoirs, furnishes a few supplementary details:

Brahms is an entirely self-reliant character who, although revered and beloved by many, seems to need no one for his own heart's satisfaction. Whatever was harsh or at times even repellingly abrupt in his Nordic nature was softened by the flowery breath of the Austrian landscape and environment and by the sunny smile of fortune and renown, but it never disappeared altogether. No one who knows Brahms well will resent his little inconsiderate acts, which occur whether he is in a good mood or bad. . . . He, who cannot put up with the slightest infringement of his personal freedom, might not have become the happiest of husbands but would definitely have been a most affectionate father. I have visited Brahms at his summer homes in Mürzzuschlag, in Ischl, and in Thun. Nowhere was there any little child who did not run toward the stocky gray-beard, or who did not wave at him from afar. . . . In addition to his good humor it is his robust health which constantly gives me renewed joy. He has already passed his sixtieth birthday, and yet he has never known the slightest sickness in all his life. He still goes on walking tours like a young student, and he sleeps like a baby.

As far as his attire was concerned, he always made himself as comfortable as possible. He no longer mended a tear in his trousers with sealing wax, as he had done in his youth (he once told Henschel about this). The solicitous Mrs. Truxa kept his wardrobe nicely in order. But his friends were by no means certain that he always wore a necktie underneath his beard, and it could happen that, while he was conducting, his trousers would begin to slide down because he had forgotten to button his suspenders.

Despite his instinctive preference for Austria he remained a confirmed German patriot. "It is hard to imagine vividly enough," Widmann tells us, "how deeply a really passionate patriotism took hold of this earnest man's soul." His years of development coincided with a period of increasing Austro-Prussian tension and rivalry within the loose-knit German Confederation. At that time the scion of the free Hanseatic city of Hamburg had no sympathy for the Prussian cause, and when open conflict erupted in 1866, he was equally critical of both sides. The patriotic fervor of 1870, however, engulfed him just as it did all Germans at the time, and his deep veneration for Bismarck, the unifier of the nation and the creator of the German Reich, stemmed from that period. "So great was my enthusiasm," he said to Henschel, "that, after the first great defeat, I was firmly resolved to join the army as a volun-

76019

teer, fully convinced that I should meet my old father there to fight side by side with me. Thank God it turned out differently." His contribution to German victory was his *Song of Triumph*, for chorus and orchestra, with texts from the Holy Scriptures; he might just as well have called it "a German *Te Deum*." This grandiose and, in many respects, remarkable work has almost entirely disappeared since the end of World War I for obvious reasons. It would be well worth resurrecting, even though it cannot be entirely divorced from its original purpose. True, its significance is surpassed by an appreciably simpler work which gives expression to an equally patriotic subject in a far calmer and less demonstrative manner: his *Fest- und Gedenksprüche*, for unaccompanied chorus, which Brahms dedicated in 1890 to Petersen, then burgomaster of Hamburg, in response to being nominated for honorary citizenship. It deserves a place alongside the most important *a capella* compositions of all time. We shall return to both works later on.

It is odd that Brahms remained the only one of the well-known musicians of his epoch who, aside from occasional trips to Italy which were devoted entirely to pleasure and recreation, steadfastly refused to travel abroad. His ignorance of foreign languages may well have been partly the reason, but on the whole it was probably some queer, old-fashioned terror of unknown surroundings, of public appearances in a strange environment—in other words, of any disturbance of his "comfort," a word that occurs again and again in his statements. He expressed himself as simply and convincingly as can be, when the question of an honorary doctorate at Cambridge came up again in 1892. At that time the same distinction had also been offered to his celebrated contemporary Verdi, who likewise politely declined it because he, twenty years older than Brahms, shied away from the trip to England, which he had frequently undertaken in younger years. Brahms wrote to Stanford, the Irish composer and professor of music at Cambridge University:

My dear and honored sir, I find it difficult to take pen in hand, for how can I speak of deep gratitude and yet say no? And still I am earnestly and sincerely thankful to you for your graciousness and to your university for the signal honor which it wishes to bestow upon me. But by next July the answer will still have to be no, even though today I would rather keep it from you as well as from myself and talk myself out of it. But please consider above all this: I cannot go to Cambridge without also going to London, and in London there is a great deal to see and to do—all this in beautiful midsummer when you also would undoubtedly prefer to take a walk with me along one of the lovely Italian lakes. I am certainly very much tempted to accept your invitation. Will it not be a very special kind of musical celebration? And would I not run the risk of being outdone and put to shame, as far as youthfulness and gratitude are concerned, by old man Verdi? But even if today I were to follow my inclination and promise to come, I know only too well that, when the time arrives, I would not possibly be able to make up my mind to undertake the trip and all that is inevitably connected with it.

It is regrettable that Brahms and Verdi never met. With all the differences in their artistic temperaments they still had much in common: manly fortitude, uncompromising convictions, and honesty of expression. Brahms, even though in later years he avoided going to the opera, was a sincere admirer of his Italian colleague, who probably never had an opportunity to hear a single note written by him. In England Brahms had a steadily growing following of admirers and enthusiasts, largely due to the tireless efforts of his friend Joachim, who spent several months there each year. But he remained adamant in his refusal to show himself there in person. Joachim beckoned: "Too bad that your antipathy toward foreign conditions keeps you away from here. Your music is known and admired here, and commands more respect than that of anyone else . . ." Brahms replied: "Many thanks for your kind remarks. It so happens that I much prefer being told of all these pretty and enjoyable things to seeing them for myself and having all the trouble that goes with it. . . . Even though I do not by any means underestimate the artistic accomplishments and joys of England, I still value my bit of independence, the fact that pounds sterling mean nothing to me, and that I can now comfortably think of a spring vacation in Sicily."

It is understandable that as a successful artist on whom riches and laurels had been lavishly bestowed, he became more or less indifferent to them. But even at an early age he was little inclined to make sacrifices for the vanities of life; this undoubtedly made him forever unsuited to court service. He could not stomach dependence. This was already true of him as a young man at the court in Detmold. During those days in 1861 he wrote to Clara Schumann: "You must have some idea of how enticing a position at this small court can be. It is possible for one to play really a lot of music for himself, but unfortunately one cannot be happy by himself indefinitely, and after a while the faces become repulsive. . . . One can enjoy the great outdoors alone, but when he makes music in a concert hall before an audience, he does not like to be lonesome either. . . ." His only closer connection with one of the German courts occurred in his later years when, through Hans von Bülow, he came into intimate artistic contact with the court orchestra at Meiningen. But even there, despite the most cordial and informal conduct of the duke and his wife, the Baroness von Heldburg, Brahms insisted on his independence. Replying to repeated invitations from the baroness to spend a summer at one of the ducal estates, he wrote her in 1887:

I imagine you must often consider me ungrateful or even disloyal, and in a certain sense you are justified. It is so when I am offered the benefits of your great and bountiful generosity and kindness. I know how to appreciate them with all my heart, as you have seen for yourself and as you cannot doubt. But often I must renounce them, and you cannot understand my reasons. Now let me confess that in such a case I am by no means disloyal, yet not entirely candid either. The really truthful answer will not come out because I do not like to speak of myself or of my idiosyncrasies. My confession is simple: I need complete solitude, not only to achieve my best but even to think of my work at all. This is part of my nature, but it can also be easily explained in another way: we "little ones" must learn at an early age that we have to renounce things, even with a heavy heart. . . . But now, with a new and larger composition [the Double Concerto for violin and cello] ready before me, I can take a little pride in myself and say: "I would never have written it if I had enjoyed life, no matter how much, on the Rhine or in Berchtesgaden [at the duke's estates]."

The simplicity and honesty in these lines, with which he shook himself free of the embarrassment of conventional court etiquette, are characteristic of him. He freely confesses that he has no time to waste, not even with these dear, noble, and generous souls. Mark the sovereign pride with which this prince includes himself among the "little ones," where by birth and origin he belongs!

It was in Meiningen in September, 1895, his last year of unbroken good health, that Brahms celebrated the greatest triumph of his life. Under the direction of Fritz Steinbach a music festival, based on Bülow's slogan of the "three great B's": Bach, Beethoven, and Brahms, was brought to a most grandiose perfection. His *Song of Triumph* took its place next to Bach's *St. Matthew Passion* and Beethoven's *Missa Solemnis*, his First Symphony and his Double Concerto next to Beethoven's Piano Concerto in E-flat major, and his chamber music next to that of Beethoven. Visitors from all parts of Europe had arrived to enjoy it. In honor of the festive occasion Brahms even appeared in white tie and tails, but he was already to be seen in this attire early in the morning. Changing for the concerts and gala receptions was too much for him: "If I am compelled to wear tails, I might as well do it right away in the morning so that I won't have to worry the rest of the day."

Shortly thereafter, in October, 1895, his *Song of Triumph* was performed, together with Beethoven's Ninth Symphony, at the opening concert of the newly constructed *Tonhalle* in Zürich, where his own portrait along with those of other giants of music looked down upon him from the ceiling. He had arrived at the summit of Parnassus while still alive, as but few before him.

But by that time he considered his life's work completed. During the summer of the preceding year his great anthology of German folk songs had been published. Significantly he called Clara Schumann's attention to the fact that one of the melodies, "Stealthily the moon is rising," had been used in his first piano sonata: "Did you notice that the very last of these songs also occurs in my opus 1? Did this give you any food for thought? It really does have significance: it represents the serpent that bites into its own tail; it says symbolically that the story is now finished, the circle closed." To Simrock he wrote similarly: "By the way, have you noticed that I have now expressly said farewell as a composer? The last of the folk songs and the same in my opus 1 represent the serpent that bites into its own tail, signifying with pretty symbolism that the story is now over."

His instinct, ever alert and ever true, did not mislead him in this. He did not want to face the truth and referred to a "little middle-class jaundice" when he was already desperately ill, maintaining the fiction of belief in his own recovery. But he knew that his hour had struck. He brought his house into order and destroyed whatever he was unwilling to leave to posterity. No trace of unpublished compositions has ever been found. With his mammon, as he called his store of wealth, he was less provident. His testamentary stipulations were juridically invalid, resulting in many years of litigation.

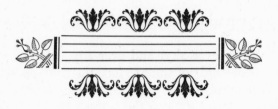

Friends

IN THE COMPLEX kaleidoscope of a character sketch, friends form an essential element. This is especially true in the case of Brahms, because he had a constant need for human contact, for exchange of ideas, and for personal relationships. This need was by no means a contradiction of his solitary habits as a creative worker and a bachelor; on the contrary, it was a necessary adjunct thereof. He had to have people around him as a counterpoise to help him recover from the ecstasies and visions of his productive labors. For this reason he was often seen in the society of others, and his correspondence with friends was extraordinarily abundant. The reader will already have noticed what an excellent letter writer he was, how beautifully precise and graphic his mode of expression, and how significant the substance of his communications remained de-

spite terseness and haste, for he hated all superfluous
expenditure of time. The fact that he did not always express himself clearly is due to his character, to a certain
diffidence which prevented him from showing his true
feelings. At times, when he quite incidentally alluded to
something as unimportant even though to him it was actually of prime importance, this almost appears as sham.
Occasionally he himself complained about his difficulties
in expressing himself. He once wrote to Clara, in connection with a birthday letter: "By the way, I really write in
half sentences only, and it becomes necessary for the
reader to figure out the other half for himself." Or, facetiously, in a letter to Bernhard Scholz: "I am aware of my
bad habit of writing briefly but obscurely."

The obscurity was no doubt always due to some inhibi-
tion; yet he was ever a true, dependable, and close friend.
"I am accustomed to taking friendships very seriously and
very simply," he once wrote to Allgeyer. His friends knew
this, and loved and worshipped him for it. But they also
feared him because one could never be certain where he
stood with him, and because Brahms knew how to hurt
mercilessly. At times one gets the impression that, in so doing, he hurt himself far more than his victims. But he simply could not bring himself to say "Forgive me," just as he
was incapable of suppressing a malicious remark whenever
one occurred to him. In his frankness there was an element
of sadism, and in his occasional aggressiveness a kind of
desire for revenge for whatever pains or injustices others
might have inflicted upon him. For this reason not a single
one of his relationships with friends remained unclouded,
and he who suffered most acutely was undoubtedly the
one who had brought about the cloud. In such cases he
could say things at whose bitterness one may well shudder.
Such is a remark which Eugenie Schumann, Clara's daugh-

ter, attributed to him: "I have no friends! If anyone claims
to be a friend of mine, don't you believe him!" And Billroth
quotes him as saying: "No man can look inside another
one." This above all contains a great deal of self-judgment.
It is for just this reason that his relationships with friends
cast such a revealing illumination on him. In many respects
each of his friends saw him in a different light, each according to his own personality; and from these complementing crosslights an image can be constructed that at
least approaches the truth.

Young people are quick to make friends. On his first excursion into the world when he was barely twenty years
old, Brahms encountered in addition to Joachim and Schumann, whom he adored above all others, two men who
remained his friends for life: Albert Dietrich and Julius
Otto Grimm. Although thoroughly competent musicians
and men of character, neither of the two ever reached far
beyond tolerable mediocrity. Young and inexperienced,
Brahms was inclined to overestimate the superior practical
knowledge of his friends, just as at the same time he overestimated Joachim's skill as a composer. But these musicians, a few years older than Brahms, had already seen the
world and had gained insight into matters concerning
which Brahms was keenly aware of his own shortcomings.
The secrets of orchestral sound and its realization in the
score, for example, were still closed books to him, and even
chamber-music ensembles presented problems for him because of the gaps in his knowledge of stringed instruments.
His imagination was entirely confined to the piano, but
this instrument he had mastered in a supreme fashion. He
therefore sought above all to learn from his new friends;
he was unbelievably ravenous for education. Early in 1854
he wrote his first chamber music to be published, the B
major Piano Trio. And during the summer of the same year

we find him—the tragedy of Robert Schumann had in the meantime gotten under way—engaged in writing a symphony which eventually, after a long-drawn-out process of growth, became his Piano Concerto in D minor. He sent Joachim as much of the score as was finished, and wrote:

As far as my score is concerned you will undoubtedly have found—and I also urgently requested Mrs. Schumann to tell you so—that whatever may be good in it is entirely due to Grimm, who stood by my side with excellent advice. That which is faulty or bad, probably not so well concealed, was either overlooked by Grimm or else left in because of my own stubbornness. . . . Do you encourage me to go on to further movements? I feel that I have the courage of ignorance. . . .

At this point a remark which he made to Joachim years later, when they were corresponding about the Double Concerto, may be relevant:

Now, however, when you see our concerto in print, please do not consider it utterly deceitful if at times I urgently requested your opinion, and then ended up by letting my own ideas stand anyway. Especially for the reconstructed [here follows a quotation from the last movement] I beg your forgiveness. For your own use you may change this passage back; I shall much prefer hearing it from you in your version than in my own from anyone else.

He might have written similar words, to Joachim as well as to others, in earlier years. He was often unsure of himself, always inclined to ask for advice, and ever appreciative of any suggestion. But it is never easy for any adviser to recommend improvements to an artist capable of thinking as profoundly and inventing as logically and organically as Brahms could. In the end his critical intelligence would decide with complete independence. The autograph score of the Double Concerto contains several places in which three different versions can be discerned: his original one, for some technical reason unacceptable; then a countersuggestion in Joachim's hand; and last, the final form which was ultimately printed and which, while utilizing Joachim's hints, represents a compromise that conforms much better to the original idea, which only the composer himself could conceive. For Brahms, Joachim was not only a lifelong and indispensable adviser as a violinist and chamber musician of consummate experience, but also one whose opinions in technical matters concerning composition he always respected highly. The fact that as a composer he never reached the heights predicted for him was attributed by Brahms, often with pronounced regret, to the single-mindedness with which he devoted his energies to his tasks as musical interpreter whether as virtuoso, as first violinist in his quartet, or as conductor. For Brahms as a young man, Joachim's help was indispensable, and for the mature artist it always remained valuable and often decisive. Both as violinist and as performing artist Joachim remained the measure for Brahms's loftiest thoughts throughout his life. Brahms wrote to him about Clara when she had gone on her first concert tour after Schumann's illness: "She plays again with her former vigor but with even greater intensity, *more like you.* Yesterday she did my F minor Sonata exactly as I had envisaged it, only still more nobly, with more quiet enthusiasm, and yet at the same time cleanly and purely and with the most magnificent tone in the more powerful passages—all little advantages which she has over me."

With his endless self-criticism and with the unattainable goals he had set for himself, Brahms, never satisfied with his results, hit upon an idea which was carried out for years by the two friends, although with incomparably greater will power and concentration on the part of Brahms than of Joachim, who after all lacked the creative impulse which drove and spurred Brahms. The latter wrote in February of 1856:

I also want to remind you and request that at long last we carry out what we have discussed: to send each other contrapuntal studies. Let each of us send the other, once every fortnight, some exercise to be returned a week later with the other's criticisms together with some work of his own; and let us so continue for a long time, until both of us will have become quite adept. Why shouldn't we two intelligent and serious people be able to teach one another better than some professor could? . . . I am hoping and looking forward to your first packet. Let's get started! It would be so lovely, good, and productive.

And a few weeks later:

I am enclosing two short pieces as a beginning of our common studies. Should you still be interested in this proposition, I would like to lay down a few rules which I consider useful. Every Sunday some work must go either back or forth. If, for example, you send me something one Sunday, I will return it the following week with some work of my own, and so forth. And whoever misses the day, i.e., sends nothing, will be fined one thaler, with which the other may buy himself some books. One is excused only when, instead of the exercise, he sends some composition, which will then be all the more welcome: a double counterpoint, canon, fugue, prelude, or whatever it may be.

And now the work began apace. But it seems that Brahms received appreciably more money for book purchases than did his partner, and his conscience began to bother him. "It seems to me that I have not yet thanked you for the lovely money. I was very pleased with it but would much prefer seeing your work and your letters more regularly to receiving your fines." He continually sent Joachim exercises:

I am again returning my canons from last time. Quite aside from the skill in them, are they good music? Do the artifices make them more beautiful and valuable? Did you notice something? I know nothing! I am also enclosing some short canons. I particularly want to request your opinion on the four-part round. I add yet another work which I found difficult, and which I ask you, or rather order you, to complete: the canonic imitation on the *cantus firmus*. Please save all the music sheets which you sent me and I returned. I will do the same. Then perhaps after a long while we can look at them together and, I hope, note great progress.

Joachim replied, with reference to the last assigned exercise:

To keep my word, here are the desired contrapuntal solutions on a given theme. . . . It was a difficult task, and, compared with your meaningful and definitive ones, my canons are rather muddy and unsure in their rhythmic as well as their melodic execution. I repeat: have patience with my lack of skill in such things.

At about the same time he wrote to Gisela von Arnim:

Some time ago I started a kind of musical correspondence with Brahms: we send each other assignments of considerable difficulty. This type of musical interchange with him means a great deal to me; I remain in intellectually close contact with someone in whom I take the most heartfelt interest. My friend, although younger than I, is already very accomplished in the manipulation of this type of composition, whereas I never occupied myself with it beyond the basic grammatical necessities. In this way I also acquire some artistic stimulation.

It can be seen that Joachim did not lack critical self-judgment any more than good will. But the principal beneficiary of this course in the most advanced skills of counterpoint was Brahms. It helped him develop his already extraordinary technique as a composer to an unsurpassed mastery discernible in every measure he ever wrote. Joachim, whose primary talent drove him more toward performing activities, was only incidentally a composer. He remained his friend's faithful adviser and admirer, and not only observed his success joyfully, without any jealousy, but promoted it most intensively by performing his works. All of Brahms's chamber music passed through his hands, and none of his orchestral compositions was sent to the printer before Joachim had scrutinized the score with a critical eye.

A tragic incident separated the two for years, and both suffered agonies because of it: Joachim's divorce proceedings, in which Brahms vehemently took the wife's part, probably in a tactless manner. How profoundly this cleft hurt, can be concluded from an incident related by Joachim's biographer, Andreas Moser. In it the honest, mature, and sagacious man said things which on quiet reflection he could not possibly have maintained. Moser reports:

When in the spring of 1885 I stayed with Joachim for several weeks in order to keep him company in his loneliness, he unburdened himself one day in the most violent manner imaginable about Brahms's "disloyalty," only to play together with Barth and Hausmann, a couple of hours later, his C major Trio, Opus 87. Deeply moved by the magnificent rendition of this work, I could not suppress the astonished question how it was possible to bring such devotion to Brahms's music while bearing so much anger in one's heart. "My dear friend," was the answer, "the artist and the man are two different beings! But quite aside from these distinctions, I cannot experience and execute this music other than with my entire self. It acts upon me like a force of nature." In a quieter mood he once expressed himself quite differently: "Whoever writes like this must be noble and good." And: "The *German Requiem* is a composition which, to me, shows Brahms as an exalted being against whom I well never cavil about petty things I might find objectionable."

Written communication between the two was, by the way, never entirely cut off during the period of their estrangement, because there were always factual matters that required an exchange of ideas. And at last Brahms found the longed-for occasion to take the first step toward a meeting and a reconciliation: his Double Concerto for violin and cello, which owes its existence to this desire. From then on, the relationship between the two friends remained undisturbed until Brahms's death, although it probably no longer had the same heartiness and warmth as before.

Incidentally, their correspondence represents a gold mine of priceless knowledge about all kinds of general musical questions. To quote from a letter by Brahms on the subject of his Fourth Symphony:

I have marked a few tempo modifications in the score with pencil. They may be useful, even necessary, for the first performance. Unfortunately they often find their way into print (with me as well as with others) where, for the most part, they do not belong. Such exaggerations are only necessary when a composition is unfamiliar to an orchestra or a soloist. In such a case I often cannot do enough pushing or slowing down to produce even approximately the passionate or serene effect I want. Once a work has become part of flesh and blood, then in my opinion nothing of that sort is justifiable any more. In fact, the more one deviates from the original, the less artistic the performance becomes. With my older works I frequently find that everything falls into place without much ado and that many marks of the above-mentioned type become entirely superfluous. But how often does not someone try to make an impression nowadays with this so-called free artistic rendition —and how easy this is, even with the poorest orchestra and but a single rehearsal! An orchestra like that of Meiningen ought to take special pride in showing just the opposite.

This last remark contains a sting which concerns yet another conflict of friendship in Brahms's life; it is unmistakably directed against Hans von Bülow, the celebrated conductor of the Meiningen orchestra, who deserved just as much credit for disseminating Brahms's music at the time of the latter's most mature mastery as Joachim did at the time of his apprenticeship and development. Bülow was a tragic figure. A pupil of Liszt, enthusiastic disciple of Wagner, and equally accomplished as pianist and conductor, he became the most successful apostle of the two leaders of the "Music of the Future" when they waged their most decisive battles. His most memorable acts in this respect were the world premières of *Tristan und Isolde* in 1865 and *Die Meistersinger* in 1868, both in Munich. Soon afterward there occurred the scandal which drove Bülow away from Munich and out of Wagner and Liszt's camp. His wife Cosima, Liszt's daughter, left him to live with Wagner, whom she subsequently married. What Bülow had to suffer at the hands of Wagner, whom he worshipped above all, was not only the destruction of his marriage, which up to then he had been justified in regarding as a happy one; it was also tantamount to a public defamation. A man of his susceptible sense of honor was unable to live down this sort of thing. The offender was of such illustrious standing that his very eminence served to render the insult even more acute, for Bülow, according to the peculiar precepts of honor of those days, would have challenged any lesser person to a duel with pistols. He

67

passed through a dangerous crisis at that time. A few years later he took up a closer connection with Brahms—up to then their acquaintance had been a very fleeting one—when he produced the latter's First Symphony in Hanover. With his love for aphorisms he had bestowed on it the title of "The Tenth," thereby proclaiming it the first legitimate successor to Beethoven's nine symphonies. When in 1880 he assumed the directorship of the Meiningen court orchestra, which he transformed with untiring and meticulous labor into an ensemble of world renown, he offered Brahms an opportunity to rehearse his new orchestral works without interference in order to discover hidden faults prior to publication. Brahms did not have to be asked twice; and from that time on, he was a frequent visitor in Meiningen, where his Third and Fourth Symphonies, both his overtures, and his B-flat major Piano Concerto all reaped the benefits of Bülow's generous offer.

Bülow, with all the passionate impetuosity of his nervous character, went all out for his new friend, under whose lack of consideration and occasional unpredictability—he was fond of calling Brahms "the bear"—he also was to smart at times. A scene with him, reported by Kalbeck, shows how raw his old wound must still have been. The three had just finished dining at the Red Hedgehog, Brahms's favorite eating place in Vienna, and were walking through the municipal park, Brahms several paces ahead. Kalbeck relates:

Suddenly Bülow clutched my arm and, gesticulating so wildly with his right hand that passers-by stood still in astonishment, exclaimed in a choked voice: "Just look at him there, how broad and secure and healthily he stalks in front of us! I have him to thank for being restored to sanity—late, but I hope not too late —in fact, for being still alive. Three quarters of my existence has been misspent on my former father-in-law, that mountebank, and his tribe, but the remainder belongs to the true saints of art and above all to him, to him, to him."

It was a peculiar sort of friendship, based on limitless respect for each other, and yet never without some latent mutual distrust. In his first joy Bülow wrote to his fiancée, Marie Schanzer:

You know how much I think of Brahms: after Bach and Beethoven he is the greatest, the most exalted of all composers. I consider his friendship my most priceless possession, second only to your love. It represents a climax in my life, a moral conquest. I do not believe that a single musical heart, not even that of his oldest friend Joachim, feels so profoundly or is so deeply immersed into the depths of his soul as mine.

But he did have some reservations:

Master Brahms has bestowed much honor upon us but has also disturbed us painfully in our work. The second week of this month had to be devoted exclusively to his new works (three quarters of the orchestra is slipshod and one quarter raw, inexperienced, and undisciplined) in order not to embarrass Meiningen in his estimation; the third week he came here, attended rehearsals every day, conducted, and played (on three occasions in the presence of the duke). This could not be helped. Last February in Vienna, in a flush of enthusiastic optimism, I extended to him an invitation to come; but we could not agree on a time more convenient for both of us, and I had to respect his position. He seemed to enjoy himself and frequently expressed not only favor, although interspersed with occasional sharply sarcastic remarks, but downright delight. He dined at court three times and accepted the *Komtur* decoration, which he also seemed to find very agreeable. I almost dread hearing about the comments he may make elsewhere, for I consider him equivalent to Wagner, both as to genius and as to kindness.

This last remark is significant, and not too much later

Bülow had occasion to remember it. The poor devil had already learned the lesson that it is not easy to get along with the great, and no doubt he had had a taste of the "bear's" inconsiderateness. The beautiful relationship, stimulating and fruitful for both parties, was shattered by a gross effrontery on the part of Brahms: in Frankfort he conducted his Fourth Symphony, with which Bülow had traveled all through western Germany and Holland, and thereby effectively snatched it from his friend's hands. Bülow considered this a deliberate snub. Bearing in mind the letter quoted on page 66, it appears quite possible that, displeased with the plodding, excessively detailed interpretative technique of Bülow, which tended to upset the continuity of the music, Brahms wanted to bring forth his own concept, more simple and robust; or perhaps he wished to offer his work firsthand to his friends in Frankfort, who were not overly fond of Bülow. He should have understood Bülow's sensitive nature better; the latter handed in his resignation and left Meiningen. His successor, Fritz Steinbach, was just as devoted to Brahms as Bülow had been, but Brahms soon came to regret his thoughtlessness. When Bülow was in Vienna to give a concert in January, 1887, more than a year after the incident, Brahms left at his hotel a calling card with a quotation on it from the *Magic Flute*, "Shall I never see thee again, beloved?" This broke the ice, and the old friendship was restored.

When Bülow deserted the Liszt-Wagner camp to join Brahms, he arrived at the right time: it was just then that Brahms had suffered a painful, almost irreplaceable loss. One of his best friends, Hermann Levi, had defected to the enemy colors. Brahms had met him in 1864 at a music festival arranged by Liszt in Karlsruhe, where Levi held the post of court conductor. Brahms had written to Joachim:

If it were worth the trouble, I could tell you all about the festival, to which I had been driven by the desire to learn—or perhaps by just plain curiosity. . . . The whole affair was made bearable by the presence of Hermann Levi, the musical director. Despite his operatic routine, this young man is so refreshing and looks with his bright eyes into such lofty heights that everything is a joy.

The immediate liking was mutual. At about that time Levi wrote to Clara Schumann:

Brahms's departure left me with a sense of emptiness which I have tried in vain to counteract by hard work. . . . The close contact with Johannes was, I believe, of such profound and lasting influence on my whole being as nothing else in my entire musical career. He is for me the image of the really pure artist and human being; this means a great deal these days. . . .

And again, after a visit by Brahms on April 18, 1866:

Now here is a man! All descendants of Adam generally bear the stamp of their time and its weaknesses on their foreheads; he alone knows how to free himself of all earthly entanglements, to remain uncontaminated by the filth and misery of life, and to soar to ideal heights where we can only follow him with our eyes but not join him. Are we to be blamed for being dazzled at times?

Brahms valued him as a keen intellect of widespread interests who in many respects shared his own views as a man and musician; but above all he esteemed his astute and sound judgment. He found him a brilliant conversationalist, full of spirit and humor, with whom he could talk shop to his heart's content, even discussing techniques of composition—about which Levi, himself by no means without talent as a composer, had a surprising store of knowledge. Levi also knew how to be stubborn about objections and, son of a rabbi, once even found a scriptural argument for convincing his friend in a discussion of the Piano Quintet:

When you enter the Talmud, just to the left of the door is written, "If a person comes and tells you that you are a mule, don't believe him; but if another person comes and also tells you that you are a mule, then buy a saddle and let yourself be ridden." In common language this means that if Mrs. Schumann or I make a remark, don't listen to us; if however, as I believe is the case, all musicians, or a friend such as Joachim, say the same thing, then don't shy away from the trouble but go ahead and cut some of the last four pages.

As in so many similar cases, Brahms declined to brook any interference, and he was within his right. At the time when the *German Requiem,* the *Song of Triumph,* and the *Song of Destiny* were created, Levi constantly looked over his shoulder, and Brahms always considered his opinions seriously even though he might let his own ideas stand. During these decisive years when Brahms's choral and or-chestral works began to find public acceptance, Levi re-mained his preferred interpreter. On the other hand he too came into conflict with the negative side of Brahms's char-acter. He wrote most disconsolately to Clara Schumann on October 2, 1867:

I am afraid that Brahms, the man as well as the musician, is now at a crossroads, and one path will lead him to destruction. If he should not succeed in snatching his better self from the demon of abruptness, of coldness, and of heartlessness, then he is lost to us and to his music, for only all-engendering love can create works of art.

At that time no serious differences between them had arisen. But when in 1872 Levi transferred his activities as conductor to Munich, the center of the Wagnerian cult, his relationship with Brahms seems to have grown more tenuous, especially since his performances of Brahms's symphonies in Munich were disastrous failures. In 1878 he wrote:

I had a very sad experience with Brahms's C minor Symphony this winter. Never have I lived through anything more painful. Perfect silence after the first movement; after the second, following a few attempts at applause, lively hissing; and the same after the third. It was a prearranged affair. The opposition was not organized by the Wagnerians but by the so-called classicists, headed by the music critic of the Augsburg *Abendzeitung*, whose enthusiasm confines itself to Lachner, Rheinberger, Zenger, and Rauchenecker, and who several weeks prior to the performance had already warned the Academy against producing the symphony, because the audience would not stand for it. None of this would have been important if I had only had some support within the orchestra. But there wasn't a single musician whose eye I could catch at any of the most beautiful passages. After the performance there appeared a flood of abuse in the newspapers and anonymous letters from concert goers who threatened to cancel their subscriptions. There was even a movement afoot to compel the Academy to publish all programs at the beginning of the season so that, in the event a Brahms symphony was to be presented, one could decline to subscribe.

Shortly afterward, on March 6, 1879, he wrote to Clara Schumann: "In the next concert I shall do Brahms's Second. I have not yet been able to make the adagio my own; it leaves me cold." But this cooling off embraced their entire relationship. A few years later Levi, by then one of Wagner's most faithful paladins, conducted the world première of *Parsifal* in Bayreuth. Brahms sensed that his friend had slipped away, and he withdrew from him.

One cannot help sympathizing with Levi in this matter when one considers the following letter which he wrote to Clara Schumann:

73

I cannot agree that my views are considered paradox and my present inclinations—as opposed to those of my past—as felonious. But then I don't think it so difficult to establish the difference between a dramatist and a musician. As a musician, Brahms certainly stands as high above Wagner as Mozart did above Gluck. But does not Gluck hold a position at least next to that of Mozart just the same? Wagner does not consider himself a musician in the sense that our classics were. I find all his instrumental compositions dull and paltry. If any pupil were to bring to a lesson the *Albumblatt,* published by Schott, I would politely show him the door. But when Wagner uses music as the servant of the drama, he produces effects as none before him. Since he is so entirely different from anyone before him or next to him, and since he is neither able nor willing to create just music but rather is attempting to establish a German drama, I cannot see why an honest and sincere admiration for his works should not be compatible with an equally honest one for Bach, Beethoven, and Brahms. Certainly the *Song of Destiny* or the G major Sextet is no further removed from me just because I consider *Tristan* a great work of art. Here, as everywhere, it is the fanatical friends and foes who generate the misunderstandings. To me the group which calls itself the Wagnerians and which, in addition to Wagner, elevates an inspired charlatan like Liszt on its pedestal, is just as repulsive as its opponents are incomprehensible.

Among artists, motivations of a practical nature can hardly be entirely ruled out in forming friendships and in bringing about estrangements. Brahms was a realist and saw these things as they were. Yet his warmest and most personal feelings of friendship were free of ulterior motives. Considering his absorption in musical matters, it can hardly be imagined that for him any friendship could possibly have developed in which music was not the decisive link. This is certainly true in the case of his dearest friend of the Vienna years, Dr. Theodor Billroth. This cele-

brated father of modern surgery met Brahms in 1866 in
Zürich. Soon afterward he followed a call to the University of Vienna, and his move coincided almost exactly
with Brahms's decision to transfer his residence to the
same city. Thus optimum conditions were given for the
rapid development of an intimate friendship.

Billroth was by nature an artist, as are so many scientists
who have the gift of imagination. His uncommon musical
talents were developed early and painstakingly. He was an
able pianist and a passable violinist and violist; music was
a vital necessity for him. Brought up in the classical tradition, he was exposed relatively late to Brahms's music, but
he obviously at once sensed an affinity to it and enthusiastically made it his own. Presumably it was he who took
the initiative in establishing the friendship. Billroth, who
combined the methodical orderliness of a modern scientist
with the impulsive temperament, the effervescent joy in
living, and the craving for beauty of a Renaissance man,
was the only one of Brahms's friends who could face him
on a basis of equality as a personality. And Brahms loved
his receptivity, his sharing experiences of a musical as well
as nonmusical nature. For Billroth, on the other hand, each
new work by his friend proved to be an exciting event
which enriched his own spiritual world. He united a passionate desire to communicate with the ability of an artistic man to put his thoughts into words in an expressive
manner. Brahms was thankful for this; without such an
echo a creative artist lives in a vacuum. Billroth wrote him,
still at an early stage of their relationship: "A pen transforms me miraculously; my tongue could not possibly speak
that which flows so readily from my heart through my
pen." And Brahms replied: "It is a beautiful thing to say
the right thing at the right time. Thus I want first to slap
my own face and then to thank you with all my heart for

doing these things so much better than I can." And many
years later: "Basically you are just as facile with the spoken
word as with the pen, and you can tell others such things
as I can only tell myself in a monologue."

It goes without saying that Billroth could never be ab-
sent from the performance of a new work, and Brahms
never failed to let him see its manuscript as soon as it
could be spared. During this time he had an urge to show
every new composition to somebody, or to play it and have
it confirmed that he achieved the effect he had sought.
"Whether or not I have a pretty symphony," he wrote to
Billroth from his vacation home in Pörtschach, "I do not
know; I will have to ask some wiser people." But Billroth,
when he received the score, wrote: "This is utter blue
sky, a murmuring of brooks, sunlight and cool green shade!
It must be beautiful on Lake Wörth." And later, when
Brahms sent him a four-hand piano arrangement of
his Second Symphony, to which the above referred, Billroth was delighted: "I have already completely immersed
myself in this piece, and it has given me many a happy
hour. I cannot tell which movement is my favorite; I find
each one magnificent in its own way. A cheerful, carefree
mood pervades the whole, and everything bears the stamp
of perfection and of the untroubled outpouring of serene
thoughts and warm sentiments."

All of the new chamber music of Brahms found its first
hearing in Billroth's hospitable mansion on the Alser-
strasse. Billroth insisted on this seigniorial right, as he
called it. An evening of this type combined the best available players (with the composer at the piano whenever a
piano was called for) and a select group of close friends
into a symposium that was, also in a culinary respect, carefully organized. Billroth was an epicure, and he loved to
play the generous host to his friends. He was especially

glad to do so following the performance of a new work by Brahms. After one such occasion Brahms wrote him:

I wish there were two words, for more wouldn't do at all, with which to tell you exactly how thankful I am to you for the days that came to an end yesterday afternoon [rehearsals and pre-mière of the First Symphony]. I don't exactly want to say that my bit of composing is nothing but a troublesome chore, a continuous irritation, and that nothing better will come; but you cannot imagine how beautiful and heart-warming it is to sense a sympathy like yours. In such a moment one realizes that this is the best part of composing and all that is connected with it.

And on another occasion, speaking of the *Song of the Fates:*

You can't believe how important and how precious your favor-able comment is to me, and how much I appreciate it. One knows what one wanted and how badly one wanted it. But actually one also wants to know what came out of it all, and this is much better said by others; one is eager to believe each friendly word. This is what happened again this time; only now am I happy with the piece, and look on it favorably.

One of the closest associates of Billroth's circle was Edu-ard Hanslick, music critic and professor of music history at the University of Vienna, who was also an intimate friend of Brahms. Because it involved certain mutual reser-vations, this triumvirate was most peculiar. What both Billroth and Brahms valued in Hanslick was his wit and brilliance as a writer, his strong character and convic-tions as a man, and his genuine charm. His weaknesses were so obvious that they could be accepted. Hanslick was as good-natured and conscientious as any man with a nar-row outlook is capable of being. But his musical percep-tion was limited and his whole feeling for music somehow underdeveloped despite his painstaking upbringing, nimble piano playing, and genuine readiness to make an honest effort. His antipathy to Wagner was at least partly due to such constitutional limitations. The fact that he invariably studied scores or piano arrangements prior to any performance, whenever such were available, failed to save him from not being able to see the forest for the trees. This was all the more true when he had to listen "at first sight," as Brahms called it.

Hanslick has made most of the fruits of his half century as a music critic available in book form, and it is interesting to note how rarely this spirited writer and master of the pregnant epigram has missed an opportunity to bet on the wrong horse. Even the waltzes of Johann Strauss, which under the influence of Brahms he later learned to appreciate as much as the latter did, provoked him at first (in 1865) to opposition, for he detected in them "that strongly pungent odor exuded by venison that smells of the past and by music that smells of the future." At first he judged practically every significant innovation either wrongly or at least in a limited fashion; this refers to Verdi and Bizet, for example, as well as to Wagner. When Brahms first visited Vienna in 1862, he was met by Hanslick with respect, almost with cordiality, but he was sufficiently astute to tolerate the friendly attentions of the dreaded critic without in any way compromising himself. Later Hanslick complained that Brahms had never said a single word to him about his numerous laudatory reviews. Of course he had a special interest in Brahms as the only possible "antipope" whom he could pit against the "musicians of the future," and his understanding of his friend's music may at times have been no more profound than that for Wagner's works. Although sympathetically inclined, he expressed himself at the outset (in 1862) with cool noncommittal:

Johannes Brahms has now introduced himself to the public both as composer and as soloist, in a concert of his own. His compositions are not among those which are immediately understandable and gripping, sweeping one off one's feet. Their esoteric effect, loftily avoiding all popular appeal, coupled with their great technical difficulties, has induced public acceptance far more slowly than was expected after the delighted prophecies which Schumann bestowed as a wayside blessing on his favorite. . . . At this time it is still a risky undertaking to give an estimate of Brahms's talent and effectiveness. . . . Especially in his most recent works there appear question marks and enigmas which will only find resolution in the next period of his creativity. This resolution will be decisive. Will his originality of invention and melodic force keep pace with the advancing development of his harmonic and contrapuntal skill? Will the natural freshness and youthful vigor of his early works continue to blossom forth without interference, to unfold in still greater and freer beauty in the precious vessel which Brahms has now wrought for them? Is that foggy turbidity of brooding reflection which frequently beclouds his latest creations the precursor of penetrating sunlight or of still denser, more inhospitable dusk?

It can be seen that the critic prudently safeguarded his retreat. Several years later, Brahms's star having meanwhile risen to such heights that it could not possibly be ignored, he no longer entertained doubts and indecisions. A contemporary caricature shows Brahms as an idol on a pedestal—perhaps inspired by Wagner's sarcastic epithet, "St. Johannes"—and at his feet, shortlegged and with pious mien, Hanslick swinging a censer.

Brahms recognized better than anyone else the shortcomings of Hanslick, who in his memoirs naively admits that for him music in the purest sense began only with Haydn and Mozart. Anyone to whom Bach and Handel were archaic and Palestrina, Lasso, and Schütz prehistoric could certainly not be considered a serious musician by

Brahms. The latter reported to Clara about one of his concerts at the *Singakademie* in April, 1864:

In our third concert the *Christmas Oratorio* (Parts 1, 2, 4, and
6) went off superbly. At least both the choir and I were pleased.
With the local critics, however, Bach has a difficult time here.
Hanslick must have suffered the pangs of Hell this week, since
two days later Herbeck performed the *St. John Passion.*

On the other hand he did recognize Hanslick's good
qualities and realized that he was a true friend. When the
critic celebrated his seventieth birthday, Brahms wrote to
Clara:

I can't help it, but I know few people toward whom I am as
warmly inclined as I am toward him. I consider it a very beautiful and very rare thing to be as genial, good-natured, honest,
earnestly humble, and what not, as I know him to be. I have
often had the opportunity to get to know this side of him, to
my great joy and satisfaction. Even though he and I represent
vastly different points of view, I may still say that he is uncommonly competent in his field. But I neither demand nor
expect anything unjustifiable from him.

Billroth felt just as affectionate toward Hanslick but
with similar reservations; at times he was in despair about
his musical primitiveness and even more about his emotional superficiality. Once after having played some piano
duets with him, of course by Brahms, he reported:

There is a transcendental loftiness in the music which to him
is like a book with seven seals. . . . I have also played a great
many other things of yours with him. But the schoolmasterly
way he performs everything, with his dry tone and without the
slightest grasp of the whole, often drives me nearly to distrac-
tion. He never warms up, and his inability to play even eighth
notes simultaneously with even triplets upsets him in the most
horrible and painful manner. All this would be comical, were

it not so incomprehensible in an otherwise very musical person. He also has the characteristically feminine quality of being utterly unable to play legato. If he were not such a good-natured fellow and if he did not have the most sincere desire to understand your spirit, I should be furious with him. Still, when I see how much he enjoys our food, I am mollified.

At times there were disturbances in their good relations, as could happen so easily with Brahms. A serious vexation, caused by Billroth in all innocence, had to do with a particular sensitivity of Brahms. He was not exactly a collector—for this he lacked the necessary obsession—but still a proud and devout possessor of precious manuscripts, among them sundry musical holographs of Schubert, string quartets by Haydn, and the G minor Symphony of Mozart. He harbored outspokenly reverent sentiments about these treasures, which after his death passed into the hands of the Society of the Friends of Music in Vienna. "Yesterday I bought," he once wrote to Karl Reinthaler, "the manuscripts of six Haydn quartets! . . . Would you not also have a pleasant feeling of inner warmth and quite some emotion if you held something like this in your hands or called it your own?" Brahms had presented the manuscripts of his own two String Quartets, Opus 51, to Billroth, to whom he had dedicated them, an honor which gave more happiness to the professor than all his citations and decorations together. On Billroth's desk was a framed photograph of Brahms, who one day noticed his portrait adorned with the title and the dedication cut out of his quartet manuscript. Mandyczewski tells, with a feeling for the humor of the situation, how Brahms came flying to him in white-hot fury: "Can you imagine? Billroth has cut up my quartets! Just think! He who should have known that I love him so well I would gladly have made a fresh copy of the entire quartet had he so desired! And now he goes ahead and cuts a piece out of it!" With a deep-rooted sense for that which in any manuscript constitutes a direct part of the author's spirit, he considered his friend's action an act of vandalism, even though it concerned "only" his own work; it was a long time before he could forgive him.

Another dissonance in the harmony of their friendship had more serious consequences because it left a pall on the last years of Billroth's life. Already fatally ill, he never found out how—or even that—he had hurt the feelings of his friend, who noticeably withdrew from him. Billroth had the habit of writing long letters to Hanslick after performances of Brahms's works, giving his impressions in an enthusiastic and freely communicative manner. Brahms, who knew of this custom, once expressed to Hanslick the desire to see such a letter, whereupon the latter sent him half a dozen which he happened to find on his desk. The unhappy man noticed too late, as he himself subsequently reported, that an entirely unsuitable letter had slipped into the pile. In it Billroth had made some remarks about Brahms's occasional inconsiderateness, ascribing it, like similar vagaries of Beethoven, to "neglected upbringing." Brahms, proud of his humble background and passionately devoted to his parents' memory, felt this accusation as a mortal insult. He replied to Hanslick, who, completely crushed, had begged his pardon and his discretion toward Billroth:

My dear friend, you need not worry in the least. I hardly glanced at Billroth's letter, but immediately returned it into its envelope and only slightly shook my head. I am to mention nothing to him? My dear friend, I do this automatically. It has ever been my experience that even old friends and acquaintances take you for something quite different from what you are (or, in their eyes, claim to be). I remember how I used to maintain a surprised and hurt silence in such a case in the old days; now my silence is perfectly calm and natural. This may seem harsh or rude to a good and kindly soul like yours, but I hope that I have not strayed too far from Goethe's dictum: "Blessed is he who can withdraw from the world without rancor."

This was just one of the many factors that contributed to Brahms's increasing loneliness as he grew older. The fact that this loneliness was often transformed into irritable misanthropy is not surprising, and his friends had to become inured to suffering through all this, especially since he was by no means always conscious of his grumpiness. Kalbeck tells of a characteristic incident in Ischl. Just as Brahms was playing some new piano pieces, Viktor Miller von Aichholz, one of his most devoted friends, timidly knocked at the door. After a roaring "Come in," Miller appeared in the doorway, but for the longest time he could not be persuaded to sit down. At last Brahms, impatiently banging the table with his fist, bellowed: "All right then, don't!" Miller, quite frightened, fled from the scene. After a while Brahms said with the utmost good humor: "That Miller is really a grand guy; if only he didn't constantly apologize for being alive. I just had to use some devilish self-control not to be rude to him." Richard Specht tells of a similar episode in which Kalbeck himself became the victim of an outburst of impatience. It was at a party at Ignaz Brüll's house, where Kalbeck was riding his hobbyhorse as a violent anti-Wagnerian and making some inflammatory speeches. Brahms suddenly turned on him: "For Heaven's sake, stop speaking of things you don't understand." Kalbeck turned silent and left the room. A few days later he met Specht on the street and complained bitterly: "What do you think! All the things one has to put up with! This is what I get for the years of labor, for faithful friendship, for active devotion! But this time I did not tolerate such a vulgar attack by the lord and master: I wrote him a long letter and told him off in no uncertain terms." Specht asked: "Well, what was Brahms's answer?" And Kalbeck smiled: "Of course I never mailed the letter."

This faithful friend, as a critic much more temperamental and impulsive than Hanslick but by the same token more erratic in his judgment, was often a victim of Brahms's sarcastic caprices. Mandyczewski was present when Brahms pointed to a passage in the newly published supplement to Beethoven's complete works, which Mandyczewski had edited, with the remark: "Look, Kalbeck, here Beethoven has written something so precious that it ought to be put under every one of your reviews." He was referring to a sketch of a song by Beethoven ("Plaint") which was first written in two-quarter time and then changed to four-quarter time with doubled note values, to which the composer had added the remark that in this way one is inclined to take the tempo more slowly than with single note values. He had then thought it over and written beneath it: "Perhaps the opposite is true." Kalbeck mentioned this sentence as being one of Brahms's favorite quotations—he applied it, for example, to Nietzsche's philosophical paradoxes—but he had evidently forgotten the occasion on which he first heard it.

The only one of Brahms's friends who claimed never to have experienced anything but kindness and consideration from him was Mandyczewski. But this was probably due largely to himself, a man of such mild and natural charm and strict objectivity that unfriendliness seemed impossible in his presence. Brahms valued the keen critical eye of his very much younger friend, who during the master's last years was the first to see his new works. His accuracy was of great service to Brahms in such details as the wording of his German folk songs or the punctuation in the *Four Serious Songs*. Brahms also appreciated his sense of humor, which was based on skeptical principles similar to his own. Thus Brahms once forwarded to him from Ischl a telegram he had received from the Viennese concert agent Gutmann, who had by chance gotten word of the newly composed Clarinet Trio and Clarinet Quintet. The telegram read: "Revered master do give the Hellmesberger Quartet and myself the happiness of letting us have the ninth [mutilated for *new*] clarinet quintet and trio most respectfully Gutmann." Brahms underscored the word *ninth* in blue pencil and wrote with it: "Hurrah!" Underneath he remarked: "I have always considered it an exaggeration to believe half of what people say."

As the reader may already have noticed, the serious, often lonesome, and grave Master had a good deal of sense for the rehabilitating force of humor. Just as it was easy at times to nettle him, so at other times he would gladly put up with a good practical joke. Kalbeck, one of the members of a bachelors' round table at the old Viennese restaurant Gause, which flourished in the 1870's, knew many an amusing story about this group. They called themselves the "Seat of the Scornful" and counted among their members some of the most popular columnists and humorists of the day, such as Ludwig Speidel, Hugo Wittmann, and Daniel Spitzer. Brahms was frequently one of the party. Each member was obliged to put up with an improvised verse at his expense, and of the many funny Gause rimes which Kalbeck has passed on to us, one dedicated to Brahms may be quoted here because it touches on an interesting point:

> *At Gause's sang Johannes Brahms,*
> *And whatever good he found he took*

Into the realm of airy spirits;
But since already there was a Master,
He became assistant master.

In those days any mention of the "Master" unequivocally referred to Richard Wagner. Understandably this did not always please Brahms. Incidentally, there is some reason to doubt the authenticity of Kalbeck's version of these poems because, as he himself reports, they were sung to the tune of *Wirtin an der Lahn,* a bawdy song still popular among students. The Gause rimes would have been badly out of style had they not contained a few juicy ribaldries; unfortunately the originals were lost to posterity with Kalbeck's death.

A prominent member of the circle was the Beethoven scholar Gustav Nottebohm, an odd character whom Brahms esteemed highly even though he enjoyed teasing him at times. When he learned that Nottebohm was seriously ill in Graz, he interrupted his summer vacation—something unheard of for him—in order to go and take care of his friend. And a few months later Brahms, who usually had an insurmountable repugnance against sickness and the sick, was at the dying man's bedside to help lighten his last days.

The creator of the *German Requiem,* who sat on the "Seat of the Scornful" and who was able to utter the most delicate and the most crude, the most cynical and the most profound sayings, was, despite all his contradictions as a human being, hewn from one piece. Mighty and gnarled like an oak tree, he made a complete synthesis of all his conflicting characteristics in only one medium of expression: his music. Here is where one finds that which all his life he avoided showing openly: his genuine humanity and kindness, which could be as overflowingly rich as his

86

covert charity. This unpretentious and frugal man, Spartan in his simple requirements, gave away in his later years, when he felt himself a Crœsus, far more than he ever needed for himself. And whenever possible he did it secretly in order not to burden the recipient with a feeling of obligation. He was tireless in finding devious ways and means when he wanted to help somebody in grand style. And if his discourtesies, inconsiderateness, and outbursts are balanced against his good works, then one must consider that a person may commit unfriendly acts for a vast number of reasons, but acts of kindness for only one: out of goodness.

Women

THAT BRAHMS was an ardent worshipper of woman-kind is in odd contrast to his enigmatic behavior as far as women are concerned, shown by everything we know about this minstrel of the tenderest love songs. Of all the riddles and contradictions in his nature, this is perhaps the most fundamental, the most central one. It is useless to search out things about which any conclusion would be meaningless because attendant circumstances are either unknown, ambiguous, or contradictory. Still, one is hardly wrong in considering this the basic problem of a man who has had to pay for the divine felicity of creative work with the lonely isolation of a solitary existence. It is hard to imagine how deeply a man of his powerful nature, his un-bounded enjoyment of life, and his emotional vivacity must have suffered during the lonesome days and nights forced upon him by his self-imposed celibacy. In this and many other respects he had much in common with his great predecessor Beethoven. In both cases it is impossible to find the reasons, although in the case of Beethoven, with his deafness and his hypochondria, this may appear less puzzling than in that of Brahms, with an entirely positive attitude toward the world and, in the earthiest sense, a craving for life.

It can be assumed as certain that his relationship with Clara Schumann was the decisive, tragically fateful experience of his younger years. But even in this case the known circumstances are more of a negative than a positive nature. The most important negative aspect of the case is certainly significant: the two agreed in 1887 to return one another's letters in order to destroy them. Clara wrote into her diary:

On the sixteenth of October Brahms passed through here. . . . We discussed the return of his letters; this was extremely hard on me. . . . He has now given me back my own letters, and it is only right that I should also return his. . . . I had wanted to extract from them everything concerning his life as an artist and a human being, because they provide a more comprehensive portrait of him and his work than any biographer could possibly hope for. I had intended to compile all this prior to the destruction of the letters; but he was adamant, and tearfully I let him have them today.

Actually she did succeed in wheedling out of him a few to which she was particularly attached, and these were thereby preserved for posterity. The rest were thrown into the Rhine by Brahms, whereas Clara burned only a part of her own. "In her work of destruction," writes her daughter Marie, "she was fortunately interrupted by me. She gave in to my urgent plea to preserve the letters for us, her children." In any event, whatever is extant of the correspondence between them has passed through Clara's censorship, and all letters written by her prior to 1858 were destroyed.

Brahms's letters reflect a steadily growing tenderness. To him Clara was not only a beautiful and attractive woman, but she was Clara Wieck, Clara Schumann, the glorious musician and universally admired artist whose sympathy and appreciation were the highest reward he knew. "Mr. Marxsen," he wrote her in 1854, "is very gratified with the improvement in my playing. For this, too, I must thank you; it is only since I heard you, and even more since I have been able to please you with my own playing, that I can communicate my true feelings to others as well." And two years later: "My dearest Clara, I wish I could write to you as tenderly as I love you, and do as many good and loving things for you as I would like. You are so infinitely dear to me that I can't express it in words. I should like to call you darling and lots of other names, without ever getting enough of adoring you."

His state of mind becomes unmistakably clear from a passage in one of his letters to Joachim, for some unknown reason suppressed in the original publication by Andreas Moser in 1908 of the Brahms-Joachim correspondence and only recently brought to light by Arthur Holde in *The Musical Quarterly* (New York: July, 1959). In it Brahms wrote on June 19, 1859:

I believe that I do not respect and admire her so much as I love her and am under her spell. Often I must forcibly restrain myself from just quietly putting my arms around her and even —I don't know, it seems to me so natural that she would not take it ill. I think I can no longer love a young girl. At least I have quite forgotten about them. They but promise heaven while Clara reveals it to us.

Thus speaks a young man who is irrevocably enmeshed in passion. Then, following two years of close association in intimate, almost daily contact, there came, after Schumann's death, the separation about whose circumstances nothing that would allow any conclusions has been left in writing. It appears like a flight, but what actually happened can only be surmised. Brahms returned to Hamburg; Clara moved to Berlin. Externally their relationship remained unchanged: they met frequently, they exchanged letters, and there was no composition by Brahms that was not shown to Clara the moment it was in shape to be communicated. She remained his faithfully devoted adviser—a relation to be reversed in later years—and he remained her most beloved being in the whole world. Clara's daughter Eugenie knew perhaps more than she divulged when she wrote her memoirs. But in them exists the only direct clue that can be found:

I did not know at that time just what Brahms's friendship meant to my mother during this most difficult period of her life. It was not until several years after my mother's death that I saw the words which, like a legacy, she had set down in her diary for us children to read, words in which she enjoined upon us a lifelong gratitude to him who had sacrificed years of his young life to her. . . . After our father had fallen ill, Brahms was filled with that enthusiastic devotion to our mother which guided his entire being and to which he consecrated—not sacrificed, since he followed his own deepest and most heartfelt inclination—several years of his existence. The realization was inevitable, however, that a task awaited him which demanded his entire strength and which could not be reconciled with an exclusive dedication to any single friendship. To recognize this and immediately to seek a way out were acts in keeping with his strongly pronounced masculinity. Even the fact that this was done in a brusque way was inherent in his nature, and perhaps in the nature of the entire situation. But it is certain that he fought a hard fight in order to steer his ship of fate in a different direction, and that the knowledge of having hurt my mother at that time long haunted him and often manifested itself in his abrupt behavior, especially since the wrong could no longer be righted. This at least is what we children came to believe.

Brahms had his work, his aspirations, and his dreams; whatever conflicts may have disturbed him then or earlier, he now started on his real career as an artist. He was confronted by new impressions, new tasks, and the immense experiences of his creative work. The really tragic figure was Clara, who still had half her life to live but whose bloom and joy had been irretrievably lost. The ghastly event which made her a widow was followed by a fateful passion, of which we know nothing except that it was the last ardent episode in the life of a woman who had barely passed her mid-thirties. She remained a priestess of her art, active until the very end, as unhappy in motherhood as she had been as a wife, for death took a fearfully heavy toll among her children. The one grandiose and magnificent thing in her life was that she was privileged to bear active testimony, supported by the most profound artistic comprehension, to the creative careers of two eminent musicians from beginning to end. That Brahms caused her much heartache is evident from her letters and diaries. He was often irritable and always unpredictable, capable of being cold and rude, and yet at all times full of love and tenderly concerned for her welfare. She on her part frequently nagged him with petty complaints, reproaches, and suspicions to such an extent that he would take offense. They tortured each other as only lovers are capable of torturing; yet they were inseparable. He often disapproved of her exhausting concert schedule and refused to understand that it was the only substance of her life, even when she put forward practical reasons: "You think, my dear Johannes, that I give too many concerts only because I must *occasionally* put a little something aside. But just consider my anxieties in providing for seven children, five of whom are still to be brought up. Next winter they will all be home again." And then followed an involuntary remark which furnishes deep insight into the soul of this unhappy woman: "Am I not to think of my own future at all? I have no way of knowing whether I may not be compelled to live for a long time."

Brahms rarely neglected to ask her opinion before publishing anything. This opinion he always valued highly, even though fully aware of Clara's limitations, above all her occasional pedantry. For example, in sending her some new songs, he wrote:

Please write me whether you like anything in them or whether one or another arouses your dislike. Especially if the latter is the case, perhaps I'll listen to you and thank you. But don't judge things harshly at first reading; do read a poem over again if you don't like it the first time, for example *Der Mädchenfluch,* which perhaps might frighten you. Forgive me; I am just afraid of being scolded.

To her he somehow remained the little boy. She was long since resigned to her fate, and at times even encouraged him:

You should establish a household of your own soon. Take some well-to-do young lady of Vienna (surely there is one whom you can learn to love), and you will become more cheerful and, despite some worries of course, get to know joys to which you were a stranger until now. Then you can embrace life with renewed vigor. The concept of earthly happiness is, after all, bound up with life in the home. I wish you would create one for yourself; the time for it is ripe [1867].

During the course of years there was much serious discord between them. At one time Clara complained to Kalbeck that to her Brahms was still as mystifying and strange as he had been twenty-five years earlier. Nevertheless, there was nobody to whom she was more intimately devoted, and her death cut the last link tying the increasingly lonesome man to the outside world. He survived her by barely a year.

The real enigma of Brahms, just as of Goethe in his younger years, was his readiness to take flight. This theme recurred in all the romantic attachments of his life, at least so far as we know anything about them, but its emotional intensity decreased as the years went by. Parallel with this continuous diminuendo in his passion—we repeat that we can only judge by what little we know for certain in this respect—there was an overwhelming crescendo in his vitality as creator and inventor. This vitality (about which we will say more later) reached its zenith around his mid-forties; it is only from this time on that his work was like a mighty river which could now flow freely and openly after having overcome all the obstacles, rapids, and cataracts of its headwaters.

One thing has already been mentioned: Brahms was and remained a worshipper of feminine beauty, easily set afire but apparently just as easily cooled off. Scarcely two years after his flight from Clara there occurred the only occasion when he almost got as far as walking down the aisle. Agathe von Siebold, the pretty, young daughter of a professor in Göttingen, got him to exchange engagement rings with her. Like most of his later flames, Agathe was a singer. It appears that a beautiful voice, like a beautiful human figure (an expression he was fond of using), was irresistible for him. In those days Brahms frequently visited Göttingen, where his friend Grimm was music director, and the close relationship between Brahms and Agathe became so noticeable that Clara, who had stopped over in Göttingen to visit friends, departed precipitately and without taking leave as soon as she became aware of this intimacy. She must have felt bitterly hurt at the time. Indeed, a year later she had nothing but reproaches for his indiscretion: "I spent some difficult days in Cassel," she wrote him, "and the thought of Agathe and of a great many other things kept haunting me. I could see the poor, abandoned girl before me, and lived through all her sufferings with her. Oh, dear Johannes, if only you had not allowed things to go that far!" Her opinion was undoubtedly shared by others; the affair had become small-town gossip. It seems that Grimm had tried to exert some gentle pressure on his friend, with the result that Brahms brusquely broke off the engagement. What he wrote to Agathe, with exaggerated expression of feeling and at the same time pain-inflicting egoism, does not ring true, but reading between the lines, one detects panic: "I love you! I must see you again, but I am incapable of bearing fetters. Please write me whether I may come again to clasp you in my arms, to kiss you, and to tell you that I love you." Grimm, who as music director in Göttingen had to listen to all the prattle at close range, was embittered; and the immediate result was a discord, fortunately of short duration, between the two friends. Later Agathe was happily married, and Brahms never saw her again. But he did confer immortality upon her: one of his most important works of this period, the G major String Sextet (1864–65), bears her name like a motto in a subsidiary theme in its first movement, a motif based on the letters of her name, A-G-A-H-E:

Many years later this theme was mentioned again by Joachim, the first interpreter of the sextet, in a letter from

Göttingen thanking Brahms for his German folk songs: "In no place could I have been more receptive to the wonderful folk songs which you have given us than in this town which brings back such lovely memories. I have read through the songs many times, and I also went over them with Agathe [here he cites her motif in musical notation], for whom I ordered a copy." And Josef Gänsbacher, one of Brahms's closest friends at the time of the sextet, remembers a remark he made about the subject: "Here is where I tore myself free from my last love." Oddly enough, Brahms's biographers have overlooked the fact that earlier he had used the same theme elsewhere but, in the light of what we know about Brahms, with words certainly significant. It can be found in the tenth of his *Twelve Songs and Romances* for women's voices, Opus 44, which Brahms had composed for his Hamburg singers to words from Paul Heyse's *Jungbrunnen*. It is a piece of soul-searching depth and expressive force but at the same time of great simplicity in form and diction. The Agathe theme recurs as an *ostinato* figure in the alto part at the words:

When passing through the church yard,
You'll see an open grave
Where tearfully they buried
A lovely broken heart.

The grave stones cannot tell you
What cause it had to break,
But soft the zephir whispers:
'Twas love that was too great.

It was a difficult decision that Brahms took upon himself at the time: he buried his heart. But he knew what he was doing, and never again did he "allow things to go that far." There was some occasional flirting in his later life but no real love. He suppressed with full consciousness whatever might too easily have gotten out of hand. Many years later (see page 45) the confession escaped him that he had "some cause to fear the gentle sex." Yet it continued to attract him irresistibly, and shortly after the Agathe episode he was again involved in a flirtation. This time it was a cheerful young girl from Vienna, Berta Porubszky, a temporary member of his women's chorus in Hamburg, who seems to have turned his head. Certainly she was not entirely unconcerned in his decision to visit Vienna, and it was her family—she was the daughter of the minister of a Protestant congregation in Vienna—who arranged for his first social contacts there. But when reading the following lines addressed to Joachim from Vienna one can practically hear his sigh of relief. "In brief, B[erta] P[orubszky] is engaged to a wealthy young man. When I first saw her here, she looked very pale and sickly, and my conscience was greatly relieved when I received her formal announcement with a few words added." Berta and her "wealthy young man," the manufacturer Arthur Faber, remained among the most devoted friends Brahms ever had in Vienna. He almost invariably spent Christmas at their house, where a private "Faber Chorus" continued the Hamburg tradition for many years and where all of Brahms's *a capella* choral works were first sung. And the Faber couple took care of him with tender affection at the time of his last illness (see page 22).

Still another lifelong friendship dates from his first visit to Vienna: with the then sixteen-year-old Elisabeth von Stockhausen, daughter of the ambassador from Hanover in Vienna and for a short time Brahms's piano pupil. It seems that he discontinued the lessons when he discovered that he was in danger of falling head over heels in love with the highly talented young girl, who was mature, both intellectually and musically, far beyond her years. Again it was his incomprehensible instinct for flight which drove him away from her. She was married a few years later to Heinrich von Herzogenberg, a young musician whose talents Brahms valued and promoted, although his development as a composer did not live up to its early promise. Brahms continued to correspond with Elisabeth, who was endowed with the most exquisite musicality, until her death at the age of forty-two; and at times she almost displaced the visibly jealous Clara Schumann as musical confidante and trusted adviser. Both Herzogenbergs adored Brahms and his music passionately, but Elisabeth did not hesitate to voice some objections occasionally. Brahms is known to have actually suppressed the publication of certain songs on her advice, which was given in all humility but without affectation when she found fault with something. But when she waxed ecstatic, she could be touching:

I would prefer to say nothing about your sonata [the G major Violin Sonata] since you must already have had to listen to a great deal of sense and nonsense about it. Of course you are aware that no one can help loving it more than anything in the world, and that one becomes addicted to it by just studying and understanding it, by listening to it as in a dream, and by becoming completely absorbed in it. The last movement utterly enmeshes one, its emotional content so overwhelming that one must ask himself whether it was this piece of music in G minor that has gripped him so or whether something else, unknown to him, has taken possession of his innermost soul. It almost seems as though it were you who invented the dotted eighth. . . . When I play the last page of the E-flat major adagio with its heavenly pedal point and keep slowing down so that it will last longer, I always think to myself that you can only be a thoroughly good-hearted man.

This type of comment, like the previously quoted letter from Billroth on the subject of the Second Symphony, has documentary value. It proves the contrary of what lately has become, as a result of so many contemporary misjudgments, almost accepted dogma: that music, as long as it is new, must necessarily sound chaotic. One can see that on a receptive and talented listener—no one denies that untalented ones exist—Brahms's music had precisely the same effect when first performed that it has on a congenial listener of today, eighty years later, and that the overwhelmingly rich humanity expressed in his music was the principal element felt in it by his own contemporaries. This, however, is only partly true for the music of his formative period, with its occasional unevenness. The Violin Sonata, Opus 78, to which Elisabeth's letter referred, the Second Symphony, and the Violin Concerto heralded the beginning of Brahms's most abundant and glorious creative period, which he entered in his middle years as an accomplished, sovereign master. In this connection let us quote from another letter by Elisabeth, written after hearing the Fourth Symphony for the first time, in Berlin. Referring to the andante, she wrote: "This is all melody from beginning to end, and continues to get more beautiful the further one penetrates into it. It is like walking through an ideal landscape at sunset; the tones become ever warmer and more crimson. When the second theme in E major returned, we blissfully looked at each another and offered thanks to you."

The other member of this "we" was her husband Heinrich, who—to his dismay as well as hers—was never able to elicit for his own enormously prolific but unfortunately not very inspired musical output more than the most grudging comments from Brahms, whom he idolized. Brahms valued him as a highly cultured and noble-minded man and musician, but he was unable to tell a lie, and he could not praise what he considered inadequate. "My enjoyment of these people," he wrote to Clara, referring to the Herzogenbergs, "is appreciably curtailed, indeed may vanish altogether, because of his composing. I would be able to deal with this situation easily if only I could get to talk to him alone some time. But the wife is always present, and it is really difficult to find the right phrases." And on another occasion: "Herzogenberg's *Requiem* undoubtedly did not cause your face to light up with joy any more than it did mine. I don't know what to say to him about this dismal piece." And again: "If only one could enjoy any of his pieces the least bit! In every respect they are now weaker and poorer than his earlier compositions. The only happy feeling one can get is a thankfulness to God for having preserved one from the sin, the vice, or just the bad habit of mere musical scribbling." Once an impatient, offensive remark escaped him which grievously wounded poor Herzogenberg. Elisabeth courageously took her dear Heini's part and respectfully, but in no uncertain terms, made her standpoint clear: "I know you don't intend harm at such moments. But there is an imp sitting on your shoulder with whom, thank Heaven, you are not usually on intimate terms, but who whispers a few words to you which, when uttered by you at the wrong time, inflict sharp pain on others. If only you knew *how* sharp, you wouldn't do it. For you are basically good-natured and would never repay love with derision." Brahms, in trying to soothe her, had trouble finding the right words for an apology:

I confess that your letter was a real blessing, for I had feared you were out of sorts with me. Now this is not so, is it? And since you yourself say that I must be a good-natured fellow, I can reassure you quite solemnly on that score. So I ask you to consider that people should never part company solely on account of other things [how discreetly he includes her husband in the "other things"], since we encounter few really good persons and good things in the brief and rapid course of life. . . . Though I do not deserve such consideration, you must take nothing I do amiss; otherwise you would never cease feeling hurt. Wouldn't it be better not to begin at all?

But he steadfastly avoided saying a single word of praise that would be insincere, even though Elisabeth begged for it so prettily. Herzogenberg had sent him his setting of Psalm 94, and Elisabeth wrote about its successful performance, trying to pry an opinion out of him: "But from you he hasn't heard a single word about his music; it would mean so much to him." His answer was a triumph of diplomacy:

Nobody can receive and examine your husband's pieces with more zeal and affection than I do. But please don't ask me to go into further detail. I can find my way neither in nor out. Add to this that since we both strive for the same goals, I would be tempted, willy-nilly, to make comparisons with my own work. This would leave nothing but the text open to my cheerful criticism; and that also would bring me no credit since it would only indicate that I am not as industrious as Heinrich, and that I sit quietly and wait until something tempts me. The words of his psalm would not have done this; they bring to my mind a fanatical religious war, and such a thing one doesn't set to music.

Elisabeth von Herzogenberg was the most fascinating and most charming of the women who played a part in Brahms's later life, and the only one to whom he was attached by a bond of genuine, lasting friendship. The rest of the history of his romantic connections is of little interest. One by one his friends got married: his widowed father remarried; Hanslick, already in his late forties, found happiness with a young wife; both Joachim and Bülow married again after their first unions were shipwrecked. Brahms found women infinitely attractive, and he yielded with rapture to any budding fancy. Above all he was enthralled, body and soul, by a beautiful voice. But he turned mute as soon as a declaration was expected of him. At fifty he carried on a lively flirtation, widely noted by all his friends, with a young and pretty singer named Hermine Spies; and when almost sixty, he was bewitched by Alice Barbi, an attractive Italian, who sang his songs more beautifully than he had ever heard them before. But he never got beyond the stage of paying court; it pleased him to be considered a harmless rake. Edward Speyer, a well-to-do musical amateur who lived in England and was married to the daughter of Anton Kufferath of Brussels, an old friend of Brahms, tells in his memoirs of an amusing episode that took place in Frankfort. Brahms was expected in town, and Clara Schumann had asked Speyer, who happened to be there, to meet him at the station. Speyer relates: "The train rolled in, and I ran to the compartment which Brahms had already opened. He flung his arms about me, and then suddenly shoved me back with the words, 'Oh, forgive me; I thought you were your wife!'"

Brahms acted as though he gladly remained single out of conviction. To quote Widmann: "He generally spoke facetiously of his bachelorhood and liked, especially when confronted by inquisitive ladies, to use the gay formula, 'Unfortunately, madam, I am still unmarried, Heaven be praised.'" But at times he unburdened himself in earnest on the subject of his celibacy, giving motivations which are plausible but in no way convincing. He said to Widmann:

I missed my chance. When I still had the urge, I was unable to offer a woman what would have been the right thing. . . . At the time when I was still willing to get married, my compositions were received with hisses or with icy silence. Now I was perfectly able to put up with this, because I knew exactly what they were worth, and that the picture would eventually change. And when I would return to my lonely lodgings, I was by no means discouraged. On the contrary! But if at such moments I had had to face a wife, her questioning eyes anxiously seeking mine, and had to tell her that again it was nothing—that I could not have endured. For no matter how much a woman may love the artist who is her husband and, as the saying goes, have faith in him, she can never know the full certainty of eventual victory that dwells in his breast. . . . And if she had tried to console me—a woman's commiseration for her husband's failure—bah! I can't bear to think what a hell on earth that would have been, at least the way I feel about it.

This may have been true when he was thirty years old, but it hardly applied five years later; and at forty he was beyond all question so secure financially and so well established as a musician that no failure could possibly have touched him. Thus there must have been other inhibitions as well. He said to Hanslick: "I feel about matrimony the way I feel about opera: if I had once composed an opera and, for all I care, seen it fail, I would most certainly write another one. I cannot, however, make up my mind to either a first opera or a first marriage." Brahms frequently expressed himself with this allusion to the parallel between opera and marriage. Despite its apparent frivolity the thought merits further scrutiny. It is a fact that in his middle years he constantly and seriously toyed with the idea of an opera, and that this field, though alien to his experience, held great allurement for him. Paul Heyse, Widmann, Turgenev—all of his literary friends and acquaintances—knew of this interest, and during the course of years he was shown a great number of opera outlines and sketches, with which at times he occupied himself seriously. At no time, however, did such a plan progress beyond a first attempt, although he earnestly discussed one possibility, *King Stag* by Gozzi, in a letter to Widmann dated 1877. But nothing further came of it. Ten years later, when Brahms spent several summers in Thun, near Widmann's home, a number of newspaper dispatches appeared, dealing with the possibility of an opera by Brahms with a libretto by Widmann. The latter expressed regret that this was not in accord with the facts. To this Brahms replied: "Have I never spoken to you about my principles? One of them is never again to attempt either an opera or a marriage." And then he tried to persuade Widmann to accompany him on a trip to Italy: "If you, my dear friend, have really liberal views and principles, you can readily figure out how much money I can save for an Italian excursion if I don't get married or buy myself an opera text this summer. Couldn't we make the trip together for all this? In Italy I don't like to go it alone."

In both marriage and opera it was the unknown element which frightened him, who was accustomed to weigh all circumstances rationally beforehand; hence the regret for not having tried them earlier. As a young man one is still sufficiently fearless to overcome any uncontrollable component of an undertaking by simply ignoring it. A dramaturgic construction is far too removed from the practical experience of a musician for him to bet on it by entrusting it, for better or worse, with his music. And a woman is such an enigmatic being that accepting the physical and moral responsibility of a life with her would have necessitated a decision to which he did not feel equal. These may of course be rationalizations of far more deep-seated inhibitions whose origins remain hidden. "He once told my mother himself," writes Eugenie Schumann, "that when still a boy he had absorbed impressions and seen things which left a dark shadow on his soul." He often made simi-

lar remarks. He had grown up literally next door to prosti-
tutes and pimps in Hamburg's slum district. Billroth, to
whom he told a great deal about his childhood and adolescence, behaved in a very cool manner, much to Brahms's
dismay, when the latter introduced his "good father" to his
Viennese friends (see page 43). He could never forgive
the old man for having unconcernedly dragged the half-
grown boy into low dives just to earn a few extra marks.
When he referred to Brahms's "neglected upbringing," the
keen-eyed physician knew or conjectured perhaps more
and deeper things than Brahms himself wanted to admit.
One horrible fact can hardly be doubted: all that Eros had
in store for this man of infinitely delicate sensibilities, with
all his yearning for true love, was the chance of the street.

The real world of an artist is that of his phantasy. Experience in imagination is far more essential than experience in reality. A longing that is never fulfilled may act all
the more intensely on the level of artistic creation. Handel,
Beethoven, Schubert, and Bruckner lived in celibacy, just
as Brahms did. The reasons may have been different in
each case; there are paradoxes of all kinds in the realm
of creative achievement, and the process of sublimation
through which they come into being defies analysis. For
this reason the entire line of questioning is fundamentally
futile: the work of art and its transcending truth are all
that matters.

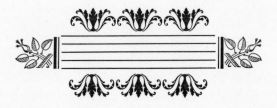

The Struggle for Mastery

THE PATHS of originality are inscrutable. There exists a staggering multiplicity of possibilities for a beginner endowed with genius to achieve mastery. They are determined by character, circumstances, and historical background, which at times may favor one, at times another manner of endeavor. However, the impression one gets from reading a history of music that the right man always emerges at the right time is almost certainly based on a fallacy. Actually the right man is invariably the one who by his own efforts succeeds in making his personal truth a universal one. In the abundance of possibilities the one and only phenomenon recurring with regularity is that such a man always begins by addressing a minority.

This is especially true of the modern artist, who no longer grows up as an artisan in the tradition of the workshop and gradually finds his own way, as his predecessors did in the sixteenth, seventeenth, and eighteenth centuries. The fate of the modern artist is to begin as an individual from the start. The conditions under which he matures depend on countless crisscrossing, mutually contradictory, positive and negative influences, which he may either accept or reject but toward which he must take a definite stand. How he does this is a question of his character, his environment, and his inner and outer development. The classical tradition which formed Brahms's background, with Bach's Well-Tempered Clavichord, with the Beethoven sonatas, with Haydn, Mozart, and Schubert, became blended with the urge for romantic expression symptomatic of the times and which at first, in his earliest published works, seems to predominate. Closer examination reveals, however, that this preponderance of sentiment is paired with an extraordinary sense of form fashioned after Beethoven. Romantic excess is an element antagonistic to form, or at least a danger to it. Young Brahms was a sleepwalker. As can occasionally be found in his early works of genius, he strode sure-footedly over pitfalls that would be dangerous to him only at a later stage when he had become aware of them. As a young musician Brahms was bursting with new ideas whose impetus carried him along, even though their quality may have been uneven. A critical analysis of, for example, his F-sharp minor Sonata, Opus 2, written earlier than his C major Sonata, Opus 1, reveals that the vibrant energy, with which a characteristic motif of Beethovenian proportions introduces the first movement, in the end leads nowhere. It exhausts itself in repetitions without developing into a true theme, as a real Beethoven motif would have done. This sort of thing no longer got by the mature and more critical Brahms. And this exciting but structurally imperfect opening is matched by a similarly incomplete ending in the coda of the finale: The movement basically does not come to an organic close; it breaks off and stops instead of ending.

Brahms later regarded his early works with mixed feelings. He loved them but steered clear of them. His principal publisher, Simrock, bought the rights to the earliest compositions from the original publishers, Breitkopf & Härtel, in order to reissue them. They had been long out of print, and Brahms upbraided him half seriously and half facetiously about his lack of acumen:

My dear Simrock, ought I to congratulate you? I can't say a word because I don't understand a word. . . . It is not my fault if you overestimate me sky-high. I certainly have not contributed to this by either word or deed. On the other hand I couldn't very well flay myself alive in front of you, could I? . . . I am touched by your kindness, but I find it exceedingly improvident that you buy things from Härtel—God knows how dearly—which may have cost them about 100 louis d'or and which in a very short time won't be worth a penny. . . . In order to show you my own kindness, or rather my compassion for your kindness, I should like to arrange right now, seriously and truly, that henceforth I receive no further payment from you but instead, as I suggested the other day, that a credit account be opened against which I can draw in case of need, and which will simply expire at the time of my death. You know my circumstances better than I do, and are therefore aware of the fact that I can get along beautifully without any further honorarium. And that I will, according to my un-Wagnerian way of life. At my death, however, I actually ought to bequeath the entire balance to you so that at least you get something out of the Härtel affair. So there, I congratulate you but wash my hands in carbolic acid and all kinds of things.

Needless to say, Simrock did not take him up on this generous offer; he knew the market value of Brahms's music better than the composer himself. And he earned a permanent place of honor by republishing Brahms's early works, if for no other reason than that this caused Brahms to undertake the highly significant revision of his B major Trio, about which we will speak later.

The artistic inheritance of the youthful Brahms included, in addition to a romantic melodic exuberance and a strict Beethovenian formal discipline, another stylistic element of fundamental significance: the folk tune, whose influence can be traced throughout his creative life. In a previously quoted letter to Clara Schumann (see page 56), he himself called attention to the "serpent that bites its own tail," to the melody, "Stealthily the moon is rising," which he used as a theme for variations in his Sonata, Opus 1, and with which he concluded his collection of German folk songs, his last effort as a composer of lieder. We don't know where the source of his lifelong enthusiasm for folk melodies is to be found: perhaps in childhood memories, perhaps in chance encounters at an impressionable age, or perhaps stimulated at least partly by a literary impression from one of his favorite books, *Des Knaben Wunderhorn* ("The Boy's Magic Horn"), an anthology of folk poetry by Achim von Arnim and Clemens Brentano. The simple, diatonic, and unsentimental folk tune remained a fountain of inspiration for him and safeguarded him from the affectation and chromatic exaggerations of the late romanticists. His passionate predilection for Hungarian folk music stemmed from the same source, as did probably a profound feeling of kinship with his younger contemporary, Dvořák, whose traditional Slavonic mode of expression delighted him. In Brahms's first collections of lieder, Opus 3 and Opus 6, a good deal points toward folk melodies as far as form and expression are concerned, and even though in his later lyricism he occasionally departed quite markedly from this archetype of the song, he always re-

turned to it. Finally, the experiences of his prolific output led to a technique in his folk-song arrangements that
bridges the difference between folk song and art song. To
what extent he must have been conscious, from the very
beginning, of the folk song as an ideal form can be seen
from a letter he addressed to Clara Schumann just after
he had arranged some folk songs for his Hamburg choral
society in 1860:

Now we get together quite informally once a week, and I believe the lovely folk tunes will amuse me most agreeably. I even
think I am learning a good deal, since I am compelled to study
and listen to the songs quite concentratedly. I want to absorb
them fully. It is not enough to sing through them once enthusiastically when one happens to be in the mood. Song-
writing is now sailing such a wrong tack that one can never do
enough to impress upon himself the ideal, which to me is the
folk song.

His youthful lyricism was dominated by the romanti-
cized folk style of the *Wunderhorn,* which played such a
large role in romantic poetry. It blossoms forth in his early
sonatas and perhaps even more abundantly in the most
ambitious work of his early period, the above-mentioned
B major Trio. Written early in 1854, it was the first chamber-music work he published. He withheld earlier chamber
music, although Schumann had recommended its publication. A letter to Schumann, written in November, 1853, explains Brahms's reasoning, and one cannot help but admire
the unsparing self-criticism of the young man:

The open praise which you bestowed on me has probably excited the expectations of the public to such a degree that I
don't know how I can come anywhere near fulfilling them.
Above all it induces me to use extreme caution in selecting
pieces for publication. I contemplate issuing none of my trios,
and to designate as Opus 1 and Opus 2 the C major and F-sharp

minor Sonatas, as Opus 3 the songs, and as Opus 4 the E-flat minor Scherzo. Of course you understand that I strive with all my might to cause you as little embarrassment as possible.

In the same letter he also mentioned a violin sonata which Schumann had proposed for publication but which Brahms set aside.

Immediately after completion of the B major Trio there occurred the tragic event which put an end to Brahms's period of carefree youthfulness. On February 27, 1854, Schumann threw himself into the Rhine and, although rescued, remained hopelessly deranged for the rest of his life. This catastrophe played a decisive role as a traumatic element in Brahms's life and further growth. The years following were a kind of incubation period for the seeds of his development; their focal point is a major work in which are concentrated all the conflicts, all the difficulties, and all the problems of the artist's maturation, from inception to ultimate mastery.

There are singular phenomena that take place in the soul of an artist, and here is one of the strangest: in Brahms's imagination the Schumann tragedy became associated with an artistic event of about the same time, forming a curious identity that defies analysis. In Cologne he heard Beethoven's Ninth Symphony for the first time, and the impact literally swept him off his feet. Perhaps the awesome experience which he had just undergone had made him ripe for the overwhelming effects of Beethoven's gigantic work. The feelings of his lacerated soul and the chaotic mood of catastrophe which he sensed in the first movement of the Ninth Symphony gave rise to an eruptive inspiration: the opening theme of the D minor Piano Concerto, which lay before him like an erratic boulder, huge and mysterious. The monumental idea challenged him to monumental treatment, but the young artist was still unsure of himself and did not know how far he dared go. The towering stature of the Ninth Symphony has caused disorder in the minds of generations. In this single work Beethoven advanced the frontiers of the symphonic form further than ever before. He solved the problem by his colossal force of will and his unfailing architectural instinct in a way that defied copying and against which all those who attempted imitation were shipwrecked. Any form can be said to be subject to physical limitations; its external dimensions are, by the principle of form itself, kept within certain boundaries which may well be elastic but by no means capable of unlimited expansion. The symphonic form—or sonata form, as we call it—becomes a monster when it outgrows its natural dimensions. A development section that runs into wide, uncoordinated episodes becomes a shapeless improvisation; a recapitulation is meaningless when it is so far removed from the exposition that the connection is no longer immediately recognizable. The principle of dramatic contrast, which underlies that form, is destroyed by such supersizes. In architecture the natural limitations are imposed by the building material; an oversized cathedral would collapse with the first wind, like a house of cards. If musical material were to react physically, many a symphony and many a tone poem would also disintegrate into dust with the very first orchestra rehearsal.

The young Brahms became only gradually aware of the problems he had conjured up. What he noticed first was really the least of the problems: it was the fact that he had not yet mastered the tools of the art. He was puzzled by the problem of projecting his idea into sound. He tried to capture it in the form of a sonata for two pianos, but found the piano timbre too neutral, too insipid for the mighty thoughts he envisioned. His imagination was powerfully stimulated by the possibilities of the orchestra; indeed an orchestral breadth of conception can definitely be discerned in the piano writing of his early works. This is what caused Schumann to refer to his sonatas as "veiled symphonies." On the other hand, his practical experience was limited to the piano, and whatever he attempted in the orchestral field was somehow encompassed within the world of piano sound. It cost him years of persistent labor before he learned to have a feeling for the true capabilities of orchestral sound. A composer's imagination is dependent on the tone combinations offered by the available instruments. Each has its specific advantages and difficulties, its technical and dynamic limitations, and its peculiarities of tone color in various registers. Only experience and knowledge of all the secrets of the craft can provide a composer with the sureness necessary for manipulating orchestration.

The opening theme of the D minor Concerto, an idea of primeval force, is a classic example of an invention in abstract space: The orchestra lacks the means for realizing what the composer had in mind. Dissatisfied with the piano effect, he attempted to turn the work into a symphony (see his letter to Joachim, page 61). Ultimately the idea of a piano concerto arose from the recognition that piano and orchestra sounds must blend together in order to achieve that for which he strove. To a certain extent he succeeded in this, but by no means without reservations. The effect of the grandiose beginning remains unsatisfying: The inner strings of the violins and cellos lack the necessary power, the consonance of clarinets and bassoons has a dull timbre, and the accompanying timpani roll ruins the picture completely unless kept so discreet that the threatening background thunder, which must have been the composer's intention, becomes ineffective. And this cannot be improved. The orchestra does not have instruments with the necessary force to do justice to the neighing, awe-inspiring trills of the theme. Brass instruments would be too strident. One must simply take the will for the deed and do his best to achieve the desired effect; this is almost possible with a sufficiently large string section. The young composer must have been conscious of these shortcomings from the very beginning, for he never tired of asking his friends for advice. "A thousand thanks for having studied the first movement in such a sympathetic and careful manner," he wrote to Joachim. "I have learned a great deal from your remarks. As a musician I really have no greater wish than to have more talent so that I can learn still more from such a friend." The further he progressed with the work, the more he became frustrated by obstacles to his attempts at doing justice to its grandiose conception. The highly charged character of the piece made it infinitely difficult for him to force the material into a mold. The classical, Mozartian formal plan concept, in which the solo instrument opposes its own thematic suggestions to those first introduced by the orchestra, results in a vast architectural breadth in which the subsidiary piano episodes appear almost like independent interludes. It cost Brahms an incredible amount of work to deal with these problems, and he spread it out over a period of four years. The task of following the passionate and tempestuous first movement with an adequate continuation in the following movement drove him to despair. He was finally successful, although not without certain questionable elements. These, however, form an integral part of this great and yet problematical work. A kind of saraband rhythm, sketched as the slow movement of the sonata for two pianos which he had originally planned, was ultimately transformed into the second movement of the

German Requiem. For the concerto he wrote a calm, dreamlike adagio, the opening of which, in manuscript, bears the device *Benedictus qui venit in nomine Domini*. This has more significance than the words themselves indicate. At that time the young musicians had bestowed the honorary nickname *Dominus* on Schumann. It is more difficult, however, to find an emotional link to the forceful, robust finale. The composer has here evaded a problem which at that stage was still beyond his capabilities; only years later did he find a solution in his First Symphony. But here he took advantage of the privileges of concerto-writing by providing the soloist with a brilliant ending. This brilliance, however, is not of a light and relaxed nature but rather of the gnarled and sometimes gruff manner characteristic of Brahms at the time. At any rate, the fact that the titanic struggle unleashed in the first movement does not in the end lead to anything more than a devil-may-care, now-let-us-live attitude, somehow bypasses the basic principle which Beethoven's concept of form had contributed to music. It is a credit to the healthy direct-ness of this finale that the hearer is scarcely aware of the esthetic question mark in it. But it is not surprising that the composition had no immediate success. It contained more unexpected and even bewildering elements than an unprepared public was willing to accept from a composer who was moreover, according to objective contemporary opinion, by no means an ideal performer of his own works.

The fact that his critical conscience was never entirely satisfied with the result is apparent from his written comments to Joachim:

I am sending you the rondo once more. And just like last time, I beg for some really *severe* criticism. Some parts have been completely replaced—for the better, I hope—others merely changed. Especially the ending was improved; it was too sketchy and did not accomplish what it set out to do. One place I left untouched, although it bears a mark on its forehead [probably a question mark in Joachim's hand]. Must it be removed at all costs? In the first movement I have smoothed out a few of the weak passages. I did not quite succeed with the first one and therefore left it alone, at least for the time being. I again enclose both movements; perhaps you can point out a few things that I can improve. . . . . In the finale several episodes are still very thinly orchestrated. I am still so ignorant, and don't know how to help myself.

Finally, just prior to the first public performance, again enclosing the manuscript: "If you are willing and able, do write me a few words to let me know whether the effort wasn't altogether futile, and whether it has a chance. I no longer have either judgment or control of the piece. Nothing decent will ever come of it anyway." Hence, the disappointment resulting from its lack of success was by no means unexpected: "I am still trying and groping," and "my second one will sound quite different." How prophetically his self-confidence asserted itself! Whoever reacts to defeat in this manner is an ideal illustration of Franz Grillparzer's definition: "A genius arises when talent and strength of character are combined."

It was necessary to deal with this composition in some detail because it occupies a key position in Brahms's productive work and in his inner development. The surprising and esthetically not entirely convincing turn of the finale into a differently oriented mode of expression is of symptomatic significance. It signals the breakthrough from the first movement's highly charged emotionalism and ponderous expressiveness and from the adagio's calmer but equally highly charged emotionalism to an objectivity and to a healthy, exuberant creativity freed of inner pressure— from the *Sturm und Drang* of the romanticists to the ideals of a new classicism that had gone through the romantic experience. Not only two styles but two artistic philosophies confront each other here. Brahms devoted half his creative life to the problem of finding a bridge between them. This circumstance explains what was touched upon in the preceding chapter: the extraordinary expense of time required by his developmental process, which actually continued into his mid-forties.

The D minor Concerto is not the only product of this tortured, disrupted period when the composer wrestled with the difficulties of forcing into a mold a substance heavy with experience and laden with passion. Passion is an inspiring but also an explosive, form-disrupting element. We are already acquainted with the Wertherian mood of the C minor Piano Quartet, which was sketched at that time (originally a half tone higher, in C-sharp minor; from this, however, he was dissuaded by Joachim because of its awkwardness for strings). And it appears that the inception of the First Symphony also harks back to this period. The piano quartet was published in 1875, the symphony in 1877; in both, the white heat had to cool and the emotional tension to ease before the composer could succeed in overcoming the problems of creating a form. The dual difficulty of learning how to harness both the form-destroying passion and the recalcitrant instruments was present everywhere. Another work of this interim period, highly charged with emotion, had to traverse a long and tortuous path of suffering before this problem was solved: the Piano Quintet in F minor, originally conceived (1862) as a string quintet and then a year later completed as a sonata for two pianos, but finally cast (1864) into a form in accord with its conception of sound. To lend the composer a friendly hand by reconstructing its lost—probably destroyed—version as a string quintet with two violoncellos, as has actually been attempted, is a naive undertaking. It is obviously not difficult to find places in it in which a string quintet would provide an excellent tone color. Brahms was fully aware of this, but he abandoned the attempt because he recognized that other passages, especially in the third and fourth movements, demanded more volume of sound and percussive force than strings are capable of providing. On the other hand he failed to find in the two-piano version that expressive, silklike string-and-bow color which was part of the original conception. For this reason he ultimately found the correct solution: a combination of piano and string instruments.

The essence of all this is his incorruptible critical conscience toward his work, his patience in letting it mature, and his iron determination to bring it to perfection. During the interim years in Düsseldorf and Hamburg, Brahms published very little, although he worked incessantly. At that time and in the following years in Hamburg, he found his footing with increasing confidence by an expansion of his musical horizon in the direction indicated to him by his already well-grounded acquaintance with the musical past. He recognized that Liszt's path of poetic ecstacy and surrender to emotions could not lead him anywhere. And now he strove for a better mastery of the textural and formal techniques, as he found them in the unattainably sublime and yet utterly natural creations of the giants of the past. His contrapuntal studies, which he carried out with Joachim, and his tireless scrutiny of works by the great masters constituted the principal elements of this endeavor. He even pored through old text books—Mattheson, Marpurg, and the like—finding stimulation everywhere, and every stimulation became productive in his teeming brain. The most striking phenomenon of latter-day music,

The youthful Brahms

Clara Schumann

Brahms at the age of fifty

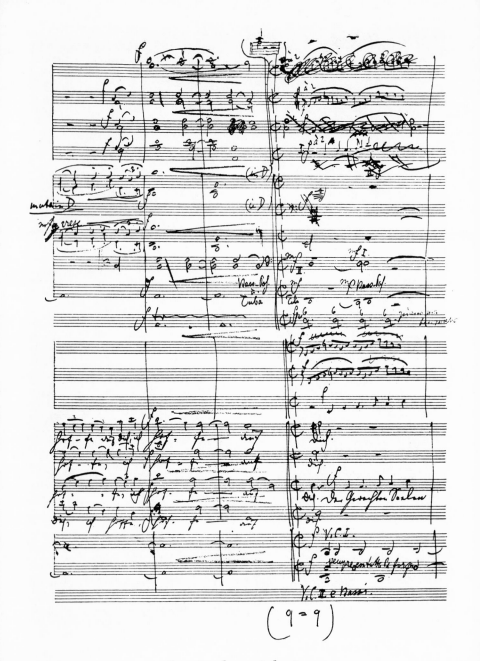

Opening bars of the fugue
"But the righteous souls are in the hands of God,"
from the third movement of the German Requiem

First page of the Double Concerto
for violin and cello, Opus 102

Cradle Song.
Music by Johannes Brahms,
words in Clara Schumann's handwriting

Johannes Brahms; last photograph (June 15, 1896)

"Want a walnetto?"

Brahms at the piano

the steadily growing posthumous influence of Bach, who was unknown during his life time, forgotten after his death, and actually discovered only a generation later, reached its climax in Brahms. For him the complete edition of Bach's works, which appeared in annual volumes starting in 1850, was a more significant artistic stimulus than any other musical event of his time. The great and permanent values of the past cannot be ignored as long as they continue to exist as a living reality. They may have been submerged or rendered unavailable by external circumstances, but from the moment they clearly enter an artist's cognizance, they become part of his universe. How he adjusts to them is a question that can only be answered individually. Brahms was the first one of the great musicians who faced this problem with full consciousness. His explorations into the realm of baroque music led him still further back: to Heinrich Schütz, to the *a capella* music of the 16th century, to Lasso, Palestrina, and their German contemporaries. Out of all this, whatever he has wrought into an integral component of his own musical consciousness was nothing eclectic, nothing adapted; it was rather a natural enrichment of his language which thereby became still more expressive, still more individual than before. What led him in this direction was originally prompted by instinct rather than by reasoning. His development consequently did not proceed in a straight line but rather in a spiral: seemingly going around in circles, he really progressed step by step. But he never entertained the slightest doubt as to the rightness of his goal, which to him was synonymous with the eternal, imperishable element in music of all time. If religion can be defined as a faith in absolute, supertemporal, and superpersonal values and truths, then this man, firm as a rock in his artistic ideals and deeply rooted beyond any conceivable shadow of a doubt, the prototype of a modern, illusion-free skeptic, was in the deepest sense religious.

Just as for Bach, who in his later works searched most intently for the mysteries in the art of counterpoint, so the ancient craft also had its mystic aspects for Brahms. When he followed its traces in joint studies with Joachim, he felt that he had found firm and unshakable ground under his feet. Among the music of this interim period which was subsequently published, there are quite a few compositions which presumably had their origin in this quest. His three sacred pieces for unaccompanied women's voices (*O bone Jesu, Adoramus,* and *Regina Cœli*) and a sacred song ("Let nothing be regretful"), all in difficult canonic settings, certainly form a part thereof, as do presumably the two *a capella* Motets, Opus 29 ("There is Salvation Come to Us" and "Make me, Lord, Pure of Heart"). The first of these is a five-part study in chorale variation. The second consists of two canons and two fugues in alternating sequence, of which the first section, a canon by augmentation, deserves special attention because it illustrates how deeply Brahms had penetrated into the innermost secrets of that venerable scholastic technique. In the exact middle of a chorale-like, dignified, and yet expressively simple movement there is a double bar line which may puzzle the reader at first. And yet it is this double bar which gives a guarded hint of the secret form construction: at this point, in the twelfth measure, the soprano melody, which is simultaneously started by the bass but sung in augmented time (with double the note values), comes to an end. Thus the bass arrives here at only the half-way point. Brahms now continues the augmented theme to the end while the soprano starts all over again from the beginning and repeats the entire melody which, as can now be seen, is in perfectly smooth counterpoint with both halves of itself as sung in doubled note values by the bass. One can almost hear the composer asking: "Quite aside from the skill in it, is it good music? Do the artifices make it more beautiful and valuable?" A technical sleight of hand is idle play if the resulting music does not flow so naturally that the contrapuntal strait jacket is not noticed. This he had learned from the old masters. Its purpose? A discipline for the imagination, which benefits by using and shaping tonal material in all conceivable combinations; a means to an end, but never an end in itself. Brahms always retained a predilection for subtle contrapuntal constructions. They can be found, for example, in his *Variations on a Theme by Haydn* and in all his symphonies. After one has just enjoyed the lovely, simple melody which introduces the scherzo movement of his Clarinet Quintet, one suddenly becomes aware that the scherzo theme itself is a contrapuntal combination of two motifs which seem to be quite unintentionally stated, one after the other, in the introduction. And when Brahms, for some reason or other, was forced to comply with the request of an annoying autograph hunter, he did so in the form of a puzzle canon in which the words present a riddle. He wrote down only the first word, "When," and at the end, "Ludwig Uhland." Those well versed in literature will find the solution in an epigram by Uhland:

> *When will this rain of albums cease,*
> *And autograph hunters give us peace?*

To him this kind of a joke was always worth some brain racking.

During the Hamburg years, in which his already masterful ability was developed, through incessant labor, into a technique of unsurpassable virtuosity, his creative output grew constantly richer and broader. Having found his way out of the distressing situation at Düsseldorf into freedom, he now began joyfully to feel his own strength. In addition to the D minor Concerto, which bore the burden of all his sorrows and frustrations and from which he wanted to escape into other, friendlier fields, there appeared an abundance of other works, every one a definite step forward. In each of these he conquered new possibilities of expression and displayed new aspects of his technique of form and texture.

Part of the depth of his nature was that any occupation with a problem of composition spurred his imagination far beyond whatever was immediately requisite; the result was the double composition, which became characteristic of most of his later work. If for example he was immersed in writing a piano quartet, his inspiration within the framework of this ensemble was so stimulated that it carried him into a second one at once. Thus he produced in rapid succession two serenades, two piano quartets, and two sextets. And in every case the second of the pairs was richer, his technique in it surer, and his form freer and bolder. By the same token, he later wrote in uninterrupted sequence two symphonies, the two String Quartets, Opus 51, two overtures, two pieces of chamber music for clarinet, and two clarinet sonatas. During that Hamburg period he mastered one technique after another through methodical effort. In so doing, however, he still seemed timidly to avoid the two challenges which to him were the greatest and most demanding in the field of instrumental music: the string quartet and the symphony.

The economy of the pure four-part setting of the former and the unlimited possibilities of the latter presented him with problems to which he did not yet feel equal. According to his own statements, his first string quartets, published in 1873, were preceded by many attempts which were rejected. He again briefly toyed with the idea of a symphony when he rearranged for orchestra a sketch originally intended for an octet. But the idyllic character of this work caused him to turn it into a serenade, his No. 1 in D major, scored for a full Beethovenian orchestra. Again Joachim became his counselor, playing it in Hanover for the first time. "What a magnificent surprise!" he wrote to Brahms after receiving the first movements. "Your orchestration is almost everywhere effective and in many places even beautifully original; only very little will have to be changed. Some of the passages must be played through before one can come to a decision. . . . So much after a first reading—do continue and finish it happily." Simultaneously the second serenade had already progressed quite far. It employs no violins—an experiment Brahms had attentively studied in Méhul's opera *Uthal* and which he tried again in the opening number of the *German Requiem*. Neither of the serenades is a fully matured exercise in orchestration, in the sense that the composer still utilized the facilities of the instruments in a somewhat hesitating manner, with chamber-music-like caution. Both lack the full force of color, the alfresco character of a genuine symphonic style. But both have the virtue of relaxed, youthful grace and charm, the D major one in a more forceful and robust, the A major one in a more delicate and lyric manner. The latter is probably the more personal and appealing of the two; the somber, subdued sound of the violinless orchestra, in which the violas predominate, lends it a peculiarly dreamlike character, more appropriate for an intimate background than for a big concert hall. No doubt the court at Detmold had some part in the conception of this music, which has such a timeless effect, and perhaps also the Göttingen idyl, the Agathe episode. With these two works, which belong to a friendlier world, the composer has with finality left the deep recesses of his *Sturm und Drang* period behind him.

It is easy to understand why he included in his early chamber music the piano, with which he felt himself in his element. The two Piano Quartets in G minor and A major—he had in the meantime discarded the *Werther* quartet—were his first masterpieces in the grand manner, which by this time he knew how to handle with assurance. Only now did he venture into the realm of pure string music with his B-flat major Sextet, which again was introduced on the concert stage by Joachim. It was through these three works, the two Piano Quartets and the Sextet, which truly signaled his initiation into full mastership, that Brahms achieved his first successes in Vienna.

At the same time the pianist in him was not idle, either, and constantly provided stimulation to the composer. At the piano he now thoroughly applied himself to the variation form. His first work in this genre had already originated during his first spring season in Düsseldorf—the *Variations on a Theme by Him dedicated to Her,* as he inscribed on the manuscript. The theme was by Schumann. In this very significant work he had already penetrated deeply into the techniques of variation writing, which he learned only later to handle knowingly and which during his last year in Hamburg (1861) culminated in the *Variations and Fugue on a Theme by Handel,* one of the most important piano works he ever created.

One problem of style remained unresolved during this developmental period of almost ten years: the juxtaposition of romantic, emotional substance and formal, classical construction. It would be definitely exaggerated to speak here of a stylistic conflict, but it cannot be denied that at times one, at times the other mode of expression predominated. In the melodious episodes the romantic element is likely to prevail, and in the lively passages the formal element, occasionally accompanied by a certain cooling off. The classical stylization at times leads to almost demonstrative archaism. In the minuet of the D major Serenade, for example, the trio part is marked *Menuetto II* in the manner of designation common in baroque times, and its style is entirely in conformity with this. The bucolic opening theme of the first section, reminiscent of Haydn, stands in contrast to a romantic, nostalgic triplet figure in the trio section; the restless, haunted first scherzo and the poetry-filled adagio contrast with a rather robust, Beethovenian second scherzo. It takes a great deal of self-confidence to venture such an experiment, and it takes an unrestrained creative imagination to fill the ancient vessel again and again with new, original material. Even though it all sounds fresh and amiable, one is nevertheless tempted to skip the two frankly archaistic movements, the minuet and the second scherzo, thereby restoring the original four-movement symphonic structure. And in the far more mature, uncommonly poetic A major Serenade an interpolated supernumerary scherzo, of a vigorous, classical style, is apt to cause more disquiet than contrast.

It is unnecessary to follow this dualism through all the compositions of this interim period. Both elements were equally important and equally fruitful in the composer's inventive process. The further he advanced, the more natural and unfettered became his style, in which every note was inspired and every detail carefully balanced as to form and expression. Whereas the classical element with its cool, light brilliance predominates by far in the variations on the ultrabaroque theme of Handel, the Trio in E-flat major for horn, violin, and piano, written four years later, is devoted entirely to romantic memories of younger days. And a counterpart to the old-style motets and the *Marienlieder* ("Songs to the Blessed Virgin Mary")—the latter in a wonderfully vigorous style inspired by the masters of the German secular part song of the sixteenth century: Senfl, Hofhaimer, and Hassler—is a work of the most delicate and warmhearted soulfulness: the Four Songs, Opus 17, for women's voices accompanied by harp and French horns. They reflect the light of the youthful, blond face of Johannes, and Clara, not without reason, was enamored of them. In even more striking apposition are the two styles in his Three Songs, Opus 42, for six-part mixed chorus. These also stem from his Hamburg period. The first two, "Serenade" and "Vineta," follow the style of the romantic part songs of Schumann, while the third, "Darthula's Lament," begins and ends like an antiphonal chorus of the sixteenth century but has a middle section in the romantic lieder style. And yet, because the musical construction flows so naturally from the words and their expression, one never has any sensation of discrepancy.

Here a remark may perhaps be interpolated. Even among the great masters, Brahms is unique in that all of his instrumental works—chamber music, orchestral compositions, and piano music—form in their entirety a part of today's living concert repertoire. This might lead to the assumption that his vocal compositions are less viable, for it cannot be denied that today far fewer of these works are to be heard than one might expect from their analogy with his instrumental music. But this assumption would be wrong. The cause of the phenomenon lies in the over-all development that music has undergone in our century. The gigantic growth in virtuosity, accompanied by an enormously increased capability of professional musicians in general and by an unprecedented availability of music in the concert hall, in recordings, and on the radio, has resulted in a progressive and evidently relentless deterioration of amateur participation in music. Certain branches of musical life have virtually ceased to function altogether. This had its effect on the music of Brahms, as on that of all other composers, which depends on active participation by nonprofessionals. Brahms's piano music for four hands is just as much affected by this as are his vocal quartets and duets and his unaccompanied choral works. The exclusivity with which lieder are today left to professional singers accounts for the fact that, because they are no longer generally known, two thirds of Brahms's songs have already become promising objects for rediscovery. The few dozen which have for one reason or another become popular, and which therefore must be in every singer's repertoire, have forced all the rest out of the race. The resulting evil is twofold. Not only have we become deprived of precious music of all ages which happens not to fit into our standardized concert pattern— music for "connoisseurs and music lovers," as Bach called it—but also of the connoisseurs themselves, who have ceased to be participating factors. If during his lifetime Brahms was already considered a worthy and equivalent successor to the great classical composers, the credit for this is due to a hundred thousand choral singers who never tired of singing his music, and to the countless amateurs, instrumentalists or singers, who have taken up his music with ever-growing affection and enthusiasm. Wagner would not have become popular, any more than Brahms, had it not been for the hundreds of thousands of vocal scores and piano transcriptions of his works, which made his music the true property of music lovers everywhere. The impoverishment of present-day music continues progressively and ceaselessly, for neither radios nor record players can be true substitutes. Anyone who has ever taken part, no matter how humbly, in the joy of making music will understand this. Only those who experience music through active participation can truly make it their own.

Brahms, himself a devoted performer of music, wrote music for people who make music. This is one of its most essential qualities; it helps strengthen its part structure and makes it stimulating for the executants. For him these were always the decisive critics, and beyond them was the public, the community of listeners. No matter how mixed, it constituted a tribunal whose competence he always acknowledged. The idea of appealing from an unappreciative present to an imaginary future would have seemed preposterous to him. When he experienced a failure, he only blamed himself; and there were failures which caused him bitter grief. The disappointment of his first great orchestral composition, the D minor Piano Concerto, was equaled by that occasioned by his last one, the Double Concerto for violin and cello. Mandyszewski was convinced that at that time Brahms had planned, and perhaps even partly sketched, another concerto for two or three instruments, in accordance with his habit of writing two compositions of kindred techniques in rapid succession. The indifference with which the Double Concerto was received at its first hearings, in Vienna as well as elsewhere, and the respectful but noticeable reserve with which his friends and even the performers themselves reacted to it, depressed and discouraged him profoundly. From that time on he often spoke of having reached the end of his road and of not wanting to compose anything further. The rapid decline of his vitality and creative impulse, which became apparent toward his sixtieth year, was probably very much a result of this. He often expressed disappointment when his compositions at times failed in their living reality to measure up to the ideal he had envisaged. For some reason the synthesis of the Double Concerto out of its component parts did not come up to his expectations, just as had happened so often with his early works.

In those earlier days, however, there were technical reasons or reasons of insufficient experience on which he could put the blame for such disappointments, and he was determined to learn how to do better. His profound sense of responsibility caused him to consider any new branch of music to which he turned as a set of challenges, which he then sought to approach in a methodical manner. In Detmold, then twenty-five years old, he gained his first experience as orchestral and choral conductor, and his women's chorus in Hamburg served as a valuable complement. In Vienna he widened his horizon by his activity as an oratorio conductor. And now a big object which spurred his imagination provided him with the impetus for a conception which made it possible for his full powers, by now matured and equal to any task, to unfold. Thus came into being the *German Requiem*, which, at the threshold of the full mastery he had acquired through fifteen years of unremitting toil, combined all the fullness of youth and all the enthusiasm of a soul thirsting for expression into a unique accomplishment. Anything in this work that may still be recognizable as a symptom of his interim period— the orchestration still may not be fully commensurate with the intended sound—is of secondary importance. Such occasional imperfections are obliterated by an infallible sense of form unhesitatingly reaching for greatness, an intense feeling for poetic expression, and a masterful handling of vocal settings. But the most essential thing that the composer achieved in this work defies all analysis: the depth of experience and its utterance, which touches the listener to his innermost soul and captivates him. This is the mysterious ingredient of those great works that tower above time.

Brahms had not made it easy for himself. A performance under Herbeck of the first three movements in December, 1867, in Vienna, was rather a failure, probably because of insufficient preparation. Afterward, Brahms "did a thorough cleanup job with his pen," as he wrote to Reinthaler. And even after the decisive victory at the performance in the Bremen Cathedral in April, 1868, he still added a magnificent movement with solo soprano. Incidentally, despite all his exhaustive experience, he remained true to his habit of thoroughly trying out any new work before he considered it ready for publication. But this was the last work with which he had to experiment. From now on he was a master.

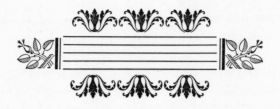

The Antipode and
the Battle of Opinions

ONE THING, however, he could not become at that time: *the* master. That title had already been awarded; that throne he found already occupied. No matter how highly developed Brahms's genuine inner humility may have been, the Wagner cult and the rivalry with Wagner that it forced upon him accompanied his entire rise to fame like a constantly recurring theme, and it must often have caused him bitter vexation. Competition between those who strive for the same goals or between artists who follow similar ideals can be a noble impulse. But rivalry can become a source of evil, uncontrollable emotions when incompatible faiths confront each other in uncompromising, diametrically opposed contradiction.

Brahms took every opportunity to express, by word of mouth or in the form of letters, his respect for Wagner's artistic stature and seriousness, and he liked to designate himself "the most ardent of the Wagnerians," with the justifiable claim that he understood Wagner's musical qualities better than anyone else. No musician of his penetrating insight could possibly look at a Wagner score without admiring the workmanship of the sovereign master. But he found Wagner's theories absurd, his arguments sophistic, his publicity and propaganda methods demagogic, and his almost pathological urge for surrounding himself with extravagant luxuries cheap and vulgar. (Concerning the last point, see a remark in the letter to Simrock quoted on page 108.)

At the time of his visit to Liszt in Weimar, when he was twenty years old, he knew nothing of all this and had probably never even heard a note of Wagner's music. But a nature as strong as his reacts with great sureness of instinct, whether positively or negatively. What he encountered in Weimar at the time remained for him simply an evil principle with which he was not prepared to compromise. The negative example of the "Music of the Future" was hardly necessary to make him a radical idealist of form, for this was part of his nature. Liszt's music and Liszt's intentions he could brush off with a clear conscience as "swindle." But next to Liszt there was someone of quite a different caliber, one whose shadow, as *Lohengrin, Tannhäuser,* and *Der fliegende Holländer* conquered one opera house after the other, would within the next decade fall more and more heavily across the stage of German musical life. Wagner could no longer be ignored.

The way the two actually met seems like a stage trick arranged by fate. Very shortly after Brahms had arrived in Vienna in the fall of 1862, Wagner appeared on the scene in order to supervise the production of his *Tristan* at the Vienna Court Opera House. This was subsequently postponed for an indefinite period of time after months of rehearsals, on account of insoluble problems of casting. Wagner's closest friends in Vienna were Cornelius and Tausig, with whom Brahms had just established amicable relations and through whom he came into contact with Wagner. He considered it by no means below his dignity to do some copying for the great man. The latter, accustomed to conducting his affairs in grand style and without regard to cost, decided to produce a series of three orchestral concerts with excerpts from *Das Rheingold, Die Walküre,* and *Die Meistersinger.* This necessitated the copying of orchestra parts, since none of these works had at that time appeared in print. For further details we may turn to Wagner's memoirs:

Both Cornelius and Tausig, assisted by a few more copyists, got down to work, which because of the necessity for musical accuracy could only be entrusted to reliable score readers. . . . Tausig mentioned Brahms to me, recommending him as a "very good fellow" who, although already famous in his own right, would be glad to undertake part of the work; he was given a section of *Die Meistersinger* to copy out. Indeed, Brahms's behavior proved modest and good-natured; only he seemed to lack liveliness, so that in our meetings he was often scarcely noticed.

The taciturnity of the guest on these occasions can be accounted for by Wagner's expansive and enormously vivacious manner and his untiring perorations and argumentations, which probably made Brahms, the reserved North German, even more monosyllabic than usual. Above all there was a fundamental conflict of character, which could hardly be bridged. In opposition to the passionately excited and restlessly driving nature of Wagner and his

insatiable need for communicating, there stood the self-
control and the coolly deliberate manner of Brahms, ob-
serving from a distance and keeping his own counsel.

The situation brings to mind another one, fifteen years
previously, which was described by Hanslick, who had
made the acquaintance of both Schumann and Wagner in
Dresden, where the latter as conductor at the Royal
Opera House had just produced *Tannhäuser* for the first
time. Wagner spoke of Schumann with respect but without warmth: "On the surface we are on very good terms
with each other. But it is impossible to communicate with
Schumann. The man is hopeless; he does not talk at all."
And Hanslick goes on: "[Wagner] talked unbelievably
much and rapidly, in a monotonous, singsong Saxon drawl;
he spoke incessantly of himself, his works, his reforms, his
plans. If he ever mentioned the name of any other composer, he did so in a disparaging manner." On one occasion, in Schumann's house, the conversation turned to
Wagner, and Hanslick asked whether Schumann had any
social intercourse with him. "No," replied the latter, "for
me Wagner is impossible; no doubt he is a spirited man,
but he talks without ever stopping. One just can't talk all
the time."

Although Brahms was taciturn in Wagner's presence, he
could at least play the piano for him. It is known that he
played his Handel Variations for Wagner, and the latter
made an appreciative remark to the effect that a good deal
could still be done using the old formulas, provided one
knows how to handle them. This incident, by the way, was
confirmed by Wagner himself, who otherwise in his essay
On Conducting had less friendly things to say about
Brahms. In it he describes the occasion with his peculiar,
inimitably malicious irony: "Objectively regarded, there
is nothing wrong with these musicians, most of whom

compose fairly well. Mr. Johannes Brahms once was good enough to play some piece with serious variations for me, from which I could tell that he is not a joker, and which I considered quite acceptable."

It is understandable that relations between the two remained cool and polite; there was no occasion for any closer *rapprochement*. Brahms took the opportunity of studying Wagner's scores in detail, and he was present at Wagner's concerts which created a sensational impression plus a massive deficit in Vienna, which Wagner, in his unconcerned fashion, left for his Viennese friends to cover. Although Wagner's junior by twenty years, Brahms could learn nothing from him. Their fundamental philosophies clashed far beyond the natural contrast between symphonic and dramatic composer. Their antagonism was already expressed in Wagner's condescending remark about the "old formulas." He as well as Liszt had so often, so emphatically, and so incontestably affirmed and proven that these patterns of form no longer had any claim to existence, that it was an oddity, to say the least, if anybody acted as though they still existed. For Brahms, on the other hand, they constituted the greatest and most productive musical heritage, the concentrated wisdom of generations, whose mastery is the first and foremost duty of every serious worker. Whatever he knew, whatever he was to attain, was the result of his immersion in the essence of his great spiritual ancestors, who had sat at the fountainhead of wisdom and who had been able to draw directly from this source. He considered himself an infinitesimal particle in this vast macrocosm. To him the *St. Matthew Passion*, the *Well-Tempered Clavichord*, *Don Giovanni*, *Fidelio*, Haydn's string quartets, and Schubert's lieder were what the Tabernacle is to the faithful: symbols of eternal truth. Compared with this artistic conception,

Wagner's becomes crudely disrespectful toward all tradition. To Wagner, despite his appreciation of certain great individual accomplishments, tradition meant something purely historical, a sequence of embryonic stages of evolution, the culmination of which was he himself, who had made a reality of the only meritorious, genuine, eternal ideal: the universal work of art. There is something grandiose in this megalomania; it led the way to the *Ring*, to *Tristan, Die Meistersinger, Parsifal,* and to Bayreuth as a shrine and an object of pilgrimage. For the full blossoming forth of his productive powers, he evidently needed the euphoria of this self-adoration. He was somehow disarmingly naive in all this; for example, when he wrote to his friend Theodor Uhlig in Dresden about the conception of the *Ring*, he concluded with the words: "The whole will then become—out with it! I am not ashamed to say so—the greatest work of poetry ever written." Small wonder that there was no poet, no composer among his contemporaries about whom he was prepared to say a single kind word.

The fact that Hanslick, who was Wagner's most obstinate and most critical opponent, again and again took the opportunity of playing Brahms against Wagner, may have led the latter to suppose that Brahms was behind Hanslick's vicious attacks. In this he was certainly unjustified. There is no record of a single anti-Wagner statement by Brahms, and Hanslick himself assures us: "I have often heard him eagerly taking Wagner's part when narrow-mindedness or stupid presumptuousness expressed itself in disdainful abuse. He recognized and fully appreciated the brilliant aspects of Wagner." But it was more than Wagner could bear to have anyone else taken seriously, and he considered it positively and completely unforgivable that Brahms irrepressibly rose to continuously greater fame following the appearance of his *German Requiem*. In 1879 the University of Breslau had conferred an honorary doctorate on Brahms. When the news was disseminated by the press, quoting the citation in the diploma which named him *artis musicae severioris in Germania nunc princeps* ("first among today's masters of serious music in Germany"), and since in addition there were coincidental special honors awarded to him on the occasion of the golden jubilee of the Hamburg Philharmonic Concerts, the Master of Bayreuth lost all patience. He published his essay "On Poetry and Composition" in the Bayreuth *Blätter*, in which he attacked Brahms in the most venomous manner without mentioning his name:

Compose, compose, even if you don't have the slightest ideas! Why should it be called composing, i.e., putting together, if invention were an essential part of it? But the more boring you are, the more distinctive a mask you must choose; this amuses the public! I know of some famous composers who in their concert masquerades choose the disguise of a cabaret singer one day [*Liebeslieder* waltzes], the hallelujah periwig of Handel the next [*Song of Triumph*], the dress of a Jewish czardas fiddler another time [*Hungarian Dances*], and then again the guise of a highly respectable symphonic composer dressed up as a Number Ten [reference to Bülow's characterization, see page 68]. You laugh. This seems easy to you witty listeners! But these others are so serious, so strict, that one of them had to be given a diploma as First Prince of Music of our Time in order to stop your laughter. But perhaps you are again laughing about this? This solemn prince of music might perchance have appeared very boring to you if you clever ones had not discovered that something not at all so dignified was hiding behind the mask but rather someone exactly like yourselves, with whom you can now turn around and play masquerade, by acting as though you were admiring him. This in turn will again amuse you when you notice that he puts on a face as though he believed you. My late colleague in the Dresden conductorship, Gottlieb Reissiger, composer of *Weber's Last Thought* [a waltz by Reissiger that had been popular], once bitterly complained to me that the selfsame melody which in Bellini's *Romeo and Juliet* had always aroused the public to enthusiasm made no impression at all in his own *Adèle de Foix*. We fear that the composer of Schumann's Last Thought [the *German Requiem*] has reason to complain about similar misfortunes. Mendelssohn's great saying [referring to Berlioz], "Everyone composes as well as he is able," constitutes a standard of wisdom which fundamentally will never be surpassed. The evil begins only when one tries to compose better than one is able. Since this cannot logically be done, one can at least put on airs as though one could do it. This is the disguise. But it still doesn't do much harm; it only becomes serious when many people—committee members and such—are fooled by the mask, and when festival banquets in Hamburg or diplomas in Breslau result. Such misrepresentation can only be rendered possible by making people believe that one composes better than others who really compose well.

Brahms did not in any way react to this outburst of temper. He knew how to differentiate between Wagner the serious artist, whom he respected, and Wagner the malicious polemicist, who by doing this sort of thing did more injury to his own dignity than to that of the persons he attacked. But toward Wagnerianism as such, toward the claim of exclusive validity for an esthetic dictatorship whose principles seemed utterly reprehensible to Brahms, one must not expect any friendly feelings from a character wrought of such hard timber as was that of Brahms, nor from an artist fully conscious of his own worth, who had for decades been compelled to maintain himself against the pressures of a powerful opposition party. He had not been able to please the conservatives any more than the progressives. Reservations similar to those expressed by

Hanslick with the best of intentions, at the time of Brahms's first concert in Vienna (see page 79), had been familiar to him from previous occasions in Leipzig and Hamburg: absence of melodies that are easily committed to memory, unnecessarily involved structures, and harmonic and contrapuntal hypertrophy. The better his image became established in the public mind since the appearance of the *German Requiem* and the *Song of Triumph*, the more virulent became the attacks against him from the publicity-conscious Wagner party. What Cornelius, normally a benevolent and objective observer, wrote to his sister in a letter concerning the *German Requiem* is characteristic of an esthetic which had not one single feature in common with that of Brahms. Despite the fact that he represented the more moderate wing of the party, Cornelius wrote: "It wouldn't tempt me in the least to sing before the public for the hundredth time, with all the beautiful and rich devices of the art, how the Middle Ages contemplated death."

Contemporary estimates, no matter how biased, are always of interest because they show how an immediate impression was formed before preconceived opinions could exist. This is true in spite of differences in receptivity and in positive or negative prejudices. Wagner certainly was nothing less than an objective observer. But the fact that he found Brahms boring and deficient in invention had deeper causes. What a dramatic composer looks for in an idea is direct appeal to the senses. Wagner would not have known what to do with a Brahms theme. If one considers, for example, the latter's First Symphony—probably the only one which Wagner ever heard—one can well imagine Wagner's impatience during the first movement while he listened for an idea, for a melody that irresistibly fills the universe with grandeur and emotion. The nobility of this first movement rests on qualities that were alien to the dramatic composer: a thematic interplay worked out to the smallest detail and based on polyphonic structure; a delicate balancing, from beginning to end, of tonal relationships; and a formal design whose grandiose dimensions only become apparent when one experiences the whole movement as a single, great continuum. It may be added here that in the First Symphony the composer was still engaged in a struggle to conquer the monumental Beethovenian principle of form. The uncertainties besetting young Johannes, the passionate nature of his innermost soul, the chaotic world of Beethoven's Ninth which he could not escape and which cost him many years of insoluble problems in trying to adapt it to his own form—all these account for certain peculiarities in this work which stamp it as a product of his interim period despite its late appearance (Brahms was forty-two at the time of its publication). Perhaps even more striking than the similarity between the hymnlike theme of the finale and the *Ode to Joy* in the last movement of Beethoven's Ninth (which "any jackass could see," as Brahms himself said, his crudeness masking a bad conscience), is the over-all emotional curve going through the whole work, which may with some oversimplification be designated as "through darkness to light," or "struggle and victory." In this respect it follows the examples of Beethoven's Fifth and Ninth Symphonies unashamedly. Billroth understood this at once when Brahms showed him the score: "The thought that the entire symphony is based on an emotional pattern very similar to that of Beethoven's Ninth became increasingly clear to me as I studied it." The universality of such musical thought precludes the slightest objection; it is an integral part of Beethoven's symphonic art to which Brahms's is closely related. One fundamental difference, however, must not be overlooked: Beethoven was an idealist and a convinced optimist; the optimistic philosophy of the Rationalists, as expressed in Leibniz's faith in "the best of all possible worlds," remained alive in him, as it did in Schiller. How far Brahms, the skeptical pessimist of the late nineteenth century, was removed from this conception! The hymnlike enthusiasm of his finale lacks the ultimate in genuine, convinced, and convincing joy. The jubilation with which the movement comes to a close is the result of a self-delusion. One can sense in it more the desire to be joyful than real surrender to joy. No doubt this finale has always been the decisive factor in the effectiveness of this symphony; it achieves victory through the magnificence of its hymnic theme and through the transcending beauty of the horn solo which enters like a first beam of sunlight during the transition from the somber introduction to the allegro. The fate of this movement, and thus of the entire symphony, appears to have been decided by this inspired idea which Brahms had already mentioned in a letter to Clara Schumann on September 12, 1868, eight years prior to the completion of the symphony:

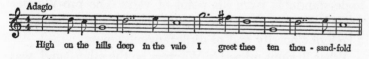

High on the hills deep in the vale I greet thee ten thou - sand-fold

The added words were of course only meant as an endearment and had nothing to do with the symphony. To a very sensitive hearer this great moment suffers from an ambiguity which one may readily admit: it is theatrical rather than symphonic. With its tremolo accompaniment, its second-inversion chord, and with the solemn chorale following it, it is unique and anomalous in the entire world of Brahms's symphonic production. By the same token, the exultation in the coda somehow seems con-

trived, not fully convincing. Clara, with her extraordinary
sensitivity, made an innocent remark which certainly hits
the nail on the head:

If I may still say something about the last movement, or rather
the very end of the movement (the presto), I do feel that musically the presto, compared with the supreme exaltation that
precedes it, falls a bit flat. To me its intensification seems to lie
in external rather than internal emotion; it somehow does not
organically evolve from the whole, but seems merely to have
been added as a brilliant afterthought. Forgive me, my dear
Johannes, but I can't help being perfectly frank with you.

Brahms was hardly ever in any mood for jubilation. Perhaps the nearest thing to it can be found in the finale of
his Second Symphony, but even there it seems somehow
modified by a classical stylization. And if one disregards
the luxuriant beards and raised beer tankards in the coda
of the *Academic Festival Ouverture*, which may be set
aside anyway as a work for a particular occasion, there is
no other place where Brahms bursts out in to such untroubled C major joyousness. If Wagner spotted certain
weaknesses in Brahms as a symphonic writer, this is quite
understandable from his point of view. The pro-Wagner
press has never ceased to accuse Brahms's symphonies of
a lack of sincerity and of direct inventiveness.

What Brahms missed in Wagner, on the other hand, was
a background perspective of the grand form, which did
not mean a thing to the dramatic composer. Brahms's most
telling and positive expression concerning his great anti-
pode is contained in a letter (1888) to Widmann: "If the
Bayreuth theatre were in France, it would not require
anything as grandiose as Wagner's works to make you
and Wendt [a philosopher and esthetician] and all the rest
of the world undertake pilgrimages there and be inspired
by such ideally conceived and created things."

Still, this estimate must be understood with certain reservations which the absolute, as opposed to the dramatic, composer found necessary to express and which are summed up in the following statement made by Brahms to his friend Rudolf von der Leyen: "One cannot do a greater disservice to Wagner than by bringing his music into a concert hall. It is created solely for the theatrical stage, and that is where it belongs." What made Wagner great, and what fascinated Brahms, was the white heat of his inventive process and the unique depth and individuality of certain of his ideas. Inspirations such as the *Ride of the Valkyries,* which Wagner performed then for the first time in Vienna, delighted Brahms again and again. But such inspiration carries both its effect and its fulfillment within itself; it is not capable of being extended or of being made symphonically fertile. For this reason such lofty heights in Wagner's inventiveness never grew beyond the stage of episodes. When it comes to larger, seemingly symphonic, forms such as the overtures to *Der Fliegende Holländer* or *Tannhäuser,* and even that to *Die Meistersinger,* the structural principle rests in the last analysis on the episodic, Weber-like form of loosely connected moments of individual invention, more akin to the potpourri than to the symphony. The subtle interweaving of the conjoined episodes only serves to bring into sharper focus the looseness of the formal scheme and the superficiality of the connecting links. In addition to all this there is an irreconcilable contradiction between Brahms, a composer of vocal music whose invention invariably flows from the voice part, and Wagner, whose voice part is often no more than just another contrapuntal melody in his orchestral polyphony, even in such significant lyrical passages as Isolde's *Liebestod* ("love-death"). For Brahms the idea of an orchestral opera was an absurdity. In this respect Wagner, wherever his fervent inspiration made him forget his theory, proved Brahms's views of him right. What Brahms always esteemed in Wagner was his serious artistry and great musicianship; what he had to reject were his theories and his intolerant claims to a monopoly of values.

This was the reason why Brahms considered Wagner's influence on the younger generation so insidious. He once remarked to Kalbeck: "It is only when one sees Wagner's imitators that one learns to appreciate Wagner himself." And he could never make up his mind, despite really live interest, to visit the party gatherings in Bayreuth, neither for the first festival in 1876 when the *Ring* was first produced in its entirety nor six years later when *Parsifal* had its première. He wrote to Bülow at that time: "The fact that I cannot come to a decision about Bayreuth is, no doubt, one indication that I just can't utter a 'yes.' I need hardly tell you that I fear the Wagnerians, and that they are capable of ruining my enjoyment of even the best of Wagner."

It has already been mentioned (see page 103) that Brahms toyed for many years with the idea of meeting his rival on the latter's own ground, that of the opera. These plans were primarily shattered by the problem of finding a suitable text. To what extent other inhibitions, of which he himself was hardly aware, played a part in this, cannot be readily determined. Josef Widmann, who was an experienced librettist (the libretto of Hermann Goetz's *Taming of the Shrew* stemmed from his pen), exchanged ideas on this subject with Brahms for a long time. He avers that the composer had in mind something in the form of individual numbers interspersed by spoken dialogue, like the German *Singspiel*. This is entirely plausible if one considers his consciousness of form. Beethoven's *Fidelio* must

have been to him a form ideal of much greater conge-
niality in every respect than any of Wagner's music
dramas, with which he could have nothing, not one iota,
in common. He expressed himself on this subject in a letter written in Vienna, 1870, to Clara Schumann. It must
be borne in mind that Clara, probably because of certain
memories of Dresden, had an insurmountable antipathy to
Wagner, and that Brahms had to respect her feelings. He
wrote:

Die Meistersinger had to be put on and off five times. Now,
however, every additional performance causes just as much
trouble. This in itself, of course, prevents the audience from
waxing enthusiastic, for which a certain momentum would be
required. I find the public much more apathetic than I had expected. I myself am enthusiastic neither for this work nor otherwise for Wagner. Still, I listen to it as intently as I can, i.e., as
often as I can stand it. Of course one is tempted to gossip a
good deal about it. . . . This much I know: in all other things
which I attempt, I follow on the heels of predecessors who
make me self-conscious; Wagner would not in the least make
me self-conscious about tackling an opera with the greatest
gusto. By the way, on my long list of wishes, such an opera
ranks even higher than the position of music director.

It is useless to speculate what the style of a Brahms
opera would have been. By the same token it would be impossible to imagine an opera by Beethoven, had he not
written one. Brahms's only work that even remotely approaches the dramatic style in its manner of presentation
is the cantata *Rinaldo,* for male voices. If something re-
sembling an operatic style has been recognized in it, nota-
bly in two elaborate tenor arias, this should lead to no
conclusions; similarly, the *German Requiem* did not sug-
gest what the *Song of Triumph* or the *Song of Destiny*
would be like. A composer of Brahms's poetic feeling ad-

justs his style to the poetic subject in the most natural way. This is certainly true in the highest degree of Wagner: how much less would we know about him if the idea of *Die Meistersinger* had not one day captured his imagination and conjured up an entirely new world! If Brahms had found a libretto that would give wings to his imagination, we would perhaps be richer by an exquisite opera—but surely poorer by several symphonies or concertos. His restless creative urge did not leave any free time in his entire life during which a work as substantial as an opera could have been produced.

It is by no means impossible that behind his desire to tackle the problem of an opera there stood his critical estimate of Wagner, who in the consciousness of his time ranked overwhelmingly high but whom he was compelled, despite all his admiration, to regard as his opponent. Whatever he had to say about Wagner he could, by his very nature, express only in a positive, artistic manner. On the other hand it is understandable that anyone not versed in the intricacies of the theatre will not carelessly plunge into the adventure of writing an opera. Brahms was already too big; he had—quite aside from his time—too much to lose.

Still, he could not entirely evade the controversy with Wagnerism. At the time of Wagner's death the outcome of the battle had long been decided in the public mind: judging from the press and from professional publications, it was a smashing victory for the forces of the Music of the Future. As always in such debates, the attack had an advantage over the defense, and the progressive and aggressive wing of the esthetic scored an easy victory over the weak, poorly organized defense. Today all this seems strange, considering the fact that Liszt's music, which had produced so much discussion and acclaim at the time and had stood in the very center of events, has long since van-

ished from the scene. His great works—the oratorios *The
Legend of Saint Elizabeth* and *Christus,* the *Missa solemnis* (for a festival in Esztergom, Hungary), and the *Hungarian Coronation Mass,* the *Faust* and *Dante* symphonies—
are today only known by hearsay. And if by any chance
one of his twelve symphonic poems happens to appear on
a concert program, one may rack his brains about why and
how such a work could ever have been controversial; nothing of its magnificence is left but trivial, formless, uninspired music of emphatic gesture. Even the once-admired
brilliance of the orchestral sound—Hugo Wolf declared
that he preferred a single cymbal clang by Liszt to a whole
symphony by Brahms—is no longer recognizable. This
simply proves that sound is nothing but an adjunct to
music, and it perishes as soon as the music itself is no
longer viable. All that remains of Liszt, the genius who
burned himself out like a sky rocket, are a few of his virtuoso and salon pieces and the great fame of a uniquely
gifted performer, a stimulating spirit, and a noble, selfless
patron of younger artists.

If one considers how difficult it is at times for any contemporary to grasp the true significance of a new and
unusual work of art, one will also understand how much
nonsense and swindle the contemporary must be willing
to swallow as long as he can be made to believe that there
is something of value behind it. For this reason, things
look quite different when seen from a distance. Time is
a judge without forbearance.

Brahms evidently had a clearer and better understanding of the situation than any of his contemporaries did.
For this reason his works today rank as a monument of
genuinely artistic integrity. He had no illusions about the
meaning of the desert around him. In the face of this, it is
easier to understand his bitterness and his occasional

lapses into injustice toward things stemming from the enemy side.

It is not surprising that critics often show poor and inept judgment. But artists—unless, like Schumann, they are great and very rare exceptions—are no better judges. What critics lack in insight, artists lack in objectivity. Only indifference, not true faith, can be entirely tolerant; and no artist would be a real artist if the path he chooses to follow did not appear to him the only possible, the only true path. Brahms was a sympathetic and generous colleague, witness the many musicians whom he helped—if he found them worthy of his help. But he was not inclined to make good-natured concessions when faced by inadequacy or by what he considered spurious. And he had no sympathy whatsoever for people who were unduly touchy. He himself had been roughly treated and saw no reason why others should have it any easier. His deadly sarcasm was feared, and anyone having dealings with him had to be prepared for it. He was on intimate terms with Carl Goldmark, for instance; in fact, he undertook one of his trips to Italy in his company. But he never liked Goldmark's music and made no bones about it. A younger colleague, Ignaz Brüll, whom Brahms esteemed highly as a musician and who was his favorite partner whenever he played a four-hand arrangement of a new work for friends, also became a victim of his biting remarks about his music, which admittedly was a little tame and uninspired. "Ignaz once wanted to modulate from F major to B minor," Brahms observed, "but his whole family was opposed to it, so he let it be." He found the early works of Max Bruch extremely worthy of consideration, and even produced his oratorio *Odysseus* at a concert of the Society of the Friends of Music in Vienna. But he was not at all satisfied with his subsequent progress and made no secret of it. Edward

Speyer tells of an incident in Frankfort, the subject of which was Bruch's newly written oratorio *Arminius*. Bruch had given the score to Brahms with the explicit request to keep it confidential. A few days later, while both were dining at the home of a well-to-do patron of music, they heard a hurdy-gurdy man in the street. "Listen, Bruch," Brahms shouted across the table, "this fellow has gotten hold of your *Arminius*."

On the other hand, such acts of inconsiderate baiting were often balanced by many friendly acts, even though their recipients may not always have satisfied the high standards which Brahms felt obliged to establish. As a member of a commission charged with submitting to the Austrian ministry of education proposals for the annually distributed state scholarships, he got direct insight into the achievements of young and talented musicians in Austria and was struck with the quite general decay of technical proficiency and of elementary knowledge of the skills of the trade. He ascribed this, probably not without reason, to the devastation wrought by faulty theories and inadequate teaching. In a letter to Elisabeth von Herzogenberg he once wrote: "The situation in our Conservatory is deplorable as far as composition is concerned. One only has to look at the teachers and not even, as I frequently must, at the students and their work." He was, therefore, all the more gratified by each and every talent that did show promise. In such a case he demanded nothing more than an aptitude capable of growth and an adequate schooling, but on these two he insisted unconditionally. It is a pleasure to read the recommendation written by him in 1879 which decided the fate of Mandyczewski, with whom he later formed such an intimate friendship:

By far the most commendable, in my opinion, is Mandyczewski, whose gifts are most earnestly gratifying. They not only show significant, quiet, and steady progress in everything that needs to be learned, but they also testify to the development of a talent far greater than we had felt justified to expect. The compositions submitted by him are so highly superior to his earlier ones that one is sorely tempted to praise every single thing that ought to be considered and examined in such a case. It must not be forgotten that, in addition, Mandyczewski pursues other studies with diligence and that his admirable father also takes care of six more children.

This case shows how seriously and how humanely he acquitted himself of his task. It brought him into contact with many talented young artists who in this way became part of his circle. The most notable among them was Antonín Dvořák, for whom he arranged state scholarships for several years. Dvořák was already past his middle thirties and still completely unknown outside the immediate region of Prague, his home. Through a recommendation written by Brahms to his publisher, Simrock, Dvořák found his way into public acceptance and, within a few years, into world renown. It is most touching to see with what tact Brahms, otherwise so apt to be ironic on such occasions, attempted to lead the younger colleague, whose talents he admired unreservedly, toward more self-critical and careful workmanship while at the same time thanking him for his offer of a dedication:

Today I will just say that being occupied with your works affords me the greatest pleasure. I would give a great deal for an opportunity to discuss them with you in detail. You do write a bit hastily. If, however, you will fill in the missing sharps, flats, and naturals, you may perhaps also take a second look at the notes themselves and at the part writing. Please forgive me; it is very presumptuous to express such wishes toward a man like you. I will very gratefully accept the works as they stand and would consider a dedication of your quartet a signal honor.

Their relationship developed into a lasting friendship. Brahms was untiring in his efforts to clear a path for the only contemporary whom he really considered worthy, especially since he felt very sympathetic toward this simple, unassuming character, who was celebrated for his taciturnity. When Dvořák's symphony *From the New World* was first performed, Brahms wrote to his friend Miller von Aichholz, to whose house he was regularly invited for Sunday dinner: "In case Dvořák should come up for tomorrow's concert [he did], and if he should be free, will you have any objection if I offer him the pleasure of coming to your house? I will share my food and drink with him, and as far as I know, he does not make any speeches."

It is worthy of mention that the *princeps artis musicae severioris,* who had once copied orchestral parts for Wagner, also did not find it at all below his dignity to read proof for Dvořák when the latter, at that time director of the National Conservatory in New York, was away from Europe for a few years. Simrock, the publisher, reported this to Dvořák, adding Brahms's remark: "Do tell Dvořák how much I enjoy his gay creativity." To which Dvořák replied in his candid, somewhat awkward German: "So Brahms is interested in my music, is he? I am very glad, but I find it hard to understand why he took on the very tedious job of proofreading. I don't believe there is another musician of his stature in the whole world who would do such a thing."

Such traits of genuine, ungrudging comradeship must be recorded in order to avoid condemning Brahms for his incapacity to establish contact with another simple, down-to-earth character and his art. Unlike Wagner, whom he always appreciated although not necessarily approved of, Anton Bruckner, in his entire mode of expression, was totally foreign to him. It is not necessary here to bring into the foreground personal feelings whose discord would be quite understandable. After Wagner's death, his party elevated Bruckner to the position of symphonic antipope to Brahms. As early as the 1880's, the very active Wagner Club in Vienna took great pains to provide noisy, hostile minority demonstrations in the standing room of the *Musikverein* concert hall whenever Brahms's works were performed. This did not bother him any more than did the articles condemning him to eternal doom, which the youthful Hugo Wolf published every Sunday in the *Wiener Salonblatt*, much to the amusement of Brahms and his friends. But party strife is an evil thing and can poison the atmosphere. It must not be expected that it made Brahms more tolerant toward the opposition. And as far as Bruckner is concerned, there existed, without doubt, an irreconcilable antagonism between two totally contradictory artistic creeds. The mystical, Catholic world of Bruckner was just as incompatible with Brahms's rationalistic, Protestant one as was Brahms's supremely homogeneous technique and consciousness of the most minute details of form with Bruckner's method of construction, which was based entirely on instinct, often erratic, and more visionary than critically controlled. Nor could the two-dimensional, expansive inventiveness of Bruckner compare with Brahms's concentrated and interlocked creativity, any more than the almost demonstrative simplicity of Brahms's expression could with Bruckner's pathos. This pathos would have irritated Brahms far less if he had not detected in it a Wagnerian phraseology which had become an integral part of Bruckner's style even though it was fully amalgamated into the substance of his invention. The string tremolo, the pompously heavy brass choirs from Valhalla, the chromatically advancing modulations (called "cobbler's patches" in the irreverent jargon of Viennese musicians), together with gigantic dimensions enlarged to double their size by substantial recapitulations—all these things which cannot be overlooked in Bruckner's symphonies and which to this day prevent him from being fully accepted in countries other than Germany, made it practically impossible for Brahms to take him seriously. Whatever favorable impression he may at times have gotten was immediately eradicated by an unfavorable one following on its heels. Mandyczewski once found Brahms earnestly studying Bruckner's Fourth Symphony which had just been published. "Look!" Brahms exclaimed, pointing to the first pages of the score. "Here this man composes as though he were a Schubert." Brahms then indicated the unisons and the chromatic passages in the closing section and said: "Then he suddenly remembers that he is a Wagnerian, and everything goes to the devil."

The fact that Brahms paid no attention to perhaps the most talented of all the young people with whom he came into contact, was probably due to his just having been in a bad mood. This, however, had its consequences. Hugo Wolf's unbounded bitterness against Brahms had its roots in a personal experience. Kalbeck reports that Wolf visited Brahms in 1881 or 1882 and brought with him some lieder (no doubt youthful works, not published until long after his death):

Brahms stated: "The compositions he brought me did not amount to much. I went through everything with him in great detail and called his attention to a number of things. There was a certain amount of talent there, but he took things far too lightly. I told him quite earnestly where the fault lay and referred him to Nottebohm for lessons. That was too much for him; he left and never came back. And now he spits venom and gall."

Against technical incompetence Brahms could be merciless. Young Wolf, completely penniless and engaged in a desperate struggle for existence, was bitterly incensed by the dry advice, for which he had no use. Much later some statements by Brahms became known from which it can be concluded that he had long forgiven the composer of the *Mörike-Lieder* for his youthful critical excesses and that he knew how to appreciate his seriousness and his poetic sense. But by that time, past his sixtieth year and increasingly withdrawn, Brahms was already hard to approach and deeply disturbed by the direction in which music had developed. Richard Specht describes a typical scene with Brahms and the youthful Gustav Mahler, when both were taking a walk along the Traun river in Ischl. Brahms, talking of the inevitable decline of music, said that he was probably the last one who was still fully conscious of musical integrity. "Suddenly Mahler clutched his arm and, excitedly pointing into the water with his free hand, exclaimed: 'Look, master, look down there!' 'What is it?' asked Brahms. 'Look, there goes the last wave!' Whereupon Brahms growled: 'That's very nice, but it also depends on whether the wave goes into the ocean or whether it loses itself in a swamp.' "

The question cannot be decided. Up to the present, however, Brahms has maintained his place as the "last classical composer," for no one has yet come to replace him.

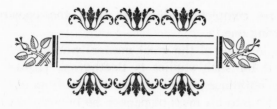

Secrets of the
Workshop

ANY GLIMPSE into a master's workshop is fascinating.
The completed work is a miracle, but it is only when one
gains some insight into the mechanism of its genesis, when
one becomes aware of the conscious element of the work
process, that one can truly appreciate the artist's gigantic accomplishment in finding among countless possibilities the one and only right one. In this way one learns
to understand that in human endeavor divine inspiration is
not a gift but the fruit of intensive, persistent labor. In his
own copy of Otto Jahn's biography of Mozart, Brahms
doubly underscored the words: "In all artistic productivity the creative, inventive force cannot even for one in-

stant be completely divorced from the constructive, organizing one."

The only one of the great masters who has left ample material for such studies is Beethoven. Thanks to his blessed untidiness, which prevented him from ever bringing order into his mass of papers, he bequeathed to us a treasure of sketches that effectively illuminate the process by which many of his works originated. Brahms showed the most lively interest in the many years of labor which his friend Nottebohm devoted to these sketches, and it was largely because of his efforts that Nottebohm's excellent work was published. It was a peculiar habit of Beethoven that he made very detailed sketches at all times. But the procedure which can thus be observed is probably quite generally typical for the creation of music, which in other cases often takes shape in the composer's head without written traces, quite aside from most artists' perfectly natural tendency to make such traces disappear.

Brahms certainly had this tendency; this is why very few of his sketches have been preserved. Occasionally one can learn something about his method of working from corrections in his manuscripts. Otherwise, one is confined to the very few instances of compositions or fragments thereof existing in different versions. One thing, however, can never be clearly determined: the various stages through which the invention itself had to pass. It is just in this respect that Beethoven's sketch material is so uncommonly rich. It shows how in the majority of cases a melody, a theme, or a motif underwent a long-drawn-out development process before finally assuming its definitive form.

That which one might call the primary idea is more or less an improvisation; the composer's imagination works over this idea, bends it, amplifies it, and changes it until it is in the shape most suitable for its purpose. This process is left to the composer's critical instinct, upon which, however, he must be able to rely unconditionally. In a conversation with Georg Henschel, Brahms once expressed himself as follows on the subject:

There is no real creating without hard work. That which you would call invention—that is to say, a thought, an idea—is simply an inspiration for which I am not responsible, which is no merit of mine. It is a present, a gift, which I ought even to despise until I have made it my own by dint of hard work. And there need be no hurry about that, either. It is like the seed corn: it germinates unconsciously and in spite of ourselves.

About one conviction, however, Brahms has never left any doubt: this element of invention is a most essential and most precious thing; it is the soul of composition.

Exactly this kind of problem is involved in the only large-scale work which he totally reconstructed after publication: the B major Piano Trio, written in 1854. The fact that this took place thirty-six years later makes this revision a veritable compendium of Brahms's most mature art of composition; the revised version is a comprehensive, practical critique of the youthful work, mercilessly exposing every weakness and drawing its conclusions from it. The result is that three of the four movements were completely plowed over. What remained in them were their beautiful, inspired initial ideas, but not much more. Only the scherzo came through the rough treatment unscathed except for a new coda. The miracle in all this—and there is no similar case in all music—is that not in a single measure of the new version does one feel a stylistic inconsistency and that, despite all the new material necessary to replace old, inadequate elements, the youthful exuberance of the original version remained completely unfettered in the revised form. Its world of expressiveness was left unchanged throughout. It invites comparison with the Paris version of Wagner's *Tannhäuser*, in which all added material, particularly the bacchanal in the opening scene, is completely different from the style of the original version.

The B major Trio is, as already mentioned, an early work. Completed just prior to the Schumann catastrophe, it brought Brahms's period of immaturity to a close. Although tremendously inspired and full of visionary romanticism, it exhibits the shortcomings of a semideveloped compositional technique insofar as it is unable to sustain the unrestrained impetus of invention throughout its broad structure. Each one of the three movements which Brahms found himself compelled to do over begins with a magnificent thematic idea, cast from a single mold, but then proves unequal to the task of continuing with anything worthy of such an inspired opening. In the scherzo this problem was appreciably less formidable because of a more compact form which finds fulfillment in only one excellent scherzo theme; and the trio section, also most happily conceived, enjoys the same advantage of a narrow, closely confined, and therefore unproblematical form. It is an indication of the master's mature vision that in this trio section he left untouched an ingenuousness which he could easily have removed: the uninterrupted, melodious homophony of the theme, especially where an orchestral violin tremolo, not at all in keeping with the nature of chamber music, accompanies the triumphal re-entry of the main melody. Candor becomes here a kind of virtue, however difficult it would be to find such anywhere else in Brahms's music. In this movement the changes were confined to insignificant technical details. What was discreetly improved is only the ending, in which the composer at first had failed to dissolve the lively scherzo motion into an evaporating, vanishing close. The original coda had been too calculated and too complicated; the natural, organic conclusion which the new version substitutes for it is a brilliant demonstration of how a master solves such a problem.

In the other movements the situation is far more complex, and here we come closer to the actual foundations of Brahms's art. How much he was possessed by his mission of carrying on what he considered his classical legacy is more apparent in his music than in anything he ever said or wrote about it. Part of this is humility, most aptly expressed in this statement addressed to Henschel: "What I can't understand is how people like myself can be vain. As we who walk upright are above the creeping things of the earth, so the gods are above us." The fact that he had a clearer grasp of Beethoven's principle of construction than either of his immediate predecessors, Mendelssohn and Schumann, is due to his better understanding of the difference between the episodic, sectionally developed form, for example the scherzo form, and the grand, truly symphonic form; he never carried the small-scale articulation of the former into the latter. The quintessence of the smaller form is that, from a single rhythmic impulse, it can develop with narrowly confined thematic material. The larger form, on the other hand, must satisfy two contradictory conditions which are equally essential and, in a certain sense, mutually complementary: it must be borne along by a continuous inventive drive that pervades its entire extent, and yet it must, by means of sufficient thematic contrast and lucid punctuation which clarifies the structural supports, fashion this invention into an impressive, well-balanced architecture. Brahms came surprisingly close to this goal in the piano sonatas that preceded his B major Trio. That in the trio itself a setback took place is due to the above principles having been jeopardized by excessive dimensions and by an inadequately established feeling for form.

In the original version, after the triumphant close of the opening section of the first movement, singing out broadly —up to this point Brahms left the substance of the composition substantially untouched in the new version—we stumble upon a halting rhythm, the thematic intention of which is defeated by its own complexity. And now, instead of arriving at an appropriately contrasting second theme or a new invention, Brahms yielded to temptation and tenaciously held on to the first theme, a procedure often adopted by Haydn, but only in a very concise structure. Here Brahms's attempt at thematic unification leads nowhere, or rather—which amounts to the same thing—to a hesitant series of repetitive improvisations. Since these are never thematically consolidated, they fizzle out in a conglomeration of short groups of measures. This not only suspends the unified flow of the inventive process, but also in the subsequent development section causes a lack of adequate melodic material because the opening motif has already been worked to death. The resultant structure falls apart into insufficiently coherent episodes.

In revising the composition, the master decided to let nothing of the original version stand except for the opening section, which occurs once more in the recapitulation. He followed this exposition of the first theme by a completely new subsidiary theme in G-sharp minor, evolving with perfect ease from a brief connecting phrase. From this theme he allows a melodic closing section to blossom forth, thereby gaining an exposition rich in contrasts and perfectly balanced in a spacious layout. Its function of introducing the thematic elements with perfect clarity is thus ideally fulfilled. The subsequent development section is now equal to its task of bringing all this material to a dramatic climax and then following it with a recapitulation of the principal ideas, which reappear practically in their original form, changed only in details of presentation. As it now stands, the entire movement is one of the summits of all of Brahms's chamber music.

Just as in the first movement it was the lack of an adequate second theme, so in the adagio it was an annoying similarity that bothered the composer. Following the broad, melodious first theme as a middle section was a new thought which closely resembled the melody of Schubert's song *Am Meer* ["By the Sea"]. The fact that "every jackass could hear this" irritated him no end. Perhaps a general observation may be permitted here. An artist possesses a thrice-blessed mechanism in his breast which guides him and sets him on the right course, just as morally sensitive people are guided by their conscience: his uneasiness. It invariably appears whenever an idea, a phrase, or any detail whatsoever does not live up to his demands, which have been sharpened by experience. The more he matures, the greater his demands on his own accomplishments; the keener his self-criticism, the more inevitable the uneasiness with which it manifests itself. Where the harm has already been done, where something remains in the finished composition that does not satisfy the artist's sensitive conscience, each new encounter with the work is a running of the gantlet, and the uneasiness is tripled if this happens in public. These are the moments about which Brahms complained bitterly at times: a disappointment in his work, which occasionally happened despite all the experience of a lifelong artistic career, and a belated realization that he had failed once again to achieve something which, in the intoxication of creativity, he had thought he had reached. It is the fear of this possibility which underlies his almost hypochondriac self-criticism and which drove him to show new works to his friends, to have them confirm that he had done well, and then at times in spite of all their suggestions to "let his own version stand." Up to an advanced age Brahms suppressed works of whose inadequacies he had become aware in time. As late as 1880 he showed the first movements of two trios to Clara Schumann and Theodor Billroth. Only one of them, the C major Trio, Opus 87, was completed and published three years later. The other, an E-flat major movement, with which both friends were enchanted, vanished.

But back to the B major Trio! The uneasiness which the composer experienced on account of the similarity with Schubert, as just mentioned, compelled him to a complete revision of the adagio movement. A new contrasting idea implanted in it led it—to its great benefit—into an entirely new direction. In the finale it was again the invention of a second subject which had defeated him in the original version. An inherent problem of the grand form consists in freeing oneself from the first idea and devising something in contrast to it, something in which the original impulse—the inspiration which had initially sparked the composition—can no longer be effective. Therefore a new act of creation is necessary, and the composer must wait for it calmly—and with the patience which a young artist is likely to lose, to his own detriment. The severity with which Brahms judged the works of his contemporaries or of young hopefuls can best be understood in the light of this habit of rigid self-criticism. Brahms was capable of any cruelty when he had the impression that someone "took things far too lightly."

As it was the lack of a second theme in the first movement and the nagging association with the Schubert theme in the adagio, so in the finale it was the weakness of a subsidiary theme announced by the cello that grated on the composer's nerves. This song-like melody—it may indeed derive from an unpublished song, as can be concluded from its whole character and from its piano accompaniment—strikes one with its sentimental affectation and its rhythmic poverty, which put it at a distinct disadvantage compared with the sharply outlined first theme. Thus a notable diminution of tension is felt. This circumstance is even more ominous because the unpleasant episode appears once more in the recapitulation, thereby again impeding the momentum of the presentation. In the revised version it has been replaced by a magnificent new idea, filled with rhythm and energy; this in turn influences the entire subsequent growth of the movement, resulting in incomparably heightened vitality and unity.

We know from several statements by Brahms that this revision brought him greater satisfaction than many a new work, and he knew better than anybody else why it did so.

While this example has shown how the composer, through a combination of critical objectivity and adaptable invention, was able to elevate an inspired but problematical work of his youth to the height of a masterpiece, another example illustrates what the master could create out of an immature idea whose capacity for expansion nobody would have suspected. Up to now this case has been neglected in the Brahms literature, but it deserves the most careful attention because there can hardly be a clearer demonstration anywhere else of the unfathomable synthesis of imagination and controlling intellect from which music is born. In the chronicles of the interim period at Hamburg there appears an occasional mention of a Brahms saraband which he had in his repertoire as a pianist and which he appears to have enjoyed playing. It was discovered, along with all kinds of other things, among Clara Schumann's papers and was first published in 1917. It is in volume XV of the complete edition of Brahms's works and is here reproduced:

One is inclined to consider this short piece of music an exercise rather than a finished composition. We know that at the time—it was in 1855—Brahms was intensely interested in acquiring a discipline of his techniques of form and composition. He wrote a number of formal studies—gigues, sarabands, preludes, and fugues—which manifest no great ambition but in which he sought, with his characteristically meticulous care, to get to the bottom of the various problems of form. The form of this saraband is the simplest imaginable: it consists of two phrases of eight measures each. This is known as the binary song form and is frequently found in suite movements of the baroque period; another example of it is the Handel theme which

Brahms used for his variations. The minuet of his D major Serenade is a similar study, except that here two such episodes are combined, giving greater scope to the form. The inadequacy of such compositions lies in the fact that form copying turns all too readily into stylistic copying, that the combination of the archaic form with the composer's personal expression appears only partly successful. Brahms wrote another saraband of this kind which, however, has an entirely impersonal effect and about which he did not trouble himself any further. The one here reproduced, on the other hand, has a true Brahmsian flavor in its combination of eighth notes and triplets, and also a characteristic quality of expression based on a peculiarly veiled tonality; it stands, without committing itself one way or the other, between major and minor.

The first half of the saraband, a formally concluded eight-measure phrase, seems like a ritual dance; the second half adds to it a sensitive, ornamental melisma, the only contrast in the piece, but it closes just as formally as the first half by reiterating the opening phrase. The weakness of the composition is its short-windedness.

The unpredictability of a creative artist's imagination is indeed singular. In 1883, twenty-eight years later, this probably long-forgotten saraband suddenly reentered the master's mind and grew into one of his most beautiful and expressive adagios. It forms part of his F major String Quintet, Opus 88, a three-movement work whose middle movement is a combination of an adagio and a scherzo-like intermezzo—a form created by Beethoven and used by Brahms again in his A major Violin Sonata. The adagio —or rather the *grave ed appassionato*—appears three times in different versions, alternating with the graceful, siciliana-like intermezzo which is also repeated in a varied form, so that the whole movement is constructed of five sections.

String Quintet in F major, 2nd movement

Grave ed appassionato

Op. 88 (1883)

What concerns us here is not the intermezzo but the slow and very stately principal section of the movement, for in it we encounter the old saraband once more. Aside from the different key signature—it is now in C sharp— the first seven bars remained essentially unchanged. But the eighth bar brings about a change which, with incredible inspiration, raises the whole composition to new heights. A comparison of the eighth measure of the saraband with that of the quintet movement and what follows it, shows what the composer has wrought here: it is one of those inimitable little devices which are peculiar to genius. He has broken down the barriers of the original, somewhat dry closing phrase, thereby setting the melody free and permitting the inspiration to flow and expand with increasing vigor and breadth, making it a joy to listen to. His ingenuity lies in the introduction, in place of the dry conclusion in the eighth measure, of a new triplet motif which complements the melody and acts as a stimulating element, begetting and unfolding new ideas. In this manner there evolved from the narrow-chested eight-bar phrase a profound and magnificent composition, filled to the brim with expressive meaning.

The first return of the episode, after the intervening charming intermezzo, is a free variation or, to be more specific, a fantasia on the opening section, broadening it still further both harmonically and melodically. After the intermezzo is once again introduced, this time with an altered rhythm accelerated to a presto, something most singular takes place: the saraband falls back into its original key of A major. This is the key of the intermezzo and now prevails over C-sharp major. With this return to the original tonality, it suddenly seems as if old memories were coming to the fore: the second half of the saraband, with its ornamental, songlike figuration in thirty-second notes, appears quite unexpectedly. By this utilization of hitherto unused material the composition now gains a new and entirely undreamed-of urge that brings the movement to an enormously impressive climax. This extremely dramatic moment immediately leads to the breaking off, to the resolution. There is a choice of two tonalities: will the C-sharp or will the A major prevail? The question is not decided until the very last moment when, with a magnificent turn, establishing beyond any doubt that nothing different could possibly have happened, the balance very gently dips in favor of the A. The saraband has found its way back to its origin.

It may be mentioned quite incidentally that not a single measure of the original saraband has remained unused. "Used" is perhaps misleading: a motif that develops into a movement is not a building block but rather a germinating sprout which unexpectedly puts forth new leaves, blossoms, and fruits. Inspiration is a permanent state, but the work of art is a living, breathing organism.

"Form is something created through a thousand years of exertions by the most outstanding masters, and yet no disciple can ever be too eager to appropriate it. It would be a most foolish conceit of badly misunderstood originality if everyone searched and groped around in his own way for something which is already perfected." This bit of homely wisdom from Johann Peter Eckermann's *Beiträge zur Poesie* ["Contributions to Poetry"] can be found in a poetic-philosophic anthology which Brahms, while still a young man, compiled for himself under the title *Little Treasure Chest of the Young Kreisler*. (Kreisler, Jr., was his self-chosen nickname among friends, after the romantic figure in E. T. A. Hoffmann's *Kater Murr*.) Brahms always revered the exalted sense of traditional form, inherited from the masters, and from this sense he drew his conclusions. He arrived at form because beyond it he saw nothing but chaos. To the "musicians of the future," form had exhausted itself; this can be the case only if the composer has misunderstood its very essence. If he treats it as a stereotyped mold, form is worthless; if on the other hand he is able to breathe living imagination into it, it becomes inexhaustible. Brahms saw form in the music of the classical composers as a natural principle for channeling ideas. What he found in a Bach fugue, a Haydn quartet, a Mozart concerto, or a Beethoven symphony was the continuous melody, the flowing series of clearly defined musical events; and participating in the shaping of these were relations of tonality and harmony, motivic technique, and counterpoint. For harmony and counterpoint there exist textbooks which may be inadequate but are sufficient for learning the basic facts. However, the divine art of dealing with form, as practiced by the great masters of the past, can only be learned from their works; no textbook could possibly approach such a complex subject except in a most superficial manner.

Brahms contemplated these facts in his characteristically profound fashion. His work therefore shows a clear

distinction between three basic principles of musical creation: the small form, which limits itself to a single, significantly formulated idea; the variation form, which transfigures such a thought by means of every known melodic,
harmonic, and rhythmic invention; and the grand, all-embracing and self-containing symphonic form, whose problems can only be approached by mastery of the smaller
forms just mentioned, coupled with rigorous contrapuntal
discipline. The essential fact, however, is that the form remains productive for a composer only as long as he has
faith in it and as his imagination is stimulated by it. The
fact that the problem of form is complicated by a number of
practical difficulties—the difficulties of an adequate treatment of the performing apparatus, for example—has already been explained (see page 113). In this respect
Brahms exercised a consciousness of responsibility and a
caution which characteristically set him apart from the
scribbler who creates with naive unconcern. It is for this
reason that, when it came to blending instruments into an
ensemble, he turned first of all to chamber music with
piano. In this genre he created his first really mature
works: the Piano Quartets in G minor and A major, composed in Hamburg. He combined in them the natural impulse of a pianist and his fully ripened and very individual piano style with an already well-developed mastery
of form treatment, resulting in a brilliance of technique
and sound which up to then had been unknown in this
type of music. But despite this brilliance he almost stub-
bornly confined himself to the range of possibilities offered
by the classical tradition. Even the finale of the G minor
Quartet, the *rondo alla zingarese,* which anticipated the
style of the Hungarian Dances he wrote a short time later,
has a classical precursor in a Haydn trio.

After this preparation, the String Sextet No. 1, Opus 18,

in B-flat major, his first attempt in the realm of chamber music for strings only, was a great and universally recognized success. At that time he did not venture into the field of the string quartet, that very soul of technical objectivity and economy. It is understandable that the pianist's imagination, deeply rooted in a rich and broadly conceived world of sound, found greater stimulation in the more abundant possibilities of a six-part setting than in the lesser ones of a string quartet. Perhaps it is significant that several years later another attempt at music for strings alone, a string quintet, proved a failure and ultimately found fulfillment as a piano quintet. Brahms had reached the age of forty before he finally published, after extensive soulsearching, two string quartets. These, however, are admittedly masterpieces. But even they are surpassed, as far as polished, genuine quartet style is concerned, by a third one, his Opus 67 in B-flat major, written three years later.

This last-mentioned work provides us with an opportunity to touch on a question of form particulary important to Brahms: the technique of variation. While still young, Brahms carried on intensive studies along these lines. His crowning achievements within the scope of piano music are the Handel and the Paganini Variations. Both deal with the problem of using a theme in a small binary song form, resulting in a procession of numerous short episodes. Beethoven, in his C minor Variations and his Variations in E-flat major *(Eroica)*, Opus 35, has shown how this problem can be resolved through linking together two or three consecutive variations by a common, unifying idea and thereby freely organizing a large number of variations into contrasting groups. Brahms successfully attempted the same in his Handel and his Paganini Variations. In this manner the variation form offers the best and most stimu-

JOHANNES BRAHMS

lating possibility for clustering a number of shorter structures into a coherent whole. In his Variations on a Theme by Haydn,[1] for orchestra, Brahms followed a different procedure which is frequently found in variations by Beethoven and also in Bach's Goldberg Variations, which Brahms loved and studied diligently. In this kind of variations the theme is a larger, self-contained structure, and each variation develops from it as a finished, independently fashioned character piece, so that the series of variations gives an impression rather like that of a suite. Consequently the succession of variations is dominated above all by the principle of contrast with its changeable tempi and varying meters.

Brahms also learned from Beethoven how to deal with the problem of the variation finale, whose function is to bring a long series of short pieces to a dynamically summarizing, broadly conceived finish. Like Beethoven, he made use of a large variety of form possibilities. In the Paganini Variations it is a greatly enlarged final variation which repeatedly uses the thematic model, and in the Handel Variations it is a fugue. In the Haydn Variations it is a passacaglia on a five-measure bass motif which, based on the theme itself, finally brings it to a triumphant apotheosis.

In one respect, however, Brahms certainly could not take a joke, though what Wagner had in mind when he made his malicious remark was hardly a joke: the integrity of the theme as a model of form was as sacred to Brahms as it was to Beethoven. However wonderfully his inventions may grow beyond the theme, its basic structure re-

[1] I hold to this title even though in recent times some doubts have been raised concerning the authorship of the theme. As long as these doubts are not more convincingly presented, I see no reason for considering the theme, which is taken from a partita for wind instruments and entitled Chorale St. Antoni, as not having been written by Haydn.

mains unchanged. In a newspaper column Hanslick once quipped about Brahms, who had sprouted a beard during his summer vacation, saying that his original face was just as hard to recognize as the theme in many of his variations. This accusation must have been made many times, but it is really unjustified. It is true that hearing the theme within a variation requires a concentration of musical memory hardly within the capacity of every listener, but such a capacity is not really necessary for the enjoyment of music whose logical coherence is convincing, even if one is not actually conscious of the circumstances underlying this conviction.

The B-flat major String Quartet, which gave rise to this discussion, assigns an entirely different and very significant task to the variation form. Like his classical predecessors, Brahms was fond of using this form in a cyclical instrumental composition, in this quartet in the finale, which consists of eight variations on a simple tune. In the last two of these variations, however, there suddenly appear motifs which hark back to the first movement but are now molded into the form of the variation theme. The theme itself then assumes the lead in a coda evolving freely from the last variation and is contrapuntally interwoven with the reintroduced opening motif of the first movement. This results in a superb closing section which embraces the entire work in a wide curve. In his last great chamber work, the Clarinet Quintet, Brahms employed a similar form device: the last variation leads imperceptibly back to the mood and the thematic material of the first movement, producing an incomparably beautiful and poetic effect. The melancholy and resignation of a farewell have never been more movingly expressed.

The variation principle exerted a much greater influence on the structures of Brahms's compositions than is evident at first glance. Kalbeck waxes rhapsodic about the "heavenly melody" of the second theme in the first movement of the C minor Piano Quartet and finds in it a "second subsidiary theme," evidently without realizing that the entire forty measures of the second theme consist of nothing but an eight-measure motif followed by four variations, each of which flows so smoothly into the next that one actually has the impression of an uninterruptedly flowing melodic invention. The true state of things becomes apparent only because a cadence is repeated five times with but little difference each time. This cadence provides an element of unruffled quiet to an otherwise extremely agitated movement. And nobody seems to have noticed up to now that the attractive, bucolic second subject in the first movement of the Third Symphony consists of seven variations on a single-measure model, again with the avowed purpose of bringing idyllic peace and quiet into very animated and excited surroundings. It must be emphasized once more that such analytical details basically do not concern the listener; what the composer has achieved by these means in his own characteristic fashion is the spontaneous flow of invention. How he has achieved it is his own affair.

This is definitely just as true for the monumental summit of Brahms's entire art of variation: the last movement of his Fourth Symphony, which treats an eight-measure phrase in the manner of a baroque passacaglia. To an even larger extent than in the other two examples just cited, the greatness of the achievement here lies in the powerful, uninterrupted continuity of invention, which is organized by means of the closing cadences of the recurring theme as though by a clarifying punctuation. The cadence, always rising to the dominant in two semitone steps, constantly changes in its harmonic relation. Brahms borrowed the passacaglia theme from the Bach cantata *Nach dir, Herr, verlanget mich* ["Unto thee, O Lord, I Lift up my Soul"], but he inserted a new note into Bach's theme: an A-sharp between the A and the B, thereby establishing the chromatic turn just mentioned. By so doing he has immeasurably enhanced the dramatic force of the theme and its harmonic variability. The variations—there are thirty of them—are divided into contrasting groups, broadened by augmentation of the passacaglia bass to double its length in a quiet middle section, and colored more richly by bringing in the major tonality—the basic key is E minor. When the last variation breaks into a freely conceived coda at an accelerated tempo, a breathless suspense is achieved in which the chromatic cadence is constantly intensified. The entire movement has the shattering force and the merciless horror of a death dance. Such suspense, such dramatic intensity have never been achieved anywhere within the confines of the variation form, which is essentially static.

At this stage of his development the variation technique had become an intrinsic part of Brahms's style, just as motivic development had in the case of Beethoven. Since Beethoven's time the variation principle has moved into the realm of the grand form; its possibilities embrace the entire gamut from brief, two-bar ostinato phrases in codas —for example, in Beethoven's Seventh and Ninth Symphonies—to the imaginative transmutation of themes in the same composer's late sonatas and quartets. With Brahms the variation form penetrated everywhere—into his sonatas, into his rondos, and even into his dancelike intermezzi. In the Second Symphony, for example, the second, trio-like middle section of such an intermezzo is in fact a variation of the first section, which had evolved out of a scherzo-type variation of the calm principal theme. The main theme in the first movement of his Fourth Symphony—a broad structure of eighteen measures—is not merely repeated with richer orchestral colors, as Beethoven would have done under similar circumstances (compare the first movements of his Third, Fourth, Sixth, and Seventh Symphonies), but as a variation with the melodic line dissolved by ornaments and with a contrapuntal accompaniment. And even in the burlesque, thematically concise third movement, a close-knit sonata form, the graceful, melodic second subject is not just repeated but instead made into a variation. Just like the *horror vacui* of ancient physics— the generally accepted intolerance of nature against empty space—there reigns in this style a *horror repetendi*, a dread of repetition. Even in the very last stages of Brahms's development—in his two clarinet sonatas, written in 1895—the variation principle became still more securely anchored in his process of invention. In the twilight mood of these lovely compositions, in their eventide weariness, their meditative resignation, this technique is almost symbolic. It seems to reflect an intensely personal thought process in which the subject is considered from every angle and contemplated with solemn wisdom. The *Four Serious Songs,* written a year later, are a miracle of this technique, by means of which the composition conforms with the greatest adaptability to the biblical text which, being prose, would work havoc with any other imaginable rhythmic form. Technically expressed, the same phrase—without some element of symmetry there can be no music—can adapt itself to any number of syllables and to any sequence of accentuation by the subtle means of variation, as the composer has done here.

Let us repeat: there is nothing contrived in this; it is a method of invention, just like Haydn's or Beethoven's "thematic work." In both cases the goal is a living continuity of musical events. Whoever seeks the principal element in the motif runs the risk of not seeing the forest for the trees. The motif is not a building block but rather the mortar holding together and strengthening a structure conceived of melodic, harmonic, and contrapuntal relationships. The opening section of Beethoven's Fifth Symphony, often cited as the classical example of thematic work, is by no means developed from dozens of repetitions of a one-measure motif, but is actually a free invention, spanning a large curve across the repeated incidents of the motif that serves as a rhythmical link adaptable to any situation. Later on, when a new, contrasting, freely invented second subject is introduced, the same motif continues to pulsate in the bass at four-measure intervals. The presentation uses it as a means for keeping the sequence of thought in a logical order. The thought itself, the real essence of the composition, emerges spontaneously and majestically from the inexhaustible gold vein of inspiration.

Seen from the standpoint of evolutionary history, Brahms's method is a later, more refined stage of composition, just as "thematic work" was a more freely manipulated and more developed derivative of the baroque fugal technique. In all this it is a miraculous phenomenon that each stage of a development extending through centuries was equally rich in artistically perfect creations. The really essential substance of a work of art is independent of its technical method.

If one observes how Brahms provided for the constant renewal of his artistic metabolism by drawing alternately on the most varied stylistic stimulants, it appears like a purposeful hygienic measure. The foe's eye is keen, but it is also hampered by hostile prejudices. When Wagner referred to the Brahmsian "masquerade" (see page 137), he

quite correctly observed just this fact. What he had overlooked, however, was the permanent element in the constant change: Brahms's unshakable personal integrity.
Brahms renewed the vitality and originality of his symphonic style at all times by going back to the root forms: to
the melody of song, to the polyphony of the motet, and to
the discipline of concentrated invention in the small form.
In this last respect, it seems that during his first years in
Vienna he had received a decisive stimulus from some
Schubert waltzes which he had discovered in manuscript
at the house of the Viennese publisher Spina and which he
studied with growing delight. Brahms at that time contributed to a new surge in the Schubert revival, as Liszt
and Schumann had done before him. "My most beautiful
hours here," he wrote to his Swiss publisher, Rieter-
Biedermann, "I owe to Schubert's unpublished works, of
which I have quite a quantity at home in manuscript. But
enjoyable and gratifying as their perusal may be, everything else about them is quite melancholy. For example, I
have a great many manuscripts here which belong to Spina
or Schneider, and of them nothing but the manuscript
exists—not one single copy! And Spina does not keep them
in a fireproof safe any more than I do. The other day a
whole pile of unpublished compositions were offered for
sale at a ridiculously low price. Fortunately the Society of
the Friends of Music acquired them. How many gems of
this type are scattered here and there in private hands
which either guard the treasures like fiends or else unconcernedly let them disappear!"

What he learned from Schubert is apparent, with certain reservations, in his four-hand Waltzes, Opus 39, which
he dedicated to Hanslick. It is amusing to see how he
politely made it clear, even in bestowing such an honor,
just how far he could entrust his friend to a sympathetic

understanding: surely the poor fellow could put up with a few waltzes! Billroth was quite a different sort of man; *he* could be entrusted with string quartets.

While he still followed Schubert's example in these waltzes within a narrower range of expression, the inspiration derived from Schubert ripened in the *Liebeslieder,* Opus 52, and in the *Neue Liebeslieder,* Opus 65, into a beautiful and entirely individual style. The fact that the vocal parts in the first *Liebeslieder* are designated as optional was a concession to a cautious publisher. In any event Brahms at first would not permit them to be printed in an arrangement for piano alone in order to make them easier for pianists. He wrote to Simrock: "The waltzes will have to appear just the way they stand. Whoever wants to play them without the voice will have to read them from the score. Under no circumstances may they be printed for the first time without the voice parts. This is how they must be brought before the public eye. And let us hope that they will become real family music, and will soon be sung a lot." This hope was fulfilled, and the *Liebeslieder* quickly became popular. It is a sad commentary on our own time that family music making, which would cherish such gems, no longer exists. There can hardly be anything more beautiful or richer, both harmonically and contrapuntally, than these pieces, which are loosely strung together like a series of Schubert waltzes and yet joined with the most delicate feeling for continuity. And in the *Neue Liebeslieder* there is a still broader finale, richly expanding and crowning the form with a concluding passacaglia raised to even higher spheres by a Goethe poem. The melodies of this passacaglia soar so freely above the foundation of a recurring bass motif that once again one can admire the master working in such a restricted scope of invention.

Just as one learns from his symphonic works to appreciate the depth of his thematic construction, one can study in the *Liebeslieder* the many possibilities of harmonic development within a narrowly confined form. In this respect Brahms stands patently and consciously on the shoulders of Schubert. But he went even further than the latter in the extension of his harmonic sphere and in his inimitable art of using the polyphonic web as the drawing to outline the painting of his harmony. Gaining insight into this secret of Brahms's workshop must be left to the experts; technical explanations would lead too far afield here.

In this chapter there has been so much reference to qualities of expression that an explanation may be called for, especially in the face of music of such an uncompromisingly absolute character as Brahms's. Expression, or poetry, whatever we may call an element which takes hold of our imagination when we, either as listener or as executant, are in contact with music, is such an enormously powerful component of Brahms's music especially, that one cannot help feeling it to be one of his music's most exalted qualities, even though it is not possible to capture it analytically or even to define it accurately. Expression is a function of music, not its content. It permeates the artist's creative act and works on the listener's receptive faculties, but it cannot be translated into a concept. To Brahms it always seemed a childish abuse to confuse the expressive content of music, which to him was so natural, with an extramusical one taken from poetry or painting—in a word, with a "program." In combating this nonsense he was of the same opinion as his friend Hanslick, who developed these principles in his book *Vom Musikalisch-Schönen* ["On the Beautiful in Music"], 1854. But in that book Hanslick fell into the opposite extreme when he defined musical content as "form moved by sounds" and denied it any connection with emotional components. His difficulty consisted above all in formulating a subject so difficult to comprehend by linguistic or conceptual means. Brahms received a copy of the book at the time. What he wrote about it to Clara Schumann is not very flattering: "I wanted to read Hanslick's *Vom Musikalisch-Schönen,* about which Sahr is so enthusiastic, but on glancing through it I found so many stupidities that I left it alone." Later on Brahms relented and became more inclined to accept the positive aspects of Hanslick's esthetics. But Hanslick himself was fully aware that his thesis was not tenable in all its implications. In his memoirs he wrote about it:

. . . On the other hand it is, as I can well see, an easily misunderstood thing simply to speak of the "lack of content" in instrumental music. This is what aroused most of the opposition to my book. How can inspired form in music be scientifically differentiated from empty form? I was speaking entirely of the former, whereas my opponents accused me of the latter.

If there was anything that Brahms profoundly detested it was theorizing. For him, music was a matter of living perception, of living experience; he considered it pointless to speculate about the conditions of its effect. That concepts such as expression, sincerity, profundity, and greatness cannot be measured in music does not alter the fact that they exist. There is another decisive characteristic of Brahms's art which cannot be grasped except emotionally: its nobility. This was the quality that stood in the way of its prompt success, that appeared "esoteric" to a small mind like Hanslick's, but was known to sympathetic contemporaries like Joachim, Clara Schumann, Billroth, or Bülow as the most exalted and essential element in Brahms's music, and that today makes him unique and revered among the greatest masters. But these considerations defy any attempt at technical analysis. Not even the immediate beauty of an invention can be analytically proven. Technical shortcomings can be pinpointed, as can poor workmanship, faulty harmony, or lack of structure. But when it comes to positive aspects, to the higher, more decisive qualities of a masterpiece, all methods fail. The skeleton of Helen of Troy would give no clue to the secrets of her charms. And under the dissecting knife a Clementi sonata is as masterful as one by Mozart, a Spohr quartet as great as one by Beethoven.

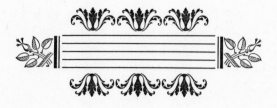

Word and Sound

WHILE BRAHMS as a symphony composer was the product of a rigorous and systematic self-discipline, as a song writer he was a primary phenomenon of nature, just as Schubert was. Whoever can create, at the age of eighteen, a masterpiece like *Liebestreu,* the opening number of the first group of lieder he published, must have been born with the gift of lyrical expression. And throughout his entire life's work, song composition flowed like an uninterrupted stream, like an ever-welcome respite after the struggles of his large-scale creations. And with the manifest slackening of his creative urge at about his sixtieth year, it was his song composition that exhausted itself first. What followed, like a conscious farewell, was in a Brahmsian sense a reproductive rather than a productive achievement: the German folk songs, whose piano accompaniments represent the most noble result of a lifetime of experience. In them the simple tonality and the simple rhythm of the voice part act as a counterfoil to the subtle individuality of the piano setting, which is utterly personal and expressive to the last detail.

With few exceptions, the song remained a form of lyrical expression for him. The epic or dramatic instinct of his soul found an outlet in other directions. Even the most extensive numbers of *Magelone,* his only song cycle of greater scope, are lyrical in nature. The *Four Serious Songs,* on the other hand, are of an entirely different cast, but then they belong to a different class of composition altogether and have hardly anything in common with what is generally referred to as a song.

A study of Brahms's lieder cannot help but show that the literary value of the poems which he set to music is uneven and often disappointing. One might conclude from this that he had poor literary taste, were it not that all the texts of his large-scale works—especially of his choral compositions—are on an extraordinarily high artistic level. The circumstances are not quite simple; they have to do with the very individual way in which he reacted to texts. In his large-scale works every thought, every line is of decisive significance and of an all-embracing importance transcending all individual considerations, just as a chorus transcends all personal expression. Here he needed the most salient and most concentrated versions of great, general ideas, such as only great masters of poetry could supply. For the composer of songs, on the other hand, it was the lyrical feeling of the poetry that was the really inspiring element. As long as a poem appealed to his live imagination and was sufficiently well conceived in wording and phrase that it would offer no resistance to composition, everything else could be left to his own in-

ventiveness. On occasion, the animating element that
acted as his inspiration can be pinpointed to a single line
and even to a single word. In the splendid vocal quartet
Heimat, Opus 64, Number 1—another bit of lost family
music!—one senses that nothing of the entire poem by
C. O. Sternau was significant for Brahms except the opening word *Heimat* ("homeland"). It opened all the sluices
of the composer's emotion and invention, and one feels
the profound ardor of a human being who loves his
homeland and yet is forced to live far away from it. Similar examples can be found in many other songs where a
single flash of feeling, a single thought, captured his imagination and gave birth to an entire composition. Everything
else is then absorbed, as it were, and less felicitous details
of diction are submerged in the music. In this respect
Brahms acted quite differently from a composer such as
Hugo Wolf. No matter how painstaking his declamation,
he was by no means pedantic and was more willing to
overlook some minor unevenness of accentuation, which a
skillful singer could smooth out anyway, than to compromise with any awkwardness or artificiality in the melody.
In a manner of speaking, here again there are antipodes at
work: Wolf's lyricism is based on poetry, Brahms's on
feeling. And his melodies have ennobled a hundred poems
which stay alive only through and in them. Just as the
poems of Wilhelm Müller would long since have gone the
way of all earthly things without Schubert's *Schöne Mül-
lerin* and *Winterreise,* so would the poems by Klaus Groth,
Josef Wenzig, Carl Lemcke, and G. F. Daumer without
Brahms's music.

The fact that in Brahms's work the large compositions
for chorus and orchestra preceded his symphonies reveals
that vocal composition lay closer to his nature. With the
smaller choral works of his Hamburg period he had tenta-

tively explored the field. Then suddenly with the *German Requiem* he appeared as a "strong man armed," for whom there was no longer any problem in the oratorio style which he could not master by his natural sense of vocal writing. The extraordinary part of his accomplishment in this composition is the whole conception and disposition as well as the choice of texts, but perhaps above all the inspired idea of countering the Catholic requiem, with its *dies irae* and its emphasis on the terrors of the Day of Judgment, with a memorial service whose inner substance is mourning but also solace. In the profound humanity of this idea probably lies the principal secret of the incomparable effect which this work continues to exert after nearly a century.

Considering the outstanding importance of the Scriptures in Brahms's creative work, it is singular that his own attitude, no matter how emotionally directed, had nothing to do with conscious religiosity. Still he must be considered, along with Bach and Schütz, one of the most Protestant of the great masters. No doubt there were childhood memories of his Protestant upbringing which had made him familiar with the Bible as soon as he could understand. Later he was not a churchgoer and made no bones about it. But he continued to read the Bible; it was and remained for him the highest revelation of human thought and sentiment. Whenever he used scriptural texts as subjects for his compositions, his deepest feeling and most concentrated power of expression were aroused.

The choice of texts for his *German Requiem* causes us again to admire the depth of his thought processes. The sequence of ideas, developed in seven partly lyrical, partly epic movements, is expressed in words of the Scriptures unsurpassed in the annals of religious music as to meaningfulness and graphic power. From the Beatitude of the

Suffering ("Blessed are they that mourn, for they shall be comforted"), contemplations of the transience of existence, of the enigma of death and destruction, and of the promise of salvation, lead to the blessing of the dead "which die in the Lord from henceforth: Yea, saith the Spirit, that they may rest from their labours; and their works do follow after them." The trumpet does not summon to judgment but proclaims resurrection. The deeply contrite prayer for mercy, *oro supplex et acclinis*, is replaced by the jubilant conviction of the spirit's immortality: "Grave, where is thy triumph? O Death, where is thy sting?"

It is remarkable how Brahms has, in this work of profoundly religious substance, avoided anything that might be dogmatic, in favor of a more general and deeper metaphysical idea. That this was due to a well-thought-out plan is apparent from the following correspondence with Reinthaler, who as a church musician and a former theologian was fully entitled to a different opinion. He wrote to Brahms:

For a performance here [in Bremen] I consider no place but the lovely Cathedral suitable. . . . I looked through your Requiem with this in mind. Forgive me, but I wondered if it might not be possible to extend the work in some way that would bring it closer to a Good Friday service. To me such an extension seems to be logical according to the basic idea of the work. . . . My idea was the following: In this composition you stand not only on religious but also very definitely on Christian ground. The second movement, for example, touches on the prophecy of the Lord's return, and in the next-to-the-last movement the mystery of the resurrection of the dead, "we shall not all sleep," is treated in detail. But what is lacking, at least for a Christian consciousness, is the pivotal point: the salvation in the death of our Lord. "If Christ is not raised, your faith is vain," said St. Paul in connection with the passage dealt with by you. Now it would be easy to find, near "O death, where is thy sting," a suitable place, either briefly within the movement itself just before the fugue, or else by introducing a new movement. In any case, you say in the last movement: "Blessed are the dead which die in the Lord *from henceforth*." This can only mean, after Jesus has completed His act of salvation.

One can hear Brahms growl: "This guy notices everything," as he replied, somewhat reservedly but with great firmness: "As far as the text is concerned, I confess that I would gladly omit even the word *German* and instead put in *human;* also with my best knowledge and will would I dispense with places like St. John 3:16 ['For God so loved the world, that He gave His only begotten son']. On the other hand, I have chosen one thing or another because I am a musician, because I needed it, and because with my venerable authors I can't delete or dispute anything. But I had better stop before I say too much."

Of course, anything ill-considered would be just as hard to find in connection with his texts as with his music. And on some occasions he did delete from his "venerable authors" when he found it advisable to exercise the ancient privilege of combining scriptural words at will. In his *Song of Triumph* such an omission was the result of necessary self-censorship. This work, suggested by the German victory of 1870, takes its text from Rev. 19:1–2: "Hallelujah, salvation, and glory, and honour, and power, unto the Lord our God: For true and righteous are His judgments." Thus far Brahms. But this was followed by words which he could not possibly let stand, even though they precisely expressed at that time the feelings of a German patriot to whom Napoleon III seemed a new Nebuchadnezzar, the Paris of Offenbach, Empress Eugenie, and the cancan an iniquitous Babylon: "For He hath judged the great whore, which did corrupt the earth with her fornication." The first seven words of this can practically be heard in the composition, but only in instrumental form. With great energy the orchestra here takes the lead, in unison, continuing and complementing the choral phrase. Brahms could not resist the temptation of inserting in his personal copy of the full score the words "for He hath judged the great whore . . ." under the respective notes (measures 89-91).

In the most magnificent of his motets, the *Fest- und Gedenksprüche,* for double chorus, there is a different type of omission which is far more questionable, for here the composer distorted the meaning of his venerable authors. As in the *Song of Triumph,* he again used biblical words as a vehicle for his patriotic feeling, and again one cannot help but admire his scriptural learning and the keen understanding with which he chose texts corresponding most closely to his ideas as well as to his form conception, a large-scale motet in three coherent movements. The subject was the German people, the German empire, and the great events just transpired: "Our fathers had faith in Thee, and Thou camest to their rescue. They cried unto Thee and were saved." We have already stated that Brahms was an ardent admirer of Bismarck, and it is easy to see that the next words refer to the Iron Chancellor: "When a strong man armed keepeth his palace, his goods are in peace." If, however, we look up this passage in St. Luke 11:21, from which it comes, we find that the "strong man armed" really signifies Satan, the Prince of Darkness. And the Evangelist continues: "But when a stronger than he shall come upon him, and overcome him, he taketh from him all his armour wherein he trusted, and divideth his spoils." If Germany in 1890 had been a despotically ruled state without any free exchange of opinion, no member of the opposition could possibly have expressed his biting criticism more sharply and yet more covertly. This certainly could not have been Brahms's intention. But his ingenuousness toward the gospels borders on the unbelievable.

It is hardly possible to deal here in more than a most general way with the question of how a large-scale vocal composition crystallizes into shape. Instrumental forms have developed as certain types of construction, evolved by plain common sense from time-tested, musically balanced relationships, such as the variation form, the sonata form, and the rondo form. Vocal music, on the other hand, knows only a single general principle and goal: the clear-cut presentation of words through music, and of music through words. While the music is responsible for expressive declamation and clarity of diction, it must at the same time remain true to its own exalted purpose: it must shape itself into a melody, a theme, into a self-contained and viable phrase, for otherwise it becomes a formless recitative. The only basic form of universal value that has become traditional in vocal music is the fugue. It derives from the urge of the individual choral part to assert itself in the polyphonic web. The means for this is a phrase which outlines the text with clear-cut articulation and which, contrapuntally applied, is taken up by all the voices. The fugue plays an important part in the *German Requiem* as well as in the *Song of Triumph:* it finds its natural place wherever an important event calls for a broadly conceived peroration. The extreme opposite of the fugue is the simple, melodic song form which, by using either choir settings or solo parts, offers a most effective contrast to it. However, a juxtaposition of contrasting episodes and their structural disposition present in each case a different problem to which the composer must address himself by selecting and arranging his text, and which he has to solve with an eye on the over-all effect. The structure of a vocal work is a task for a musical architect who must be constantly aware, over and above matters of detail, of the whole work and of the interrelationship of its parts.

The *German Requiem* derives its effect from a scrupulous sense of form and from the rich power of invention with which the composer has wrought its seven movements into a succession of deep-felt, stirring images, in which the depth and solemnity of thought and the beauty and breadth of the musical setting are of equal importance. Any weak spots appearing here and there are primarily the results of the amalgamation—not everywhere perfect —of the vocal and orchestral parts. As far as orchestration is concerned, the composer of the D minor Concerto and the two Serenades had not yet entirely outgrown the experimental stage. The area where this disadvantage is most apparent is the closing fugue of the third movement, which was responsible for the failure of the first, still fragmentary performance in Vienna and which has remained problematical in spite of certain subsequent changes made by the composer. Since then, experience has shown ways of coping with the problem. The essentially fortunate and profound idea of symbolizing the steadfastness of the "righteous souls to whom no pain nor grief shall come nigh" by a pedal point which underlies the entire fugue— the D held by timpani, trombones, double basses, and contrabassoon—falls flat on account of the dull monotony of the timpani sound, the diffuse resonance and uncontrollable overtones of the heavily scored double-bass note, and a certain stiffness of the contrapuntal setting that is apparent not only in the somewhat mechanically trotting eighth notes of the orchestral accompaniment but even in the inner voices of the chorus. At times, counterpoint becomes more noticeable than is good for the expressive lyricism, which, after all, is the basic mood of the entire work. The beautiful, lyrical warmth of "How lovely is thy dwelling place" is cooled off in a not very convincing manner by a somewhat dry fugal episode, "They praise Thy name evermore." One must really admire the healthy instinct of Clara, the sensitive musician without technical prejudices, who got to see this movement—the first to be completed—as early as 1865. She immediately seized on this passage and made it the object of her criticism: "The chorus from the *Requiem* pleases me very much; I imagine it must sound beautiful. I am especially fond of it up to this place [here she inserted the notes] which, as it goes on, is not so much to my taste." Mandyczewski recalls that Brahms himself was critical of quite a few details in his *Requiem*. In this connection he referred particularly to the "lovely dwelling place" movement, but for practical reasons he despaired of ever being able to improve a work that had already been widely distributed and whose original version could not possibly have been recalled, even if he had attempted a revised version. One can put up with such shortcomings, considering the overwhelming wealth of beauty known only in those very rare and fortunate cases where a young artist, for the first time in full possession of his forces, creates something surpassingly great which had inspired him in the highest degree.

With the experience gained in the *Requiem*, Brahms had overcome his last remaining difficulties in handling an orchestra. In his compositions for chorus and orchestra—*Rinaldo, Song of Triumph, Song of Destiny,* and the *Alto Rhapsody*—which represent his main efforts during the years between the *Requiem* and the symphonies, the orchestration became an integral part of the concept, and the sound was identical with what he had imagined. Of these works, the *Song of Destiny* is the most powerful and has at all times occupied a preferred position. Here again the master's sense of form withstood all the misgivings voiced by his friends, misgivings which are entirely understandable. In the cases mentioned before, the composer deleted certain parts, but here he added something which expanded the concept of Hölderlin's text far beyond the poet's imagination. The poem contrasts in two different, grandly conceived pictures the blissful repose of the gods ("Ye walk on high in light on downy ground, ye blessed genii") and the desperate, hopeless struggle of mortals who know no peace and no respite, "tossed from cliff to cliff, as are the floods, for years on end, into the dark unknown." Hölderlin's vision ends here. The music, like the poem, depicts two worlds in sharp contrast to each other. But this does not provide the kind of form that could satisfy the composer. The two opposing images—the beatific calm of the gods and the restless bustle of mankind—do not complement one another to form a harmonious entity. But the composer created such an entity in his own musical manner by the use of a recapitulation: He restated as a coda the most precious substance of his invention, the orchestral introduction to the image of the gods, but with changed tone coloring which dematerializes the substance in a most striking manner. The E-flat major of the gods' world and the C minor of mankind's dark confusion are followed by a C major of ethereal radiance. It seems as though all that is divine, now freed from the fetters of reality, confronts our soul like a purified idea. No poem, no painting could possibly express what the music has done here. The effect is so compelling that one is not even aware that the composer has here continued and enhanced the poem without the use of words.

Hermann Levi, who as a witness of its genesis took a great interest in this work, had some misgivings. It seems that Brahms, at his suggestion, had added another choral setting to the recapitulation, using the opening verses of the poem. A sketch for this is actually in existence. But then he decided against it, and the subsequent success proved him right. The following letter to Reinthaler, which deals with this matter, sounds somewhat annoyed with his own lack of decision: "The *Song of Destiny* is in print, and in the final adagio the chorus is now silent. It was probably just a silly idea, but think what you may, it just couldn't be helped. I had already gone as far as writing something for the chorus, but it didn't work out. It may turn out to be a miscarried experiment, but such grafting would only result in nonsense." But by that time a performance had already proved his musical intuition right. The letter continues: "In Karlsruhe the piece has made a remarkable impression."

The magic that takes place when an immortal poem receives its final apotheosis through music which without such a poem would probably never have been born, has hardly ever become more strikingly apparent than in this case. As everywhere, the decisive factor here was the ability of the composer to penetrate deeply into the heart of the poem and to bring forth a richly perceptive creation, compared with which the poem itself was but a shadow.

The fact that by the time he had become a symphonic composer he had already passed through the experience of being a tone poet, has incalculably enriched his background of expression. But it would be a sad mistake to consider his vocal works as merely a preliminary or developmental stage. They represent the first complete synthesis of his potential abilities, the first magnificent fulfillment of Schumann's prophecy. A part of these abilities, and by no means the least part, was his sense for the depth of feeling and the imagery of a poem. One need hardly mention how much a composer is dependent here upon his own emotional reaction. Brahms's broad knowledge of literature, acquired through persevering self-education, stood him in good stead in his constant quest for poetic material. And he was forever searching. The following letter to Elisabeth von Herzogenberg provides a little insight into this endeavor: "Please try to get me some texts [for choral compositions]. To have them made to order is something one must get used to while still young. Later one is far too spoiled by good literature. The Bible is not pagan enough for me; now I have bought myself the Koran, but I still can't find anything."

Brahms had at that time (1880), in the period between his two pairs of symphonies, returned to composing for chorus and orchestra. The result of this was *Nänie* and the *Song of the Fates*. The latter, a fragment of Goethe's *Iphigenie*, stands in its over-all concept somewhat in the shadow of the more forcefully inspired and more stirringly formed *Song of Destiny*. *Nänie*, however, deserves a place among the master's most characteristic and poetic creations. It is a dirge consecrated to the memory of a friend, the painter Anselm Feuerbach, who had died while still young. Brahms dedicated it to the artist's mother, Henriette Feuerbach. "The beautiful, which conquers gods and men, must also die"—like so many of Schiller's poems, this one too suffers from an excess of mythological allusions. But when Thetis rises from the floods to mourn her son Achilles, one feels how profoundly these glorious verses have touched the master's soul:

> *Behold, the gods, the goddesses weep*
> *That Beauty must perish,*
> *That even perfection must die . . .*

195

The monumental classicism of the music grows and is woven into a miraculously calm expression of deepest sentiment.

The hold that poetry had on his imagination is apparent everywhere in his vocal music. And next to the Scriptures, it was above all Goethe who brought to life his most profound emotions and his most characteristic imagination. It was he who inspired such a serious work as the *Song of the Fates* and a work of such singular character as the *Alto Rhapsody,* a strange, profound, and in many respects enigmatic composition which would be heard more frequently if the combination of alto voice, male chorus, and orchestra were not so unconventional and so contrary to ordinary concert-hall usage. The fact that the poet's magic power to inspire the composer to his highest achievement failed in one case (*Rinaldo*), shows how very much a musician's reaction depends on his spontaneous emotional grasp of a poem. *Rinaldo,* a broad cantata for tenor solo, male chorus, and orchestra, was composed for a special occasion, a prize competition about which we know nothing except that Brahms failed to make the grade—which of course says nothing against the intrinsic value of the work. Brahms always vehemently defended this stepchild of his muse, even against Billroth, who quite openly called the Goethe text "repulsive." The poem itself was also written for an occasion, and it suffers from too many allusions to Tasso's *Jerusalem Delivered.* The reader is either well acquainted with that work, or the allusions are incomprehensible. The beautiful, typically Goethian phrases and the poem's suitability for a work for male chorus—this was probably one of the conditions of the contest—caused Brahms to put himself into a trance of enthusiasm. But this enthusiasm was more of the head than of the heart; this is betrayed by the music, which displays more color than substance and a certain artificiality of perception. Probably for this reason the work has never received more than a respectful acceptance. Brahms wrote to his publisher, Simrock:

You are probably most interested in the reaction of the audience and the critics, but as usual there is nothing much to boast about. *Rinaldo* wasn't energetically hissed as was my *Requiem* last year [that unfortunate première of the three opening movements, in Vienna], but I still can't call it a success. And this time the critics listened "at first sight" and then concocted quite some writeups. It is a matter of long experience that people always expect something very definite, and it is just as true that they get from us something entirely different. Thus they hoped this time to get a crescendo like that in the *Requiem*, and definitely some nice, exciting *Venusberg* affair for Armida, etc.

A letter to Reinthaler, however, seems to reveal that his own conscience wasn't quite clear as far as this work was concerned. In it he who was usually contemptuous of all superficialities in instrumentation tried to hide behind the sound effects:

I can temporarily spare the enclosed piano arrangement [of *Rinaldo*] and am forwarding it, although with some diffidence naturally! I mean that you can't see the best parts in it, but I can't send you the orchestral score just now. I would be greatly pleased if you derive a little pleasure from it. If you do not, then believe me, it is in the orchestration.

This sort of thing would never have occurred to him with regard to the *Requiem*. Still and all, *Rinaldo*, although not a masterpiece, shows the master's hand everywhere, especially in the grand, three-dimensional layout, which is a general characteristic of Brahms's choral creations.

In this respect and insofar as objectivity and mighty, superpersonal expression are concerned, the *Four Serious Songs* belong in the realm of great vocal works, although they are written for a single bass voice accompanied by piano and thus technically fall into the class of lieder. There exists a monumentality which lies in expression rather than in size or in expenditure of material. This is Brahms's kind of monumentality, and for this reason it is often—for example, in his symphonies—misjudged. He never found it necessary to raise his voice in order to say something of moment; the significance of a statement lies in its substance, not in its emphasis. In the *Four Serious Songs* it is the tone poet himself who speaks; the words are an avowal of the most profound thoughts that can be expressed by one who has already cut all ties and abandoned all motives of human consideration. It is a work of conscious farewell if ever there was one. Certainly "sufficiently pagan," and far from anything dogmatic, it has at the same time a humaneness which rises above the most desperate pessimism and skepticism. Once again the Holy Scriptures offered him everything that—in the most clear-cut precision —he needed to express himself.

In these four pieces—one can hardly call them lieder— everything seems larger than life: the concept, the vocal style, the phrasing, even the range, which makes enormous demands on a bass voice that must have sonorous depth coupled with an effortless high register reaching up to G above middle C. We pass from the merciless wisdom of the preacher Solomon, through Jesus of Sirach, to the First Epistle to the Corinthians, along a curve of emotion that ranges all the way from desperate suffering and commiseration to the gospel of love as the highest knowledge. Throughout the entire group runs a profound fervor, a despair which the composer had to sublimate by creating this work, thereby freeing himself from it. There is no other work of Brahms which is such a direct reflection of experience. To produce this powerful achievement, the artistic discipline and the self-restraint of a lifetime were necessary.

"For that which befalleth the sons of men befalleth beasts; even one thing befalleth them; as the one dieth, so dieth the other; yea, they have all one breath." A breath of icy air exudes from these words as well as from the music, and cold despair overflows all bounds in a dire outburst of anguish: "All go unto one place; all are of the dust, and all turn to dust again." And the only solace we gain is the knowledge that "there is nothing better than that a man should rejoice in his own works, for that is his portion." How a magnificent, large, and perfect composition, cast from a single mold, could grow from such words, is one of the riddles so often posed by music. But each of the four songs answers this description and each is an individual of the most intrinsic personal character, both in form and in expression.

"So I returned, and considered all the oppressions that are done under the sun; and behold the tears of such as were oppressed, and they had no comforter; and on the side of their oppressors there was power." In this passage, too, there is despair: the despair of compassion that is unable to help. When the Preacher continues, "wherefore I praised the dead," we sink into an abyss; and with the knowledge that "better is he which hath not yet been, who hath not seen the evil work that is done under the sun" and that the evil in this world is ineradicable, the emotion becomes heart-rending, the misery greater than can be borne. What the Preacher proclaims is inexorable fact; it is the music which changes it into an expression of overwhelming compassion; everything turns into pure expression and flowing melody.

Still, the third piece rises to even loftier heights. Here we find the emotional climax of the whole work, the feel-

ing out of which it was born. Never before had Brahms
written a phrase of such boldness as the one which opens
the piece without preamble:

The lyrical and symphonic composer needed the experience of a long lifetime to arrive at such a point. A man
had to be free of everything that tied him to life, to be
able to behold his own open grave without any illusions
and without terror, in order to perceive that which is con-
veyed in this work. The moment when this phrase about
the bitterness of death suddenly changes and death appears
as a savior, is unique beauty removed from all reality: "O
Death, how welcome thy call to him that is in want, and
whose strength doth fail him, who hath nothing to hope
for, and cannot look for relief." Suddenly a bridge spans
the space of many years when, at this point, sleep's brother
brings in the closing bars of the *Cradle Song*, which
Brahms had once sung when still in his youth and which
in the meantime had almost become a folk song.

It is difficult to see how, from here, any path could lead
further, could lead in a different direction, or to a more
positive attitude toward life. We stand where, in the *German Requiem,* a desperate voice asks: "Now, Lord, what
do I wait for?" The answer is the noblest wisdom ever
put into words: "Though I speak with the tongues of men
and of angels, and have not love . . ." Love, in its most

exalted, all-encompassing sense, is the purpose, the justification, and the only hope of human existence. Here the
mightiest of the four pieces becomes the equivalent of a
symphony movement in the majestic grandeur of its
thought and contrast. The symphonic second theme is
formed, with a beautifully shaped melody, to the words:
"For now we see through a glass, darkly." And this melody
recurs at the very end where, from the knowledge that
"now abideth faith, hope, and love, these three," the ultimate knowledge, the highest of all, issues forth: "But the
greatest of these is love." He who never in his life permitted anyone a glance into his inner being has here delivered his confession of faith. Here speaks the eternal
longing of a human being who could never express his
noblest and innermost feelings other than in his music.
And here we have in the most literal sense his last word,
the last and most profound thought which he, as artist and
as man, had to express.

The
Artist's Four Seasons

Measured in terms of time elapsed during Brahms's total period of creativity, which approximately equals that passed between Wagner's *Rienzi* and his *Parsifal,* his style development kept within remarkably narrow limits. This is above all due to the unusual precocity of his talents, very much in contrast to Wagner's. Brahms started as a fully mature artist. Schumann judged quite correctly when he saw in Brahms "one who would not bring us mastery in gradual developmental stages but who, like Minerva, would spring fully armed from the head of Jove." Similar observations might have been made of Schumann himself, as well as of his contemporaries Mendelssohn and Chopin. In all three cases the early works show such a fully developed style that comparatively little significant change took place during the further course of their creative lives. Brahms, whose life and career extended far beyond theirs, underwent appreciably more change of style than they. Still, so much of his distinctive character is already apparent in his earliest works, and his entire production shows such a gradual and steady development, that it is hardly consistent to speak of different style periods in his work as has been done in the case of Beethoven. What one can observe in Brahms is a changing psychological attitude toward his work, which by its very nature had an influence on his style. Anyone closely acquainted with his music will have no difficulty in determining with some measure of accuracy the time when any one of his works was created —at least, within a decade.

A differentiation of three creative periods, such as can be made in the work of Beethoven and others, cannot be made in the case of Brahms, primarily because his spiritual maturation took an extraordinarily long time and his inner growth did not reach full completion until late in life. This kind of evolution is by no means unique among artists. Just as in the case of Brahms, it took place in Wagner and Verdi, and to a certain extent in Haydn and Handel also. In such cases a division corresponding to the general physiological development process seems more appropriate. For this the annual cycle of nature provides a most illustrative analog. A springtime of coming to life and blossoming forth, a summer of mighty growth and ripening, an autumn of rich harvests, and a winter of gradually diminishing vitality: these are the periods according to which Brahms's work can most readily be classified parallel with his life story.

The springtime of his life, which reached its climax but also its end with the B major Trio, came to a close when the overpowering catastrophe of Schumann and its sequels completely uprooted his course. This traumatic experience cast a shadow on his life as well as on his work for many years, providing us with a simple method for dating his works; it was linked to his First Symphony, the last work still rooted in that period although not completed until his forty-second year. This symphony thus spans the years of his ripening, the summer of his life—a sultry, stormy, often tempestuous and indecisive summer, a restless time of conflict, wavering, search, oppression, alternating successes and failures, and distressing inner and outer circumstances. It must have been a period of torture, although no one ever heard any complaints to that effect from him. At that time he developed a stoicism, an ability to suppress his feelings and to tame the chaos within him, just as he mastered the art of channeling into a form the tumultuous, explosive natural forces of his music. This summer time of his life and work was divided into two parts by his decisive first trip to Vienna. The demarcation, denoted by the year 1862, can be easily spotted in his style. It was characterized by a fresh impetus, which gave wings to his productivity through richer opportunities and a more congenial atmosphere; his ambition was enhanced by the higher level of competition in Vienna. The difference in style is most noticeable in his two String Sextets in B-flat major, written in 1860, and in G major, written in 1864. Also a greater sureness of style can be discerned in such works as the Horn Trio and the Piano Quintet, whose history (see page 117) teaches us that in every growth process there are bound to be relapses. But these works already prepared the way for the *German Requiem,* the creation most characteristic of this period of constantly increasing maturity. Here, between the *Requiem* and the later great choral works, we find the *Hungarian Dances* which played such a remarkable role in his rapid rise to fame during these years, several vocal quartets, the *Liebeslieder,* and more than sixty lieder, including such gems as *Von ewiger Liebe, Der Schmied, Wie bist du, meine Königin, Die Mainacht, Sonntag, Der Gang zum Liebchen,* and *Wiegenlied.* And at long last, after much hesitation, there followed the string quartets, the Haydn Variations, and the C minor Piano Quartet, which ushered in a period when complete mastery of invention and formation attained sovereign heights.

The last-named composition is, however, not entirely free of certain inhibitions. Brahms himself made some hints about its connection with the Wertherian mood of his Düsseldorf years, and we know that he carried the work around within himself for years before deciding to complete it. An idea so heavy with passion can be compulsive and will not leave the artist in peace until he has embodied it into his work. It had an emotional significance for him which may have transcended its actual value. "I no longer have either judgment or power over this piece," Brahms wrote in connection with a similar case, the D minor Piano Concerto. In the Piano Quartet in C minor, certain parts of the first movement suffer from a sullen gloominess of invention which is probably connected with this circumstance and which somehow paralyzes its driving force. Clara must have sensed this—the good soul had no idea how intimately all this concerned her—when after a first hearing she wrote to Brahms:

I have given a great deal of thought to your quartet. The last three movements have touched me deeply, but if I may be permitted to say so, I do not find the first movement quite up to the same level. I miss the fresh drive in it, although admittedly it is to be found in the first theme. I should have liked to hear it once more, to help me determine why it is that I could not

205

warm up to it. Couldn't you, who so often carry music around within you for a long time, somehow contrive to change it? Or perhaps create a new movement altogether? You have already shown on several occasions how readily and how beautifully you can re-create a mood. Forgive me; what I am saying is probably stupid.

She had no way of knowing what the "mood" meant to him and under what pains he had labored with this movement. But she did get to know it in connection with another work, the last one in which his youthful conflict was still evident: the opening movement of the First Symphony, which she was allowed to see, practically before the ink was dry, fourteen years before its completion. In a letter dated July 1, 1862, she wrote to Joachim: "Johannes sent me the other day—imagine my surprise!—the first movement of a symphony, with the following bold opening: [Here she wrote down the opening bars of the allegro]." Albert Dietrich also got to see the music at the time; according to his statement, it was still without its slow introduction. Joachim, very much interested, wrote Brahms:

Dear Johannes, I would consider it a genuine token of our unalterable friendship if you would let me know something of your new symphony, about the first movement of which Mrs. Schumann wrote me some time ago. Will it be possible to have it performed in Hanover before it goes to Hamburg? Are you considering a Hamburg performance at all, etc.?

Joachim was already thinking of a performance! But Brahms in the meantime had left for Vienna and had put the symphony aside. "I have been in Vienna for almost two weeks," he answered, "and thus your letter arrived too late for sending a reply to England. On the other hand there was really no need for a speedy answer because you may for the time being put a question mark after 'Symphony by J. B.'" The next mention of the work was the salute to Clara (see page 141), with the horn solo from the last movement. But this was six years after the completion of the first movement, and only in 1876, another eight years later, was the score finished after a thousand scruples and reservations. He knew what he risked in entering the lists with a symphony: his own critical conscience, which had always been strong, was now joined by an awareness of his high standing, which he had to defend. And he saw with perfect clarity that this symphony was not a work which would instantly appeal to a listener. He wrote to Carl Reinecke, conductor of the *Gewandhaus* concerts in Leipzig: "And now I have to make the probably very surprising announcement that my symphony is long and not exactly amiable."

The oppressed, haunted mood of crisis that dominates the first movement has resulted in a restlessness of musical idiom such as can probably not be found anywhere else in Brahms's music. It is true that the opening movement of the D minor Concerto was born in a similarly tragic vein, but there are after all extended interludes of lyrical peace in it. These are completely lacking in the first movement of the symphony, in which one brief thematic episode (second subject) for the oboe hardly affords more than a fleeting moment of quiet. Even Billroth, that most enthusiastic of all friends, expressed certain reservations concerning this movement in a report to Hanslick after he had attended the first rehearsal:

Although everything reverberated in the large, empty hall, the effect of the symphony was grandiose. With all the boldness of its construction, nobody can possibly complain of a lack of formal clarity, not even in the first movement, which storms along like a hurricane. To me, the motifs of the first movement, despite all their energy and passion, do seem to lack a certain appeal. They are rhythmically too long-drawn-out and harmonically too defiant and harsh, although at times there is an intense nostalgia; it is a kind of Faustian overture. The entire first movement can almost be considered an introduction to the whole work. The second movement, in E major, which I once played for you, was not interpreted with sufficient delicacy by the orchestra to allow the listener to arrive at the pure, sky-blue beauty which inspired its invention. The third movement is simply charming and just beautiful. But the last movement is overwhelming. When the horn solo is heard, every heart vibrates with the strings.

Here is another illustration of how the effect of a brand-new work corresponds to the impressions we get today. Brahms, fully conscious of the unusual severity of the first movement, showed how accurately he was able to estimate the emotional dimensions of the whole work by treating the two middle movements as lyrical interludes and by devoting the last movement to an extraordinary profusion of themes of immediate appeal. It is interesting to note that two such discriminating judges as Clara Schumann and Hermann Levi were at first to misunderstand this formal idea. The latter wrote to Clara: "The last movement is probably the greatest thing he has yet created in the instrumental field; the first movement comes next. But about the two middle movements I have certain doubts. Even though in themselves they are truly beautiful, they seem to belong in a serenade or a suite rather than in such a broad symphony." How difficult it is to grasp the whole of a grandly conceived work as an entity! Incidentally, it is characteristic of the passionate nature of the entire symphony that the compulsive imagery of the first movement, that ominously clenched chromatic motif which uninterruptedly burrows on and allows no respite, penetrates even into the serene melody of the andante where it occurs, like an uncanny visitor, in the fifth measure. A tormented, passionate suffering is one of the peculiarities of the whole composition and sharply distinguishes it from the three subsequent symphonies, in which the composer has finally left all *Sturm und Drang* behind him, having found his peace and his balance. The flowering landscape of the Second Symphony, the charm of the Violin Concerto, the tender, melodious depth of emotion of the G major Violin Sonata—these three signal the beginning of the master's fullest maturity. They sprang from three happy, productive summers spent in Pörtschach in 1877–79, which also gave us the Piano Pieces, Opus 76 and 79, and the two Motets, Opus 74, not to forget some two dozen lieder, a type of composition with which Brahms always filled any time gaps. In all of these works one can sense the inner peace which the master, now at the ultimate height of his productivity, had at last achieved. And this brings us to his autumn, his period of abundant ripeness.

The towering peaks at this stage were his symphonies, which evolved in two pairs and represent the apex of his life's work. Only one year separated the Second Symphony from the First, which stood at the threshold of this autumn period. The Third and Fourth Symphonies also came in close succession, originating in 1883 and 1885, respectively. The four are completely different in character, different in style, and different in effect. Herein lies a part of their greatness. Brahms's symphonic form is carved out of granite; it is the very essence of an instrumental style intensified to monumental proportions. This is true not so much because of the dimensions of his symphonies, but rather because of the concentration of thematic substance and of the living energy exuded by them. Compared to an opening subject by Bruckner, for example, one by Brahms is simple and unobtrusive. But it unleashes gigantic, space-filling forces because of its infinite fecundity. Here the dynamics of polyphony is of decisive importance. In both the Second and Third Symphonies, just as in the First, it is the principal motif of the first movement that seems to give rise to the entire work. In all three cases this principal motif is a contrapuntal invention: Two phrases in counterpoint, contrasting with each other like the two subjects of a double fugue, not only dominate the movement itself but extend thematic tentacles throughout the entire work. In the idyllic Second Symphony the contrapuntal element is introduced in a discreet fashion: the principal motif of three notes acts, at its first appearance in the bass, as though it were only an accompanying phrase to the broad melody intoned above it by the horns and the woodwinds. But this bass phrase turns out to be the real, vital, germinal motif, recurring throughout the movement in countless metamorphoses. New blossoms of melody burgeon forth from it continuously, and we encounter it again in the adagio, in the intermezzo-like third movement, and even in the finale, but each time it is in a different form. Perhaps the most superb moment in the entire symphony is in the coda of the first movement, when the double main theme of an already extended and richly developed composition unexpectedly grows into a cantilena of such magnificent breadth that it seems there can be no end to its singing.

The double theme of two phrases in counterpoint is as typical for Brahms's symphonic compositions as the concentrated rhythmic pattern was for Beethoven's. What is apparent in it is his typical blending of classical and baroque style elements. But a more romantic component is also added: an element of harmonic suspense which creates another peculiar relationship between the two contrapuntal phrases. In the first movement of the Third

Symphony the heroic, passionate melody announced by the violins seems at first to be the principal subject. Actually it is nothing but a counterpoint to the unbelievably powerful basic motif of three notes, F A-flat F, first stated broadly as a motto and then as a *cantus firmus* in the bass and the inner parts. This motif supports the entire structure like a system of flying buttresses:

The basic motif, however, acquires its peculiar tension from an enharmonic duality which characterizes the opening bar: the A-flat in the melody functions unmistakably as a G-sharp in the harmony. That is to say, the A-flat has the character of a leading tone; and the resulting harmonic duality becomes an uncommonly vigorous and colorful element in the forceful construction. The entire movement grows from this nucleus, which is charged with living force and acts as a source of energy. But when the basic motif recurs in the tempestuous finale, it comes as a harbinger of peace and indescribably transfigures the coda.

211

It is interesting to note that just at this juncture—the dynamics of polyphony—the two antipodes met one another. The spirit of improvisation which caused Wagner's love for contrapuntally telescoping his separately conceived motifs would hardly have been acceptable, in a symphonic sense, to Brahms. But where the original invention is actually contrapuntal, a kinship between the two contemporaries becomes apparent. Few who listen to the introduction to the third act of *Die Meistersinger* will recall having already heard the opening theme—the *Wahn* motif, which plays such an important role in Hans Sachs's soliloquy that follows—in the preceding act. But this motif was conceived as a contrapuntal accompaniment heard for the first time in the third stanza of Hans Sachs's "Cobbler Song." By the way, the reader will look in vain in his vocal score for this passage; the arranger has neglected this detail:

A beautiful symbol, when the cobbler and poet, clinging to the past but open to the future, turns scholar as he philosophizes.

It was one of Wagner's peculiarities that his vocal invention was rarely on the same high level as his instrumental invention, and that the concept of his most inspired moments was of an orchestral rather than of a vocal nature. His musicodramatic theories were certainly influenced by this circumstance. Brahms, on the other hand, blended together his vocal and instrumental conceptions as naturally as Mozart or Schubert, for example; and a *cantabile* quality is the common denominator of his grand choral works and his symphonies.

In view of the close-knit polyphonic structure of his symphonies, this may sound like a paradox; yet it is possible to sing every Brahms movement from beginning to end as though it were a single, uninterrupted melody. Through all its polyphonic intricacies the clear flow of invention always remains distinctly recognizable as the mighty main stream of events. It certainly requires a great deal of concentration on the listener's part to grasp a whole movement as a single unit. By the same token, only a superlatively mature interpretation will escape the temptation of building up the whole from its component parts instead of letting every detail emerge from an intense perception of the main stream. A conductor who permits the chorale phrases in the finale of the First Symphony, which in the introduction had followed the horn melody and which recur as a dynamic climax in the coda at an accelerated *alla breve* tempo, to blare forth with pompous grandeur in double augmentation, has completely lost this continuity, even if he does achieve a momentary effect. But whatever the listener and the performer accomplish in this respect is but a reflection of what the composer did and what— let it be said once more—was an act of creation equally driven by inspiration and guided by the most critical, deliberate artistic intelligence.

The creation of a language capable of such an achievement was the result of many years of gradually expanding mastery. And now, at the summit, everything that used to require infinite patience for the slow ripening seems to come to the master without effort. The same applies to the problems of orchestration which, as we have seen, had caused the young artist many painful hours of doubt. In the days when feelings pro and con ran high, a great deal of nonsense was written about Brahms's orchestral style. Its sparse, sometimes ascetic coloring admittedly invites criticism, especially if one considers Wagner's brilliant palette as the only criterion. However, the dim gray tints are just as characteristic for Brahms's sound effects as the purple ones are for Wagner's. Brahms just had a different ear, and the structure of his music was thus of an entirely different cast. If the ideal of orchestral sound is to be that which most closely brings the design of a composition into reality, then nothing can possibly be improved in Brahms's instrumental coloring.

The difficulties of orchestration encountered by the youthful Brahms were, incidentally, neither entirely of a technical nature nor entirely due to any lack of practical experience. They were perhaps even more due to the deeply rooted imagination of a pianist for whom sound is projected on a plane, in black and white as it were, and who has no understanding for the solid, three-dimensional sound structure of an orchestra. This shortcoming is quite obvious in his D minor Concerto and in the two Serenades, and to a certain extent even in the *German Requiem*. The First Symphony, however, is already pure orchestral music, drawn from the perspectives of orchestral sound; and in the subsequent symphonies the use of color acquired still greater sureness and immediacy. The joy of creative freedom which he had achieved by his own exertions expressed itself in all the music he produced during these blissful years of increasing fame and of comfortable outer circumstances. It becomes perhaps most apparent when he retraces his steps to a form which he had attempted only once during his earlier days, and then only with ambiguous success: the concerto. What he had lacked at that time was the ability to relax and be happy in carefree play—by now perhaps the most precious reward for his hard struggle for freedom. It goes without saying that as a symphonic composer he did not have to make any concessions as far as structure and development are concerned. The difference lies in the problems of artistic technique, not in the substance.

Whereas in a symphony the music in the highest and most demanding sense is its own hero and its own sole purpose, a concerto has a special and attractive additional purpose: it projects a brilliant performer, an interesting and capricious personality, into the limelight as soloist. When, as is the case in virtuoso concertos, this secondary purpose becomes the main purpose—in other words, when the concerto becomes the soloist's showpiece—the artistic result suffers. When, on the other hand, the opposite happens, i.e., when the concerto turns into a symphony with an obbligato soloist, then it lacks an essential element of its playful charm. Brahms's concertos have often been accused of the latter, but this is pure nonsense. An artist who had penetrated as deeply as Brahms into the very nature of all musical combinations was immune to this danger. In fact he even escaped it in his D minor Concerto although here the danger was more acute because of the symphonic character of its original conception. But Brahms was not only an artist who was always critically conscious of his work; he was also a pianist. As such he was incapable of thinking of a piano concerto without identifying himself with the soloist and of reshaping the concept accordingly. What is lacking in the D minor Concerto is certainly not the necessary projection of the solo part as the focus of the work, but rather the relaxed joy of playing which forms a characteristic part of this type of composition, and for which not even the final rondo brings the necessary lightness. In its ardor there is an almost sullen determination; its humor is grim and unfriendly. It was its sincerity and its love of truth, its almost desperate honesty, which gradually paved a way for the concerto and won friends for it, however slowly. "My second one will sound quite different!" he had written at that time, and he was true to his word. His Piano Concerto No. 2 in B-flat major, written in 1881, twenty-two years after the première of the first, represents the opposite pole in Brahms's world of expression, just as it signifies the opposite pole in his artistic career: the zenith as against the nadir.

There is something grandiose in the patience and the methodical planning with which Brahms allowed problems that he found challenging to wait until he considered himself ready to tackle them, and also in his unfailing instinct at the right moment for what was most in harmony with his nature and most apt to extend the frontiers of his art. After concentrating all his powers in the two symphonies, he needed, as it were, a change of climate and of environment. He found both in two concertos which, like the two symphonies, rank alongside the greatest accomplishments of their kind. His Violin Concerto was completed barely one year after the Second Symphony, also in D major, and emanated from the same enchanting landscape. Billroth might have written, "It must be beautiful on Lake Wörth," just as he did with reference to the symphony. The concerto became the crowning glory of a friendship which had already existed for twenty-five years by the time Brahms considered himself ready to write it. When he composed a violin concerto, it could only have been for Joachim. And, as so many times before, the latter freely gave him encouragement and technical advice.

Their correspondence at the time is of interest because it shows the lack of confidence in his own accomplishment with which Brahms regarded his works while they were still in progress. He sent his friend the solo part of the concerto, which was originally sketched in four movements, with this accompanying note, dated August 22, 1878:

Now that I have copied it out, I can't imagine what you will do with the bare solo part. Of course I wanted to request you to make corrections, and I did not want you to have scruples of any kind—neither a respect for music that is too good nor the excuse that the score isn't worth the trouble. I will be satisfied if you will let me have a few words, and perhaps even write some in the score: difficult, uncomfortable, impossible, etc. The whole affair has four movements; of the last I wrote out only the beginning so that you can at once discourage any clumsy passages.

To which Joachim replied:

I have immediately gone over what you sent me, and here and there you will find a notation or a suggestion for change. Of course, without a score I couldn't really get any full enjoyment out of it. Most of the material is playable—some of it, in fact, quite originally violinistic—but I wouldn't care to say whether it can be comfortably played in an overheated concert hall until I have once played it through to myself without stopping.

But Brahms was by no means satisfied with himself. In November he wrote to Joachim that he had eliminated the two middle movements altogether—"of course they were the best"—and that he had substituted a "poor adagio" in their place. It can be seen that he had worked hard. The task of writing a cadenza, which is primarily a matter of instrumental technique, he left to his friend. Classical tradition places it near the end of the first movement and designates it as *ad libitum*. Brahms never felt entirely sure of himself as far as violin technique was concerned, even though this work speaks from the instrument's very soul. Nine years later he wrote to Clara about his Double Concerto, which he had just completed:

217

I ought to have left the idea to someone better acquainted with the violin than I (unfortunately Joachim has given up composing). It is quite a different story to write for an instrument of whose peculiarities one has only a smattering and which one can only hear mentally, than for an instrument with which one is thoroughly acquainted, as I am with the piano, where I know exactly what I am doing and why I am writing one way or another.

This feeling of sovereign security of form and sound and of unlimited creative freedom is evident in every bar of the B-flat major Piano Concerto which, composed three years after the Violin Concerto, is in many respects the counterpart of the latter. Both display characters as personal, unique, and contrasting as those of his symphonies. The entire conception of the piano concerto, however, is more monumental and broader. If one compares the orchestral works written between 1876 and 1887, i.e., between the First Symphony and the Double Concerto, they will be seen to rise symmetrically, as does a mountain chain, toward towering summits in the center: the B-flat Piano Concerto of 1881 and the Third Symphony of 1883. What these two works have in common is Olympian calm and breadth, and origins in the fullness of a rich imagination. At the same age, around his fiftieth year, Wagner also attained in *Die Meistersinger* the greatest and freest unfolding of his personality.

The expression almost invariably visible in the numerous Brahms portraits of the period is one of solemn, calm reflection. Nowhere is there a more beautiful evidence of this mood than in the opening horn melody of his B-flat major Piano Concerto, which seems to lose itself in deep meditation. The profundity of the thought corresponds to the directness and the vastness of the inspiration. Here is a musical counterpoint to Michelangelo's *Pensieroso*:

The concerto character, with a solo part of overwhelmingly rich vitality, contributes here an element of unbounded fullness and free improvisation, which would burst the framework of any form if it were not for the superlatively wise architectural intelligence at work. One can sense the composer's satisfaction with the successful giant throw—it is the most voluminous but also probably the most meaningful of all piano concertos—when one reads the diminutive terms with which, true to his habit, he described it to Elisabeth von Herzogenberg (July 7, 1881): "I want to tell you that I have written a tiny little piano concerto, with a tiny little scherzo. It is written in the key of B-flat major, but I fear that I have made too heavy and frequent a demand on this udder which has on many other occasions provided such excellent milk." Indeed, B-flat major was one of his favorite keys and nearly always the one of his most serenely happy inventions; it is the key signature of the Handel Variations, the Haydn Variations, the first Sextet, and the third String Quartet. How deeply this comfortable feeling was rooted in this key is shown by the fact that three of the Second Piano Concerto's four movements are in it. Only the capricious scherzo—for this very reason a necessary interlude between the first movement, which despite some forceful episodes is essentially calm, and the adagio, which is lyrically enraptured—contributes a basic change in color by means of its D minor tonality and its passionate restlessness. And the connoisseur will admire the subtlety with which the composer veiled the tonality in the adagio and the subsequent finale: the latter makes its entrance disguised as a subdominant and does not reveal its true tonal relationship for several measures. By the way, the scherzo is the only one during this period of full maturity in which he reverted once more to the classical, Beethovenian scherzo type in three-quarter time. Brahms, who in his early works often used this form of movement—it can be found in his B major Trio, in his E-flat minor Scherzo, his Piano Quartet in A major, as well as in his two Serenades and the Horn Trio —got away from it more and more as he grew in stature. He seems to have realized that the quick pulse of the rhythmic and dynamic scherzo did not quite suit his more melancholy, contemplative nature. Brahms's art was more in the spirit of Apollo than in that of Dionysus. He was even less likely to be satisfied with the minuet form, which in Beethoven's day was already deliberately archaic (e.g., in the Eighth Symphony), and with which he had experimented in his two Serenades. Still, he felt the need for a more lightly woven movement which would provide a breathing space in the four-movement structure. This need was filled by an allegretto–intermezzo form entirely of his own making. The First, Second, and Third Symphonies contain such graceful allegretto movements which, though in form related to the minuet, are just as far removed from it in character as they are from a Beethoven scherzo. With their quiet, graceful meditation they furnish the necessary relaxation between the great musical events. The capacity for expression in such a movement is just as unlimited as in any other Brahmsian form; it may range the gamut from the graceful to the melancholy, and even to the comic or the ghostly and mysterious, but it will always remain within the framework of a lyrical composition. His more knowledgeable friends seem at first to have objected to the lively, robust burlesque substituted for such an allegretto in his Fourth Symphony. By this substitution he had replaced the usual alternating scherzo–trio–scherzo form with a concise sonata form. But even this movement, placed between the very serious andante and the gigantic finale, plays the role of a relaxing intermezzo and has an almost dancelike character, marked by a splash of color provided by the triangle which is used only here. What is admirable time and again in such feats, is Brahms's incredibly keen feeling for proportion, for the subtle elements which govern the over-all course of a cyclical structure. In this respect he was the only legitimate heir of Beethoven.

The calm majesty of Brahms's mature style stands in relationship to the kind of expression characteristic for some of Beethoven's works of his middle period, such as the andante of his Fifth Symphony, the G major and E-flat major Piano Concertos, and the grand B-flat major Trio. In the case of Brahms, this contemplative quiet is definitely a decisive characteristic of his whole being. But in dark, dramatic outbursts such as those in the first and last movements of his Fourth Symphony, something apocalyptically grandiose and superhuman takes place. He had outgrown the passionately romantic extravagance of subjectivity; free from illusions, he could now face the world from the remote viewpoint of a stoic, without illusions and without self-pity. The fact that the classical form, used with perfect freedom, allowed a distinctive, fully appropriate development of character in each one of his works, is probably the most decisive criterion of its vitality.

Between and around the great works of these harvest years there sprang forth his chamber music: the three Violin Sonatas, the second Cello Sonata, the Piano Trios in C major and C minor, and the two String Quintets, the second of which, opus 111, in G major, represents just as high a peak of inspired abundance in chamber music as the B-flat major Concerto does in orchestral music. It goes without saying that Brahms, whose origins were deeply rooted in the piano, did not neglect this instrument either; but his large-scale efforts were devoted to the orchestra and to chamber music, the more so as the latter involved the piano time and again. After the piano sonatas of his early period and the variations of his developmental years, the piano piece in one movement became the favored medium for his most intimate personal expression. It is music that is turned inward, and with a few exceptions it does not fit the perspective of a concert hall well. He called these pieces capriccios or intermezzi, depending upon whether they were lively or lyrical. The Eight Pieces, Opus 76, written at the same time as the Violin Concerto, are monologues of the most intense expressiveness and of a delicacy of structural texture which one must experience as a player in order to appreciate it fully. Alongside them, as the only large-scale piano pieces created during this period, there are the two Rhapsodies, Opus 79, with whose dedication he expressed his grateful devotion to Elisabeth von Herzogenberg. They owe their title to their wildly impetuous character. When Liszt wrote a sonata, it was bound to be rhapsodic throughout; but when Brahms wrote two rhapsodies, they must needs be in rondo and in sonata form, respectively. He was unable to express himself other than in a consistently shaped form of classical balance.

Just as in his instrumental music, his style in the various branches of vocal music ripened into a complete identity of form and substance. His romantic part songs, in which he had followed Schumann's example in his younger years, matured into the Choral Phantasies, Opus 104. With their exquisite refinement, their contrapuntal wealth, and their wide range of tone color, they are fully equivalent to the old madrigal. Especially the two *Nachtwachen* on words by Rückert and the *Letztes Glück* on a poem by Kalbeck are incomparable gems of choral lyricism. Opposite his madrigal style is his motet style, which found its ultimate and most exalted realization in the previously mentioned *Fest- und Gedenksprüche.* In them Brahms, the first in more than three centuries of instrumental ascendancy to do so, returned to the very fountainhead of innocence in musical intensity, to true vocality, to a style of clearcut depth as peculiar to him as his instrumental style and yet as different from the latter as, for example, Dürer's woodcuts are from his paintings. What changed least in style from beginning to end were his lieder. They remained pure lyricism; while the piano accompaniment grew more and more refined, the vocal part remained true to his love for simple, diatonic, and at times almost folklike melody. Any Brahms song of his late period is a jewel set in filigree, and his melodies grew increasingly sweet with maturity. Some of his lieder, such as *Minnelied, Vergebliches Ständchen, Feldeinsamkeit, Sapphische Ode, Wir wandelten, Wie Melodien zieht es, Immer leiser,* and *Auf dem Kirchhof,* achieved their popularity with astonishing rapidity, and deservedly so.

Toward his sixtieth year Brahms began to age very rapidly in his appearance; in his music, too, one can sense a decisive change of feeling, a decline of vitality which took place soon after 1890, the year of the G major String Quintet. At that time he often spoke of having arrived at the end of his career. "I have worked enough; now let the young folks take over," he was wont to say. But the joy of music making overcame him once more. His acquaintance with the talented clarinetist Mühlfeld, whom he had met in the Meiningen orchestra, stimulated him to two more sublime pieces of chamber music: the Clarinet Trio and the Clarinet Quintet. Both contain pages among the most formally accomplished and most impressive that Brahms has ever written. But it is impossible not to sense that this is the music of an old man expressing the mild melancholy of retrospection and resignation. Imperceptibly the first day of winter had arrived; the sun was low over the horizon. In the year 1891 the music of his last period began. Its artistic value is by no means diminished; what it may lack in gushing fullness is replaced by an indescribably noble, spiritual concentration of technique and expression. But the will to live and the overwhelming urge to create were a thing of the past. The man had calmed down and withdrawn into himself. What followed was more or less a gleaning. Twenty piano pieces, which may in part be of an earlier date, were published in four series, Opus 116 to Opus 119. The most precious of these, beautifully serious and pensive monologues, were probably written at that time, in 1892-93. He then took leave of the lied (see page 56) with seven times seven German folk songs arranged for voice with piano accompaniment, a labor of love by one who had always been enchanted with the folk tune. In a letter to Joachim he wrote: "Never have I written anything with so much love —nay, with so much being in love—and I need not be ashamed of being in love with something not my own." But from that time on, everything he did was a labor of love. This is certainly true of his two Clarinet Sonatas, which followed the Trio and Quintet by three years as an additional offering to "Miss Clarinet," as he dubbed the bearded Mühlfeld on account of his sweet tone. As on other occasions, the sonatas were again a pair, homogeneous and yet contrasting; and the second one, in E-flat major, is the more intense in expression, the more appealing in melodic detail and more stirring in the sunset mood of its finale, a succession of pensive variations on a dreamy, songlike tune which at the very end rallies to an energetic affirmation of life. Here the master of the variation once more demonstrated his inimitable art by allowing the almost casual thematic cadence to blossom forth into a freely developed finale.

This was the last work which he himself helped introduce on the concert stage. After an extended lull he completed, early in May of 1896, the *Four Serious Songs* in a last but magnificent burst of splendor, just before the onset of his final illness. His accompanying letter to Mandyczewski, the first to see this latest work, is very characteristic: "I am letting the enclosed ungodly ditties make the detour via Vienna because I hope they may convey a message to Simrock or to you. [Mandyczewski was to forward the manuscript to the publisher.] Otherwise I would prefer to show you with some other little trifles how contritely I do my penance." The "little trifles" were chorale preludes for organ, eleven of which he was able to complete during May and June in Ischl. They were his only posthumous work. He labored on them, already gravely ill, perhaps indeed as "penance," as a stoic exercise in concentration. They were probably intended to be part of a more extensive collection, a kind of spiritual counterpart to his folk songs. The chorale melodies woven into them had been sung in church by Brahms during his childhood, and they were another retrospective glance at the beginning—"the serpent that bites into its own tail." One of these chorales he even used a second time, as though he could not get enough of the beloved melody.

These chorale preludes are a significant epilogue to his work. With their studied concentration on the essential, the contrapuntal presentation of the chorale melody, they are a final, simple expression of faith in that most noble of all the possessions of an artist: his craft. Yet the writing is so personal that every detail of the counterpoint is filled with meaning. Every one of these preludes is a masterpiece, and some of them—*O Gott, du frommer Gott, Es ist ein Ros entsprungen, Herzlich tut mich verlangen, O Welt, ich muss dich lassen*—are of a particularly delicate, spiritual beauty. The last-named, No. 11 of the collection, is the very last composition Brahms ever wrote. It is touching in its simplicity and in the pensive manner in which the cadential phrases of the chorale are repeated like a double echo. The state of contemplation is here almost transformed into a reality: it is as though the lonesome dreamer, seated at the console of an organ, were to let every turn of melody ring again and again in his memory, as if his departing soul wanted to cast yet another look at the world he was about to leave. And again it seems like a profession of faith when the composer finds his way from a melody, shopworn by constant use in the Protestant service, back to its original source, Heinrich Isaak's *Innsbruck, ich muss dich lassen* ["Innsbruck, I must leave thee"], with its wondrously heartfelt, archaic closing cadence. Thus a bridge spanning four centuries connects the late descendant with a master of the primeval age in which genuine polyphony had its origins.

Then he dropped his pen. Perhaps because of physical exhaustion, but certainly because he was tortured by the dull discomfort that accompanies all serious illness, he who had never been sick in his life could no longer rouse him-

self sufficiently to concentrate on his work. It is impossible not to assume that he must have been fully aware of the significance of that last page of his music. Like Brahms, Bach had bid farewell to the world with a chorale prelude: *Vor deinen Thron tret ich hiemit* ["Before Thy throne I now must step"].

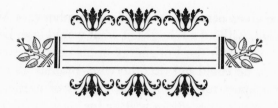

Contemporary World
and Posterity

In a certain sense every art has a practical purpose. No artist can be entirely separated from the surroundings in which and for which he creates; his work becomes part of this contemporary scene. Neither Bach nor Haydn ever thought of claiming a greater significance for the work which they created day by day than that of an honest fulfillment of duty. The fact that ultimately their work became immortal was a byproduct of its artistic integrity. The modern artist, however, must bear the fetters of his ambition. He is no longer an artisan, a slave to daily obligations. But on the other hand, he has lost the magnificent innocence with which Bach would write a church cantata for some given occasion, or Haydn a symphony, or Mozart a serenade, without a thought of what would later become of it but still with the full energy of his entire personality —because he could not do otherwise. Brahms also had a healthy respect for the practical aspects of music. From the numerous compositions written for his women's chorus in Hamburg all the way to the late clarinet sonatas, he again and again created music that was prompted by everyday considerations and destined for practical use. An "art for art's sake" point of view was foreign to him. His friends were his critics, and the public his tribunal from which there was no appeal. If the judgment were unfavorable, he would try to do better next time.

How this took place, in what indescribable loneliness the creative artist worked, dependent entirely on his own instinct and his own conscience, may best be illustrated by his Fourth Symphony. He had returned in September of 1885 from his summer sojourn in Mürzzuschlag with the finished symphony, and his urge to try the effect of the newly created work was so strong that he did not hesitate to prepare a two-piano arrangement in order to play it for a few selected friends, with Ignaz Brüll as his partner. Kalbeck, who was present, tells of this event without sparing himself—in other words, surely with authenticity. What may be considered questionable in the story is the performance on two pianos by the undoubtedly highly nervous composer, who had long cruelly neglected his piano practice, and a partner who, although very talented, was completely unprepared and had to read at sight. After the first movement a dead silence was followed by the only audible reaction, an explosive sigh from Hanslick, surely the least intelligent among those present, who ejaculated: "Throughout the entire movement I had the sensation of

being flailed by two fearfully ingenious persons." Let Kalbeck continue:

The strange sounds of the melodious andante pleased me exceedingly, and I ventured—since nobody else opened his
mouth—to utter some resounding banality which probably had
a still more disagreeable effect than the uneasy silence that preceded it. The shaggy, grimly joyful scherzo seemed far too insignificant in comparison with the preceding movements, and
the mighty passacaglia of the finale, the crowning glory of all
of Brahms's variation movements, did not appear to me a proper
conclusion for a symphony.

After a sleepless night, the good soul took his courage into
his hands, visited Brahms, and implored him to withdraw
or at least to revise radically what was so manifestly a
failure.

If things were to go according to my taste, I would throw the
scherzo, with its abrupt principal and trite subsidiary themes,
into the wastepaper basket, publish the grand chaconne as a
separate work, and invent two brand-new movements that
would go better with the others.

Brahms, just for once, did not even get angry.

He did not want to defend the third movement, on the grounds
that about the value of melodies one cannot argue. . . . The
finale he wanted to justify with a reference to the finale of the
Eroica, not by comparing the value and substance of the two
movements but merely with regard to form. Beethoven had not
hesitated to conclude his symphonies and sonatas with variations.

Brahms's confidence was limitless as long as a form sanc-
tioned by Beethoven was involved, and in this he was certainly not mistaken. A part of this confidence, however,
was his own infallible sense of form, his capacity for realizing the general architectural principle underlying each

individual, inimitable case. He knew better than any of his critical friends. Ever since its very first appearance on the stage, on a concert tour of the Meiningen orchestra through western Germany, the Fourth Symphony has made a profound impression, admittedly more so after closer acquaintance. In this instance the public was more perceptive than the experts. The latter, however, succeeded in arousing doubts in Brahms's own mind. "It is very questionable," he wrote to Elisabeth von Herzogenberg shortly after the above episode, "whether I will ever again expose the public to this piece. Bülow, however, wants to get started with it as early as November 3 in Frankfort." It was only a public performance that finally convinced him. But this conviction was final, not so much on account of the audience, even though he was by no means indifferent to its reaction, but because he himself was able to experience his music objectively and detached from his own person only when it was publicly performed.

His unsparing self-criticism, which knew no criterion other than the perfect accomplishments of the greatest masters, rarely permitted him to feel a more than very temporary and limited satisfaction with his own work. Whenever he expressed himself on the subject, he did so in a skeptical, derisive manner. When, for example, he had recommended that Clara play a Mozart piano concerto in Hamburg and she voiced the objection that the public did not evince enough interest in this sort of thing, he replied: "The fact that the public in general does not understand and appreciate the really fine works is our bread and butter and brings us fame. If they only knew that from us they get in driblets what they could otherwise drink to their heart's content!" While talking with Hans Koessler about the transitoriness of music, he remarked: "I know perfectly well what position I will one day hold in the history of music: the position in which Cherubini found himself and which he occupies to this day. This will be my fate, too." In this he was mistaken, but it shows that he did not lag far behind his most critical opponents when it came to skepticism about his own work. On the other hand, it would have been unnatural had he not rejoiced in the avalanche-like growth of his fame. If he felt that he did not deserve it, it was because he could never see himself but against the background of the giants of the past. And between the following lines of dry humor addressed to Clara (from Vienna in October, 1879) a certain contentment can be discerned:

On Sunday I am to conduct my Requiem in the court opera house here, preceded by the *Athalia* Overture [by Mendelssohn] and followed by the *Eroica* Symphony; so now, in your imagination you can listen, too. Actually the concert manager wanted an all-Brahms evening, but I made up this improved program. November 1 and 2 are, as you know, All Saints' and All Souls' Days, when everybody goes to visit graves and in the evening wants to hear "The Miller and his Son" [a popular melodrama] or some requiem.

By the way, the length of the program is astonishing but, in this respect, no exception. Less spoiled with performances than we are today, the public then evidently had a more voracious appetite.

It is difficult to form an opinion about how much or how little the enormously lively critical opposition to Brahms meant to the public at large. For Wagnerians everywhere —and in the 1870's they were increasingly in the ascendancy—disparagement of Brahms was a basic principle of musical politics. To them he represented an average talent without significance, brought into the limelight by fortuitous circumstances, but in any event a hidebound reactionary. Jean F. Schucht, Leipzig's most respected critic, expressed his regret in a discussion of the *German Requiem* that Brahms lacked the courage of rising to the freedom of form, especially as far as rhythm and declamation are concerned, which Wagner, Berlioz, and above all Liszt had pioneered in such an epochal manner. Louis Ehlert, an important critical voice in Berlin, declared: "Brahms's music has no profile; it only has an *en face* ["flat face"]. It lacks the forceful features that give definite shape to the expression." A French critic quoted by Weingartner said: "He works exceedingly well with ideas which he does not have." And George Bernard Shaw, who was a music critic in his younger days and a staunch Wagnerian, called the *German Requiem* an advertisement for an undertaking establishment. Romain Rolland considered Brahms a charlatan, a ridiculously overestimated nonentity.

Such critical expressions, just like the boundlessly venomous anti-Brahms outbursts of Hugo Wolf, have only historical interest now. A judge of the prominence of Felix von Weingartner, however, offered more food for thought in a lecture entitled *The Symphony after Beethoven* (1897), subsequently published in book form. In it he soberly presented a far better informed summary of public opinion at the turn of the century and, an excellent musician and already well-known conductor himself, he had a much more legitimate right to express himself authoritatively. At that time Weingartner represented the moderate, objective wing of the "neo-German" party, loyal to Wagner and Liszt. He wrote:

Brahms's music regarded as a whole is, if the expression may be permitted, scientific music, a play of sounding forms and phrases, but no longer that abstract and yet most expressive and most intelligible universal language that our great masters were both able and compelled to speak, a language that touches and stimulates our innermost souls because in it we recognize ourselves, our joys and sorrows, our struggles and victories. Their music is artistic while Brahms's music is artificial. It is not related to Beethoven; in fact it is its polar opposite, exactly that which Beethoven's music is not. Its character is essentially abstract, and it repels you if you long to approach it. Its effect is therefore one of coldness.

And in a different context:

Whenever I encountered the artistic productions of Brahms, I have refrained from abuse and from shutting my ears, as other Wagnerians do, and also from parrotting sections of Wagner's collected writings. I have repeatedly and diligently studied the greatest part of his work. When dissecting this music, my intelligence always remained unruffled; I was able to admire its workmanship and construction and to derive the same type of enjoyment from it that a physician may experience in laying bare the musculature of a well-grown corpse. If, however, I tried to submit to a spontaneous impression, I would experience that paralyzing disillusion which would befall the physician who had the temerity to try to bring the corpse back to life.

Weingartner, who was here visibly at pains to judge objectively and dispassionately, radically changed his opinion later on. At that time, however, at the turn of the century, it seems to have been impossible to belong to one party without unreservedly condemning the other. Such cases show that no objective criteria exist when the essence of a judgment of artistic value is at stake. Opinion is confronted with opinion.

Under these circumstances it is not easy to say how an artist, at last removed from the battleground of opinions, finally becomes a classic. If the estheticians of progress had been right, Brahms, along with Mendelssohn's *Songs without Words,* Spohr's symphonies, Cherubini's Masses, and Meyerbeer's operas, would have been relegated to the

lumber room half a century ago. There must exist somewhere below the surface of public knowledge a process
which, far more than the self-appointed oracles, has an
effect on the formation of opinion. This process regulates,
as it were, the relation between supply and demand in the
markets of the musical world and creates, as time goes on,
a more or less permanent valuation, regardless of whether
or not the oracles are in agreement. In the case of Brahms
this definitely took place.

By the beginning of our century Brahms had taken root,
although by no means unambiguously, in the German-
and English-speaking countries only. Since then his stature
has grown immeasurably, and his music has conquered the
whole world, very gradually and without any discernible
external reasons. Today it stands where Bülow had envisaged it: on a level with the works of the greatest masters of all time. This was not brought about by the esthetes,
by the critics, or by the self-appointed oracles. It came
about spontaneously, through the multitude of people for
whom this music had become a necessity and through the
countless musicians who, in order to satisfy this need, have
accorded loving attention to these works and seen to it that
this music remained alive through deserving performances.

Such an act of sanctification is certainly not irrevocable.
The plebiscite continues as long as there are music lovers,
and it has often dethroned some who had once been considered great. But any music that has survived nearly a full
century with undiminished vigor should, to judge from our
experience, have some reasonable claim to immortality
insofar as this term has any justification at all, considering
the brief time span covered by European music history.
With today's publicity methods, celebrities are quickly
created. They vanish just as quickly. The real, genuine
patina of fame takes long to develop, because the process

that gives rise to it requires a great deal of time. It proceeds with perfect calm and seems to be almost independent of the conscious forces working pro and con, forces which of course exist all the time. Individual opinions are of no importance. Richard Strauss, who grew up along classical lines but later radically switched to the opposite camp, loved to talk about Brahms, whom he rejected unconditionally, referring to him in his hearty manner with such picturesque phrases as "woolen shirt" and "lentils in his beard." A celebrated musician now living avers that he glances at a Brahms score every other year in order to reassure himself that his music is really as bad as he remembers it. But half a century ago there were already fists raised against Bayreuth, and Bayreuth continues to live. And thirty years ago a famous composer published a widely read article in which he claimed that Beethoven, although a man of respectable character, was unfortunately no musician at all. Beethoven's prestige has not suffered.

Individual judgments are erratic, and everybody has the right to make his own. But they signify little. The plebiscite goes on invisibly, inaudibly, but is stronger in its effect than anything written or proclaimed. It is the "connoisseurs and music lovers" who exercise it, whether they are few or many; they are the ones whose opinions have a cumulative effect and are decisive because all of them tend to go in the same direction. And they do this because it is in the consciousness of the connoisseurs and music lovers that the true qualities of a work of art come to life and exert their influence. The compass of public opinion oscillates, and it may take a long time ere it finds its true pole, imperceptibly but irresistibly led by the strong views—strong because they are sure of their convictions—of those whose judgment rests upon living ex-

perience with a work of art. Whoever has had the sensation, at a certain place near the end of the andante in
Brahms's Third Symphony, that the Heavens were opening up and that encompassed within the space of a few
measures were the most profound thoughts that music
can express; whoever found his eyes grow moist during the
first movement of the *German Requiem* at the words "they
that sow in tears shall reap in joy"; whoever, during the
adagio of the Clarinet Quintet, the andante of the B-flat
Piano Concerto, or the first movement of the Horn Trio,
has sensed a reflection of the noblest perfection that
human endeavor can fashion, the perfection of classical
sculpture or of Goethian poetry—that person may well
smile at the "lentils in his beard." So long as there are
those who respond to music with full and spontaneous
fervor, and so long as Brahms's music evokes such fervor
in them, his music will live. And whoever is capable of
penetrating below the surface of things will find in
Brahms's life and work that steadfast, uninterrupted single-
ness of purpose inherent to greatness. From the early piano
sonatas to the *Four Serious Songs,* from the ecstatic, romantic youth to the bitterly earnest stoic and pessimist of
his later years, the man and the world which he created
are homogeneous—cast from a single mold. Everything
wrought by the artist, everything experienced and suffered
and consummated by the toiling, searching, and occasionally erring human being, becomes one single, miraculous testimony to a great soul in whom a godless century
has once more found an expression of the highest that can
be realized by the spirit of man.

Selected Bibliography

Barkan, Hans: *Johannes Brahms and Theodor Billroth.* Norman, Okla.: University of Oklahoma Press; 1957.

Brahms, Johannes: *Briefwechsel* (Correspondence). 8 volumes. Berlin: Deutsche Brahms-Gesellschaft; 1908–14.

———: *Briefwechsel mit Clara Schumann.* Leipzig: B. Litzmann; 1927.

Drinker, Henry S., Jr.: *The Chamber Music of Johannes Brahms.* Philadelphia: Elkan-Vogel Co.; 1932.

Drinker, Sophie: *Brahms and His Women's Choruses.* Merion, Pa.: Sophie Drinker; 1952.

Fuller Maitland, J. A.: *Johannes Brahms.* New York: John Lane Co.; 1911.

Geiringer, Karl: "Johannes Brahms im Briefwechsel mit Eusebius Mandyczewski." *Zeitschrift für Musikwissenschaft,* No. 8, May 1933.

———: *Brahms—His Life and Work.* 2nd edition. New York: Oxford University Press; 1947.

Grasberger, Franz: *Johannes Brahms.* Vienna: Paul Kaltschmid; 1952.

Hill, Ralph: *Brahms.* New York: A. A. Wyn, Inc.; 1948.

Kalbeck, Max: *Johannes Brahms.* 8 volumes. Berlin: Deutsche Brahms-Gesellschaft; 1908–14.

Mason, Daniel Gregory: *The Chamber Music of Brahms.* New York: The Macmillan Company; 1933.

May, Florence: *The Life of Johannes Brahms.* London: William Reeves; 1905.

Niemann, Walter: *Brahms.* New York: Alfred A. Knopf; 1929.

Schauffler, Robert Haven: *The Unknown Brahms.* New York: Dodd, Mead & Co.; 1933.

Specht, Richard: *Johannes Brahms.* Translated by Eric Blom. London, Toronto, and New York: J. M. Dent & Sons, Ltd., and E. P. Dutton & Co.; 1930.

Thomas-San Galli, W. A.: *Johannes Brahms.* Munich: R. Piper & Co.; 1922.

List of Compositions

(Numbers in parentheses indicate the year of publication.
Numbers following refer to pages
on which the composition is mentioned.)

A. *Orchestral works*

First Symphony, C minor, Op. 68 (1877), 56, 68, 73, 77, 115, 117, 122, 139–41, 204, 206–8, 210, 213–14, 218, 220

Second Symphony, D major, Op. 73 (1878), 15, 73, 76, 98–9, 122, 142, 175, 209–10, 216, 220

Third Symphony, F major, Op. 90 (1884), 68, 174, 209–10, 218, 220, 238

Fourth Symphony, E minor, Op. 98 (1886), 21, 66, 68, 70, 99, 174–5, 209, 221, 230, 232

Serenade No. 1, D major, Op. 11 (1860), 122–5, 165, 191, 214, 220

Serenade No. 2, A major, Op. 16 (1860), 122–3, 125, 191, 214, 220

Variations on a Theme by Haydn, Op. 56a (1874), 121, 172, 205, 219

Academic Festival Overture, Op. 80 (1881), 19, 68, 122, 142

Tragic Overture, Op. 81 (1881), 68, 122

Three Hungarian Dances (arrangements, 1874)

Piano Concerto No. 1, D minor, Op. 15 (1860), 12, 60, 111, 113–117, 122, 128, 191, 205, 214–15

Piano Concerto No. 2, B-flat major, Op. 83 (1882), 4, 68, 216, 218–19, 221, 238

Violin Concerto, D major, Op. 77 (1879), 99, 209, 216–18, 222

Double Concerto for Violin and Cello, A minor, Op. 102 (1888), 55–6, 61, 66, 128–9, 217–18

B. *Chamber music*

1. WITH PIANO:

Quintet, F minor, Op. 34 (1865), 21, 72, 117–18, 171, 204

Quartet No. 1, G minor, Op. 25 (1863), 122, 124, 170

Quartet No. 2, A major, Op. 26 (1863), 14, 122, 124, 170, 220

Quartet No. 3, C minor, Op. 60 (1875), 11, 117, 174, 205

Trio in B major, Op. 8 (1854; revised version, 1891), 60, 109–11, 157–63, 203, 220

Horn Trio, E-flat major, Op. 40 (1866), 125, 204, 220, 238

Trio in C major, Op. 87 (1883), 65, 162, 221

Trio in C minor, Op. 101 (1887), 221

Clarinet Trio, A minor, Op. 114 (1892), 85, 122, 224

Violin Sonata No. 1, G major, Op. 78 (1880), 98–9, 209, 221

Violin Sonata No. 2, A major, Op. 100 (1887), 166, 221

Violin Sonata No. 3, D minor, Op. 108 (1889), 221

Scherzo for Violin and Piano (posthumous, 1906)

Cello Sonata No. 1, E minor, Op. 38 (1866)

Cello Sonata No. 2, F major, Op. 99 (1887), 221

Clarinet Sonata No. 1, F minor, Op. 120 No. 1 (1895), 122, 176, 224, 230

Clarinet Sonata No. 2, E-flat major, Op. 120 No. 2 (1895), 122, 176, 224, 230

2. WITHOUT PIANO:

String Sextet No. 1, B-flat major, Op. 18 (1862), 122, 124, 170, 204, 219

String Sextet No. 2, G major, Op. 36 (1866), 74, 95–6, 122, 204

String Quintet No. 1, F major, Op. 88 (1883), 165–8, 221

String Quintet No. 2, G major, Op. 111 (1891), 221, 223

Clarinet Quintet, B minor, Op. 115 (1891), 85, 121–2, 173, 224, 238

String Quartet No. 1, C minor, Op. 51 No. 1 (1873), 81, 122, 171, 205

String Quartet No. 2, A minor, Op. 51 No. 2 (1873), 81, 122, 171, 205

String Quartet No. 3, B-flat major, Op. 67 (1876), 171, 173, 205, 219

C. Piano music

1. SOLO:

Sonata No. 1, C major, Op. 1 (1853), 56, 107, 109–10, 159, 222
Sonata No. 2, F-sharp minor, Op. 2 (1854), 107–8, 110, 159, 222
Sonata No. 3, F minor, Op. 5 (1854), 62, 159, 222
Scherzo, E-flat minor, Op. 4 (1854), 32, 111, 220
Variations on a Theme by Schumann, Op. 9 (1854), 124
Variations on an Original Theme, Op. 21, No. 1 (1861), 222
Variations on a Hungarian Theme, Op. 21, No. 2 (1861), 222
Variations on a Theme by Handel, Op. 24 (1862), 124–5, 134, 165, 171–2, 219, 222
Variations on a Theme by Paganini, Op. 35 (1866), 39, 171–2, 222
Four Ballades, Op. 10 (1856)
Eight Piano Pieces, Op. 76 (1879), 209, 222
Two Rhapsodies, Op. 79 (1880), 209, 222
Seven Fantasias, Op. 116 (1892), 224
Three Intermezzi, Op. 117 (1892), 224
Six Piano Pieces, Op. 118 (1893), 224
Four Piano Pieces, Op. 119 (1893), 224
Hungarian Dances (2 volumes, 1872; arrangements of the piano duets)
Two Gigues (posthumous, 1927)
Two Sarabands (posthumous, 1917)
Fifty-one Keyboard Exercises (1893)
Cadenzas, arrangements, etc.

2. PIANO DUETS:

Variations on a Theme by Schumann, Op. 23 (1863)
Waltzes, Op. 39 (1866), 178
Hungarian Dances (4 volumes; 1869, 1880), 17, 137, 170, 204
(*Liebeslieder* Waltzes and *Neue Liebeslieder*, see F, 1 below)

3. FOR TWO PIANOS:

Sonata, F minor, Op. 34 (1872; same as the Piano Quintet), 39
Variations on a Theme by Haydn, Op. 56b (1873; also for orchestra)

D. Organ music

Two Preludes and Fugues (posthumous, 1927)
Fugue, A-flat minor (1864)
Chorale Prelude and Fugue on *O Traurigkeit, O Herzeleid* (1882)
Eleven Chorale Preludes, Op. 122 (posthumous, 1902), 225–6

E. Works for chorus and orchestra

1. MIXED CHORUS:
A German Requiem, Op. 45 (1868), 4, 17, 41–2, 46, 66, 72, 86,
    115, 123, 129–30, 137–9, 145, 186–8, 190–2, 197, 200
    204, 214, 233–4, 238
Song of Destiny, Op. 53 (1871), 46, 72, 74, 145, 192–5
Song of Triumph, Op. 55 (1872), 52, 56, 72, 137, 139, 145, 188–
    190, 192
Nänie, Op. 82 (1881), 195
Song of the Fates, Op. 89 (1883), 77, 195–6
Funeral Hymn, Op. 13 (with wind instruments, 1860)

2. WOMEN'S CHORUS:
Ave Maria, Op. 12 (with orchestra or organ, 1860)

3. MEN'S CHORUS:
Rinaldo, cantata for tenor, male chorus, and orchestra Op. 50
    (1869), 145, 192, 196
Alto Rhapsody, with male chorus and orchestra Op. 53 (1870),
    192, 196

F. Polyphonic vocal music without orchestra

1. FOR MIXED VOICES AND ACCOMPANIMENT:
Sacred Song, Op. 30 (with organ or piano, 1864), 120
Three Vocal Quartets, with piano, Op. 31 (1864), 205
Three Vocal Quartets, with piano, Op. 64 (1874), 185
Four Vocal Quartets, with piano, Op. 92 (1884)
Six Vocal Quartets, with piano, Op. 112 (1891)
Liebeslieder Waltzes, with piano-duet accompaniment, Op. 52
    (1869), 137, 179–80, 205
Neue Liebeslieder, with piano-duet accompaniment, Op. 65
    (1875), 179
Gypsy Songs, with piano, Op. 103 (1888)

Table Song, Op. 93b (1885)
Little Wedding Cantata (posthumous, 1927)

2. FOR MIXED VOICES WITHOUT ACCOMPANIMENT:
Marienlieder, Op. 22 (1862), 126
Two Motets, Op. 29 (1864), 120
Two Motets, Op. 74 (1879), 209
Three Songs, Op. 42 (1864), 126
Seven Lieder, Op. 62 (1874)
Six Lieder and Romances, Op. 93a (1884)
Five Songs, Op. 104 (1889), 222
Fest- und Gedenksprüche, Op. 109 (1890), 52, 189, 223
Three Motets, Op. 110 (1890)
Fourteen German Folk Songs (1864)
Twelve German Folk Songs (posthumous, 1927)
Canons, etc. (posthumous, 1927)

3. FOR WOMEN'S VOICES AND ACCOMPANIMENT:
The Twenty-third Psalm, with organ or piano, Op. 27 (1864), 230
Four Songs, with two French horns and harp, Op. 17 (1862), 126, 230

4. FOR WOMEN'S VOICES WITHOUT ACCOMPANIMENT:
Three Sacred Choruses, Op. 37 (1866), 120, 230
Twelve Songs and Romances, Op. 44 (1866), 95, 230
Thirteen Canons, Op. 113 (1891)

5. FOR MEN'S VOICES WITHOUT ACCOMPANIMENT:
Five lieder, Op. 41 (1867)

G. Songs for solo voice with piano accompaniment

Six Songs, Op. 3 (1853), 109, 111
Six Songs, Op. 6 (1853), 109
Six Songs, Op. 7 (1854)
Eight Lieder and Romances, Op. 14 (1860)
Five Poems, Op. 19 (1862)
Nine Lieder and Songs, Op. 32 (1864)
Fifteen Romances from Tieck's *Magelone*, Op. 33 (1865–9), 183
Four Songs, Op. 43 (1868)
Four Lieder, Op. 46 (1868)
Five Lieder, Op. 47 (1868)
Seven Lieder, Op. 48 (1868)

Five Lieder, Op. 49 (1868)
Eight Lieder and Songs, Op. 57 (1871)
Eight Lieder and Songs, Op. 58 (1871)
Eight Lieder and Songs, Op. 59 (1873)
Nine Lieder and Songs, Op. 63 (1877)
Nine Songs, Op. 69 (1877), 209
Four Songs, Op. 70 (1877), 209
Five Songs, Op. 71 (1877), 209
Five Songs, Op. 72 (1877), 209
Five Romances and Lieder, for one or two voices, Op. 84 (1882)
Six Lieder, Op. 85 (1882)
Six Lieder, Op. 86 (1882)
Two songs, for alto with viola and piano, Op. 91 (1884)
Five Lieder, for low voice, Op. 94 (1884)
Seven Lieder, Op. 95 (1884)
Four Lieder, Op. 96 (1886)
Six Lieder, Op. 97 (1886)
Five Lieder, for low voice, Op. 105 (1889)
Five Lieder, Op. 106 (1889)
Five Lieder, Op. 107 (1889)
Four Serious Songs, for bass voice, Op. 121 (1896), 20, 85, 176, 183, 197–201, 225, 238
Eight *Gypsy Songs* from Op. 103 (arrangement; originally for vocal quartet)
Mondnacht (1854)
Regenlied (posthumous, 1908)
Forty-nine German Folk Songs (seven volumes, 1894), 56, 85, 95, 109, 183, 224
Twenty-eight Folk Songs (posthumous, 1926)
Fourteen Folk Songs for Children (1858)

H. Vocal duets with piano accompaniment

Three Duets, for soprano and alto, Op. 20 (1861)
Four Duets, for alto and baritone, Op. 28 (1864)
Four Duets, for soprano and alto, Op. 61 (1874)
Five Duets, for soprano and alto, Op. 66 (1875)
Four Ballades and Romances, for two voices, Op. 75 (1878)

Index of Names

i

A Note about the Author

SINCE 1945, Hans Gal has been a lecturer in music at Edinburgh University, where he received the degree of Doctor of Music in 1948. Born in Brunn, Lower Austria (now a suburb of Vienna), in 1890, he was educated in Vienna, where he received his Ph.D. in 1913. During World War I, he served for more than three years in the Austrian Army. After lecturing in music at the University of Vienna from 1919 to 1929, he was Director of the Municipal College of Music in Mainz (on the Rhine) until 1933. Thereafter, he became the conductor, in Vienna, of the Bach Society, the Vienna Madrigal Society, and the Vienna Concert Orchestra for a period of five years. He has also been active in the realm of musical composition, with some eighty published works to his credit, including operas, symphonies, choral works, chamber music, and piano music. *Johannes Brahms* is his fourth book. Mr. Gal is married, and the father of two children.

January 1963

A Note on the Type

THE TEXT of this book is set in CALEDONIA, a Linotype face designed by W. A. Dwiggins (1880-1956), the man responsible for so much that is good in contemporary book design and typography. Caledonia belongs to the family of printing types called "modern face" by printers—a term used to mark the change in style of type-letters that occurred about 1800. Caledonia borders on the general design of Scotch Modern but is more freely drawn than that letter.

Composed, printed, and bound by
The Haddon Craftsmen, Inc., Scranton, Pa.
Typography and binding design by
VINCENT TORRE